A MEETING OF MINDS

A MEETING OF MINDS

A Hartman Family Novel

JEZABEL NIGHTINGALE

Join the reader newsletter for more authors that have taken a stand against the use of AI-generated content: https://www.authenticityinitiative.com/for-readers

ISBN 978-0-6458061-3-7 (Paperback)
ISBN 978-0-6458061-2-0 (e-Book)

Edited by Sarah Baker, The Word Emporium
Proofread by Cheyenne Sampson, Frogg Spa Editing
Cover art by Kristin Barrett, K. B. Barrett Designs

jezabelnightingale.com

For everyone who's been misunderstood by their family.
You are loved.
You are seen.

Love is the music that transcends time and echoes through eternity.

Unknown

Content Warning

A Meeting of Minds is a book about two men finding love. Just as in real life, there are some tricky situations in the book which some people may find bring up emotions they would rather avoid. And that's cool. Please reach out if you need clarification.

So... topics talked about or alluded to include gay conversion, non-acceptance of sexuality by parents, some racism, use of alcohol as a crutch, and the death of a parent (not a Hartman). Medical procedures are described as well as life working in a hospital—it's not all sunshine and roses.

Ken's parents are fundamentalist Christians. I've tried to be sensitive towards people of faith, however no punches are pulled with those who don't practice what they preach. And speaking of punches being pulled, a character is subjected to family and domestic violence.

This may seem heavy, but there's also some fun stuff, including lots of music, three other Hartman siblings, two Gala Balls, and a happily ever after.

Sensitivity readers have read the book and offered valuable insight.

Before you start...

This book is set in the Southern Hemisphere where seasons are back to front compared to our European and American friends. School and university years start in January/February and end in November/December with the summer holidays happening over Christmas. There may be 'Australianisms' that make little sense to you, please feel free to reach out in my Facebook group, or via email, if you need clarification!

Playlist

All You Need Is Love — *The Beetles*
Love Is In The Air —*John Paul Young*
Need You Tonight — *INXS*
The Horses — *Daryl Braithwaite*
Throw Your Arms Around Me — *Mark Seymour*
Can't Get You out of My Head — *Kylie Minogue*
Plans — *Birds of Tokyo*
Gimme! Gimme! Gimme! (A Man After Midnight — *ABBA*
Mamma Mia! — *ABBA*
Why Do I Keep You? — *Telenova*
One Crowded Hour — *Augie March*
Can't Help Falling In Love — *Pentatonix*
Dance Monkey — *Tones And I*
Wish You Well — *Bernard Fanning*
Torn — *Natalie Imbruglia*
Into My Arms — Nick Cave
Am I Ever Gonna See Your Face Again? — *The Angels*
Truly Madly Deeply — *Savage Garden*

Available on Spotify

Chapter 1

Henry

'All You Need is Love' blared through my headphones as I sat at the airport departure gate and waited to board a plane home to celebrate my parents' thirtieth wedding anniversary. Some people listen to motivational podcasts or read self-help books. I listened to playlists of songs about love.

"Is this seat taken?" A tall brunette woman spoke as she pushed her breasts together, heaving them in my face.

"Go ahead," I said, hoping my headphones might put her off making small talk. Women hit on me a lot, so much that I'd considered wearing rainbow scarves or tattooing "I'm gay" across my forehead.

"I'm Krystal with a K. You're heading to Cassowary Point?"

I might as well put away the headphones. I hate ignoring people and went out of my way to make others feel comfortable. Some may say it's my bedside manner shining through into the rest of my life, but it's probably more the example set by the way I was raised.

"Henry. And yeah, it's my parents' thirtieth anniversary on Valentine's Day, and they're having a large gala to celebrate. It will raise money for the cardiac unit at the hospital, too." Although my aim had been to have a chat with Krystal with a K, she seemed more intent twirling her hair around her finger and chewing gum.

"I'm starting a new job as an exotic dancer. You should come and see me sometime. I'll give you a lap dance for free." Krystal batted her eyelids so rapidly I expected her fake lashes to launch across the terminal.

"My boyfriend might complain," I said with a smile as I leant away from her advancing chest.

"Oh... Oh." Krystal's eyes might have doubled in size, and then she simply stood and moved on to her next victim. Straightening up in my chair, I let out a sigh of relief that the small talk was over and replaced my headphones in my ears.

If only I had a boyfriend. It wasn't for want of trying. Sure, I'd dated over the years, but the longest relationship I'd had was twenty-seven days. I thought he was the one. I thought they all were. Every time there was a second date, I was convinced this was it. I was getting my happily ever after.

But it was never meant to be. I'd lost track of the number of guys I'd introduced to my family. I'd taken them to events with my parents and brunch with my brother and sister-in-law, but they'd all ended it, telling me it wasn't me, it was them, and they were too young for a relationship.

Manuel, Mr Twenty-Seven Days, was five years ago. We were twenty-one. He married last year.

"You made it." I glanced at my watch as my sister, Val, plonked herself next to me in the seat vacated by Krystal with a K.

"I knew I shouldn't have worked today," she replied, letting out a moan, "but I forgot to say I wasn't available. Then there was an accident on the way out here. Thanks for checking my bag for me. You're the best brother in the world."

"You say that to Giles and Boyd, too." One side of my lips raised as I bumped shoulders with my sister. We were a close family.

"Sometimes, but you're really the best. And you know it."

I was the second of four children to parents who were still supremely loved up, even after thirty years of marriage. Giles was the eldest. He married Bridget almost five years ago, and they have two beautiful daughters.

Next to me is Boyd. He's been with Emily, his childhood sweetheart and best friend of my sister, for over six years. Boyd and Emily stayed in Cassowary Point to study medicine, not moving to Brisbane as Giles and I had done.

Then there's Val, the long-awaited daughter. Our parents are both doctors, as are Giles, Bridget, and me. It wasn't that it was expected of us to pursue the same field as our parents and our grandfather, but the joys of medicine were pointed out from a young age. Val was determined from an early age to be a rebel and study law.

Our brothers took her choice as an affront, but I can see Val as a lawyer. She's always loved a good argument.

"Well, Hammy. It's you and me at this gala thing, probably chasing the same men." My niece, Millie, started calling me Uncle Hammy, and the nickname had stuck.

"I'm seven years older than you, stinky. I doubt we'll be chasing the same men."

Val rolled her eyes. "As long as they can provide at least one orgasm, I don't really mind how old they are."

I shook my head, preferring not to contemplate my sister's sex life.

I hadn't had an orgasm except by my hand for weeks.

It was my second year out of uni, and I'd chosen to do another house doctor year. My goal had been to specialise in general surgery. Last year, I'd spent a rotation in orthopaedics and, whilst I somewhat enjoyed it, I preferred to be up inside someone's abdomen than screwing and plating broken bones or fixing hip fractures on oldies.

Except, now I'd finally made it to my general surgical rotation, I was hating it. It wasn't helped that the week of leave I'd planned to take around my parents' anniversary gala ball was cancelled, and I had to argue to get today off at all. I was now flying home today for a ball tomorrow and then back home on Sunday to work Monday, so it hardly felt like a holiday at all.

Then there was Mr Coltrane. He was not only old school in that he wanted to be called mister instead of doctor, but he thought the sun shone out of his every orifice. Yes, even his dick. He had a reputation for screwing the nurses in the operating room after cases, despite parading his trophy wife around at hospital fundraisers.

I was surprised he wasn't solely working in private practice. He received bonuses for working in the public system and enjoyed torturing younger doctors such as myself.

Finally, the announcement came over the PA that we were boarding. Krystal had latched onto a man in an ill-fitting suit, and they were trying to arrange with the airline staff to change seats so they could sit together. I shuddered at the scene they were creating.

"Dr Hartman, welcome aboard." The flight attendant read my boarding pass as if it was her favourite novel and contained the meaning of life.

"He's with me," Val said as she snatched our boarding passes from the attendant. "Aren't you, lover?"

"Brother, Valerie." I rolled my eyes at Val's joking behaviour. I just wanted to put my headphones back in and zone out for a bit.

"Stepbrother, baby, and our parents aren't going to find out."

The attendant had gone from biting her bottom lip between her teeth to looking as if she might vomit.

"You're wicked," I scolded Val as we took our seats. She'd conned me for the window, forcing me to sit in the damn middle.

"Yeah, but she won't be harassing you all flight now."

My sister had a point.

I had a knack of attracting crazies when I flew. When I went home for New Year, having been forced to work over Christmas, I sat next to a Swiss tourist who wanted to tell me all about his dairy farm. Flying back to Brisbane, I'd had a grandmother who feared flying and wanted to tell me all about her children and grandchildren. She also wanted to get my number to give to her granddaughter, as she thought we'd make a lovely couple.

Perhaps this flight would be different. Boarding was almost complete, and I was hopeful the aisle seat would be unoccupied. Val's eyes almost popped out of her head, and I would swear later that she started drooling when the man in the navy suit boarded the plane.

Whereas Krystal's friend looked cheap in his off-the-rack number, this suit was well tailored. I'd worked in men's fashion whilst I studied, and I knew a decent suit when I saw one. This was magnificent, but it was more the body that was wearing it. It was muscular. The face attached to the body was gorgeous. As much as I teased Val that she drooled, I was drooling, too. His dark, wavy hair sat effortlessly on his head. He had plump, soft-looking lips that I wanted wrapped around my cock, and when our eyes met, a smile had crept across them. He was Mr Tall, Dark, and Handsome.

His left hand had been in his pocket, a messenger bag slung over his shoulder. As he removed his hand and his long fingers came into view, the spell was broken when I saw a black-and-titanium band on his ring finger. Just my luck. Despite the ring, I still fantasised about undoing his pants and reaching for his cock as he leaned above us and placed his bag in the overhead locker.

"Well, hello," the stranger exclaimed as he unbuttoned his jacket and took his seat. "I'm Tom, and this is going to be a great start to my weekend." Tom had reached out and taken my hand in his, his eyes looking straight into mine as if he could see into my soul. "And is this your girlfriend?"

"I'm his sister, and I don't think Hen's ever had a girlfriend. He's into cock."

Bloody hell, Val.

"I've had a threesome with sisters before, but never a brother and sister. This could be a great weekend."

"Open marriage?" I nodded towards his ring.

"In my mind, yeah, and what she doesn't know... But yes, you reminded me." Tom removed his wedding ring and reached into his suit jacket to retrieve his wallet before placing it in a zippered compartment.

I'd been burnt last year, strung along by a man who wanted to hook up for sex, yet, as I discovered later, he was married to a woman with a child at home. This was the end of me bottoming. I was no longer prepared to be used by guys. At least Tom was upfront, I suppose.

I almost yearned for a grandmother with a fear of flying to have taken the spare seat next to me over a sleazebag who was looking to score for the weekend. Tom and Val continued talking. Tom was a lawyer who was flying to Cassowary Point for a case next week and hated the idea of spending a weekend with his wife and two children.

I placed my headphones over my ears again and hid myself in my playlist. A cover version of 'Can't Help Falling in Love with You' serenaded my eardrums. While the music drowned out his voice, I decided that I'd wasted too much time on unavailable men like Tom. Now I needed to find someone who was both available and willing to accept me for me.

Closing my eyes, I let out a sigh. It had been a long week. I didn't get to spend a lot of time in the operating room, ending up mainly on the ward writing up drug orders and ensuring there were no post-op complications. Except there had been with one patient, and Mr Coltrane had tried to blame me for not catching a small internal bleed that meant the patient had to go back to theatre.

I tried not to think about work as the plane taxied down the runway, but work was all-consuming. There were still eight weeks to go on this rotation, and then I was off to gastroenterology before heading to gynaecology. Neither rotation excited me. I'd avoided both until now. Perhaps I should just throw it all in and this was a message that medicine wasn't for me.

In my head, I reasoned there wasn't anything else I could imagine myself doing. There were aspects of my retail job I'd hated too, but I'd stuck it out through medical school, knowing I'd be a doctor and could make a difference. Now I was a doctor, and I had no idea if I was making a difference or not. I didn't know what I wanted to specialise in, but I wanted something different to what I was doing now.

No, I needed to block out work and make the best of the two nights at home with my family and celebrate my parents' love.

As the plane landed and we were told we could switch our phones off flight mode, my phone filled with messages from my family. I was surprised no one had instigated a family group chat, but there was no way I would suggest such a thing. As I read through the messages, I learned it was raining, and Mum was fretting over the marquee that had been erected in our yard for the gala ball. Val showed me a message from our older brother, Giles. He was teasing her, suggesting that there would be plenty of available medical students at the ball. He also reminded her it wasn't too late to change her degree to medicine or marry a doctor. Val simply rolled her eyes.

There was a family fascination with doctors, which was why I decided long ago never to hook up with a colleague. Even through medical school, where I knew I wasn't the only queer student, I avoided dating, or even fucking, anyone I might see regularly.

Sure, I hooked up with a nurse last year at the end of a medical rotation, but we both knew it was a one-night thing. Perhaps I could find someone to hook up with at the gala. It had been weeks since I'd been with anyone else, and my hand was getting a little boring.

Before I knew it, we were off the plane and walking through the terminal. I laughed as Tom pulled the carry-on bag of the flight attendant who had tried to chat me up.

"There they are." Emily, Boyd's girlfriend and Val's best friend, and my younger brother had come inside the airport to meet us.

Hugs were exchanged, and Val and Emily linked arms as we walked to the car.

"Dude. How's surgery?" Boyd was as upbeat as he always was.

"Shit. I hate it. The consultant's a wanker, and the registrar isn't much better." My shoulders tensed as I once again thought about work.

"Knew it wasn't for you. You're too sensitive and kind and caring to be a surgeon. You should try psych. I did the best placement there last year. If I wasn't so hell-bent on paeds, I'd be leaning that way myself. I mean, it's like a puzzle, and—"

"Yeah. I get it. But I actually wonder if medicine is for me. I mean, have I only done it because I'm a Hartman? Look at how happy Val is. Perhaps I was meant to do something else too."

Boyd looked at me as if I had multiple heads. "Like what?"

"I don't know. Perhaps it's just a quarter-life crisis. Christian hates working at the mines and is thinking about packing it in."

Christian had been my best friend since school. He'd studied engineering and taken a job on a mine site. The pay was amazing, but he hated the isolation. He also hadn't been able to swing his roster to get the weekend off for the gala.

"What does Christian want to do?" Boyd asked as I lifted my suit bag into the boot of my brother's car.

"Medicine. It's fucking baffling."

"Where's your next rotation? Have you got something to look forward to?"

"Gastroenterology. So no."

"I would have thought bums would be right up your alley." Boyd high-fived his girlfriend as if he'd cracked the joke of the century.

If only it were that easy, I thought to myself. Studying had always interested me. I'd sit in the library for hours and read journal articles on the latest medical breakthroughs. I had no time now to read. Work, overtime, sleep, repeat. I hadn't exercised in months. No runs and no gym sessions. Through school and at uni, I was on the cricket team, but I'd been unable to find a team in Brisbane to join that would fit with my work hours.

DAD HAD BAKED a lasagne for dinner, and Giles, Bridget, and their daughters had joined us. Giles and Bridget had moved home to Cassowary Point just before Christmas and were raving about their new home that was almost ready for them to move into.

Millie, their eldest, was asleep on the couch, and I held Mia as she played with my short beard. I missed having my brother in Brisbane. Despite Val moving in with them when Bridget was pregnant with Mia, I often babysat Millie when she was younger. Giles had always said he wanted to be the cool uncle before he met Bridget, and now here I was destined to fulfil this role.

I kissed Mia's head as I tried to coax her to sleep by stroking her back. My brothers were partnered up, and my sister, although seven years younger than me, had a steady stream of boyfriends. She didn't care if a relationship worked out or not. I knew she was in no hurry to marry or even settle, but I felt like I was. I wanted stability, and I wanted to be loved. Yes, my family loved me, but I wanted more. Surely I was worthy of that.

Chapter 2

Ken

"**B**ut, Kandiah, we'll never see you. First, you refuse to be an accountant, then you decide to work on the other side of the country." My mother was crying, but this was nothing new.

"*Am'mā*, your and Father's parents left their families and moved to another country. I'll still be in Australia. This is a great opportunity. Cassowary Point is the home of tropical medicine and, who knows, I might be able to transfer these skills to Sri Lanka." Not only was I excited to be able to practice my passion, I was also giddy with the thought of breaking away from my parents.

"Kandiah, there's a girl I want you to meet. Her parents are also Tamil, and she is very beautiful." My mother's emotional blackmail was not new. It was one of the reasons I needed out of here.

Kandiah, Kandiah, Kandiah. My mother used my name whenever she could. I preferred to be called Ken. I was born in Australia, as were my parents, not that you'd know it. My grandparents weren't exactly refugees, but the political situation in Sri Lanka meant staying was near impossible for them. They left family and friends and started a new life in a new country. Now I was trying to do the same, albeit in the same country, but in a different state, and my parents were objecting.

I didn't care a great deal about tropical medicine. I cared even less for women, but my parents didn't understand. Being the long-awaited son after two daughters made me *special* in their eyes. My sisters married young, both marriages arranged by my parents. They seemed happy, and my brothers-in-law were nice enough men, but I knew I would never be happy with a match designed by my folks.

When I was fifteen, I declared my love for a schoolmate in a note I left in his locker. My parents threatened to send me to conversion therapy. I'd heard stories of the barbaric practice and decided it was easier to conform to their ideals.

My parents had grown up religious but had been indoctrinated into a fundamentalist church that was very traditional in its family values. Their church didn't accept homosexuality, believing it was a sign that you had been influenced by Satan. Instead, I told them I was joking and had been dared by some Australian boys to write the note, and it was all a big joke.

My parents found a new school for me. Well, my father did, and my mother went along with whatever he decreed. I wouldn't be surprised if Mum handed Dad her ballot papers on election day and let him cast her vote as he decided everything else in her life. A shudder went through me when I remembered the time I approached Mum when I was about twenty-one and told her that Dad was controlling her, and she was in an abusive marriage. She told me to mind my own business.

After all these years, I was sick of minding my own business.

When my parents caught me out with the note at school, I pretended to be attracted to women, but I wasn't. Every so often, I'd go on a date to appease them, but there was never any spark. I pretended to date an Australian woman for a while at uni. We'd had sex, but I never found it that fulfilling, and she knew I only got into it when I was thinking about men.

Even though I accepted there was no way I could stand up to my parents about my sexuality, I'd been able to put my foot down about my future career almost three years into an accountancy degree. I'd failed three subjects and told them I was going to drop out and stack shelves at the supermarket if they didn't let me study my passion. They relented and accepted I wanted to be a doctor.

Medicine was an alternative they sort of approved of. I remember my father shaking his head as my mother told me I should take over the family accountancy business. When I pointed out my father had wanted to return to the family tea farm in Sri Lanka when he was my age, they soon shut up.

After failing several subjects, I was made to undertake a bridging course before starting medicine. This meant I was now almost thirty years old and only just starting my intern year. I'd chosen to apply inter-state because I needed to put some distance between me and my family. I wanted to go somewhere I could discover who I was. I'd never been with a man before, despite crushing on colleagues and guys at uni. In the back of my mind, I worried that my parents would find out and punish me by making me pray for hours and read my Bible. It wasn't lost on me that I was more concerned about my parents' views about me than I was about God's. Probably because I wasn't even sure there was such a thing as God these days, anyway.

I still lived with my parents, being unable to afford to live close to campus. Although I'd turned away from organised religion in my teens, my father read the Bible to us every night after dinner. They hosted a regular Wednesday evening house group, which I got out of by finding an after-hours job cleaning offices. That was acceptable to them. Working in a bar, or a takeaway shop, or even a supermarket was totally beneath our station. I never told them I was expected to clean on Friday evenings and instead cleaned on Sunday mornings to get out of worship. It suited me.

My family thought my move was quick, but I simply hadn't told them until a week before I left. It was a crazy week filled with emotional blackmail from my mother and my oldest sister. My father had ignored me, which suited me just fine.

I needed this change in my life and told my parents that I was inter-ested in tropical medicine, picking a spot on the map that was as far away from Perth as possible. My mother cried as I boarded the plane. My father had been stoic, but I could see the disappointment on his face.

The guilt I felt as the plane soared higher in the sky and further away from Perth changed to a feeling of relief. I knew I was doing the right thing for me. I had to be. It was time for me to start living my life.

FINDING AN APARTMENT HAD BEEN A CHALLENGE, but Billie, a second-year-out doctor, took a chance on me and let me take the spare bedroom in her home. She hadn't planned on staying in Cassowary Point beyond her first year, but she had failed to secure a position back in Brisbane. Billie was outgoing and determined to be an obstetrician. My first rotation was in obstetrics and gynaecology, rather ironic seeing I wasn't that interested in vulvas and vaginas. Billie and I would spend time in the evenings talking about what I'd experienced. She lent me textbooks and sent me journal articles. It was a huge help to get on top of the subject matter.

"Kenny." Billie bounded in one evening. "You're coming to the Cardiac Gala Ball, aren't you?"

I'd seen posters around the hospital advertising it. "I wasn't planning on it, no."

"Come on. It will be a chance for you to meet some guys and, who knows, maybe do some of that exploration you seem to want to do. Micky has a spare ticket, and I told him you'd take it."

Micky was Billie's boyfriend and a nurse in the emergency department. He all but lived with us.

"I don't have a suit."

"We'll find you one. You can hire one if all else fails." The idea of wearing a suit worn by others saw me shudder. "It's the party of the year, bigger than the Junior Doctor Ball in August. So, I'll tell Micky you'll take the ticket. It's all for a great cause."

Great cause or not, I'd always avoided formal dos. I'd never gone to prom at school or balls organised at uni. I owned a cheap grey suit, but I'd only worn it at graduation and for my interview to work at Cassowary Point.

There was no way of arguing with Billie, though. The vibration of my phone stopped our conversation.

I'd kept my phone on silent, but it didn't prevent the irritation from my mother's daily pestering. She left messages, and one of my sisters had shown her how to text. In all caps, she told me that there was a daughter of a client of my father's in Cassowary Point, and we needed to meet up.

Moving across the country hadn't stopped her harassing me. I would never be who she wanted me to be. There was no way I was marrying a Sri Lankan woman and adding to the family lineage like she wanted me to. My sisters each had two children. I would have loved to raise a child and show them how unconditional love truly worked, but that was unlikely.

I turned my attention back to Billie. "Fine," I huffed. "I'll go, but I'm not wearing a suit someone else has worn. I may not be able to get a dinner suit in this town, but I can get a black one and a shirt and a black tie and maybe even shiny shoes."

There was something about shiny shoes that appealed to me. I'd never been into fashion, but the thought of looking nice and maybe even finding a man to kiss appealed. Fuck, what was I thinking? Thinking back to the sloppy uncomfortable kisses I'd shared with women, I doubted anyone would want to kiss me. Clearly, I was the world's worst kisser. Plus, how would I know if a man was interested? I'd never hung out in the gay crowd, and my education on such matters had been from online searches and, well, porn.

I hoped that once the time was right, I'd know how to suck a cock or prepare an arsehole. Fuck, I hoped my partner knew how to prepare mine. I fantasised about both screwing and being screwed. Being away from the confines of living with my parents, I'd even browsed websites selling butt plugs, but I was yet to pull the trigger and order one. I pretended to look at my phone, realising I'd caught myself fantasising about butt plugs in front of my housemate. I hoped she didn't notice the heat that crept up my face from my neck.

Naïve and innocent. That was me. I was basically an almost thirty-year-old virgin. I'd told myself that one bonus of being on obs and gynae was that I was unlikely to meet patients who I might see if I found myself at a gay bar. One of the first babies I'd been involved in bringing into the world had been for a gay couple and their surrogate. The scared part of me couldn't see that new parents would be unlikely to be out at a gay bar, let alone that they would recognise me. I wasn't out. I hated the idea that I would somehow out myself prematurely and people would judge me like my parents had done.

I'd opened up to Billie on my first night in town, telling her about my parents and my sexuality, and she was determined to find me someone. Micky had a colleague in the ED who was recently single, but there was nothing there when he showed me a photo of him. I'm sure he's a nice guy, and looks aren't everything, but he did nothing for me.

Perhaps I was picky. I knew from the porn I'd watched I liked the idea of a man who was, well, like me. Leanish and fit. I had nothing against body hair, and my chest was covered in it, but I wanted someone smooth. Well, hard and smooth. Although, at this stage, I wondered if I might need to accept what I could—the whole beggars can't be choosers thing.

"I TAKE it I'll be seeing you all Saturday night?" Bridget Hartman was the registrar on our team. She was a no-nonsense kind of woman, and I would hate to be the one to be told off by her.

The department was abuzz with talk of the Cardiac Gala Ball, with several people referring to it as the Hartman Gala. I suspected it was run by her family, probably her parents. People talked about the Hartman home being impressive, with amazing views of Cassowary Point. Others had complained you could get anywhere in this hospital if your surname was Hartman. Gossip had never interested me, and I really didn't mind who was with whom in the department and which other staff members to butter up or avoid. I'd rather take people as I found them and learnt long ago I caught more flies with honey than with vinegar.

"It sounds like a good cause, and I'm going, but, to be honest, the idea of Valentine's gives me the... Sorry, Dr Hartman. It's important to your family, and that was insensitive of me."

"Kandiah." Bridget preferred to use my full name, despite my protests. "You sound just like my husband used to. I hope that one day you can be proven as wrong as he was. Love can be very special. Now, on maternity..."

Bridget proceeded with our rundown of inpatients and those in the birthing suites, even though as interns, we rarely got to help catch babies.

I HAD ten weeks to go on this rotation. Then I'd be in psych. This was what I wanted to do. I'd loved my psych placements as a student. Sure, I'd met some people with severe delusions and horrible life experiences, but I also saw hope a lot of the time. I didn't want to pursue it to piss off my parents, but I knew it would bother them. Well, it would bother them more than being a surgeon or working in the emergency department.

My first two weeks as an actual doctor had been eye opening. It was nothing like medical school. Now I was writing prescriptions and making decisions that could be life or death for my patients. Bridget was a great mentor. I knew little about her, but I liked her attitude. She always advocated we spend time away from the hospital and sent me home if I tried to stay around too long after my shift had ended.

I would have preferred to stay longer today.

"C'mon, Ken. The shops await." Billie had found me at a computer after my shift had ended.

My shoulders slumped as I thought about shopping for a suit for Saturday night. It had been a rough day. Fourteen-year-olds should not be having babies; they were children themselves.

"One guy Micky knows says there are lovely black suits at Central." Cassowary Central was the largest shopping centre in town.

"Whatever. Let's just get this over with." I pushed myself away from the desk after shutting down the computer. Discharge summaries could wait until tomorrow.

It didn't take long to get to the crowded shopping centre. Despite Billie's enthusiasm and joy at finding a car park straight away, I had trouble finding any form of excitement.

Going to a Valentine's-themed ball when single and in the closet did not sound like my idea of fun. I kept reminding myself that it was for the hospital, and the funds would be well used.

"Well hello. Aren't you the most delectable package of man-meat! How can I help?" An older man, complete with a tape measure slung around his neck and a limp wrist that he held in front of himself, greeted us when we entered the menswear section of the local upmarket department store. "No, don't tell me, black suit for the ball Saturday night?"

"Nolan, act nice." Billie slapped his chest and gave him a kiss on the cheek before straightening the name badge across the pocket of the white button up the sales assistant wore. "This is Ken, Micky's friend he was telling you about, and he's a little shy, but he needs to be the beau of the ball."

"Well, Kenderella, I am your fairy godfather. Now, we don't have any dinner suits, but there's some new Hugo Boss just landed today. You don't mind wearing Hugo, do you?" Did I? I had no idea. "Now you need a white shirt to show off that stunning complexion, and what about a tie? Royal blue or red would suit you."

"Black will be fine." Billie elbowed me in the ribs at my shortness with the sales assistant.

"Boring, but whatever. And shoes?"

"I don't suppose…" I swallowed. "Have you got shiny shoes?"

"Oh, honey, for you, I'll shine them myself. But yes, we have shoes."

For all his flamboyance, Nolan put me at ease. He measured around my neck and across my shoulders. When I asked if he needed to measure my inner leg, he winked and told me he could guess.

Sure, he was flirtatious, but it felt harmless. If anything, it made me feel more comfortable with the whole situation.

The suit looked alright. Ideally, the sleeves would have been an inch or two longer, but I had orangutan arms and often found it hard to find clothes that fit well.

Before I could change back into my usual clothes, Billie was in the change room with more shirts for me to try on. I instantly decided they were too loud and out there, shaking my head at her.

"Kenny, try them on," she begged. "You're the only person who doesn't wear a tropical shirt on Fridays, and your wardrobe needs brightening." I wasn't the only person, but I didn't dress for Tropical Friday.

"I like my plain shirts," I replied.

"They're boring, aren't they, Nolan?" Billie called through the curtain, and I heard the lurking sales assistant chuckle.

Perhaps that was me, though. Perhaps I was just boring. I was the plain guy wanting to shrink into the background. This was strange, seeing I usually stuck out like a sore thumb with my Sri Lankan heritage.

"Your shirts are two sizes too big. You have a lovely body; you should show it off." Nolan whipped open the curtain and undid the buttons on the shirt I was wearing.

My cheeks flushed, and I felt a heat spreading down to my chest. I wasn't a slob, but I wasn't in the best shape. I wanted to join a gym and get back into cricket, but work was keeping me too busy. Well, that was the excuse I used. I'd only been here a month, and the first few weeks, especially the ten days of orientation and training, had taken their toll.

A lot of the new doctors had studied together. I was the only person from the West Coast, and I didn't know anyone. It wasn't like I had friends back home either, though. The friends my parents had allowed me to have there were from the local Tamil community and were married and fathers. They'd listened to their parents' dreams and followed them. I'd rebelled.

"That is hot," Billie exclaimed as she fanned herself with her hand as I buttoned up a blue-and-green floral shirt and rolled the sleeves to my elbows. It was too warm to wear long sleeves.

Standing in front of the mirror, it looked, well, different to what I was used to. I looked different, less conservative. What struck me most was the grin on my face as I saw the transformation a different wardrobe could make. Nolan produced two more shirts in unique patterns, and I tried them on, each one making me smile a little more. I bought the three of them—a deep-red paisley print and a purple-and-yellow floral on white as well as the original I had tried on. They'd all go with the chinos I regularly wore.

Nolan had come through with shiny shoes in my size. My parents would have said they were an extravagance, as I couldn't wear them every day. I didn't care. For once, I was getting what *I* wanted.

I baulked at the total and hoped Nolan received a decent commission. I had money from my first paycheques, and although I wanted to save, at least shopping now would mean I could avoid it for another year.

When I got home and hung my purchases in my wardrobe, I discovered he'd thrown in some rainbow socks to go with the shoes. Perhaps Billie had said something to him, but I wondered if other people detected my queerness despite me hiding in the closet. Despite my parents, I wasn't ashamed of who I was. This simple act, a pair of socks, brought tears to my eyes, and I was determined to wear them to the gala.

I realised that there was no need to hide in any closet in Cassowary Point. I came here to be me, and perhaps I just needed to practice the whole putting myself out there. Fuck. I was too old. I would scare men off.

"Get out of your head, Kenny." Billie leant against my door jamb.

"It's just... I want to get out there and meet someone, but I don't know how." My head hung as I closed the drawer, hiding the socks.

"Just talk to someone."

She made it sound so easy. "But how will I know if they're, like, interested?"

"Oh, honey. Trust me, you'll know. I don't think you realise what a catch you are. I mean, you're fucking hot as, but also, you're a genuinely lovely person. Now, are you going to cook tonight, or will it be pizza?"

I loved to cook. I'd stocked the pantry with plenty of spices when I moved in and often whipped up a curry for Billie, Micky, and me after work. There was a chicken in the fridge, and cooking would help me relax.

Billie was right. I was too far in my head. I made the decision that Saturday night was going to be it. I was going to talk to a man and see where it led. Who knew, it might lead to something special.

Chapter 3

Henry

Mum and Dad's was crowded. Giles, Bridget, and the girls were living here whilst they waited for their new home to be finished. Boyd and Emily had moved out when Giles and Bridget moved in, but they still hung around there more often than not.

I'd suggested Boyd host dinner at their new digs, but Emily laughed. It was apparently a tiny flat with one bedroom and a living area that only had room for a couch that was less than a meter from their television. The picture Boyd painted was one of living in a doll's house, but he and Emily appeared to be as loved up as ever.

I sat around the pool with my younger brother as Giles bathed his daughters upstairs and Val caught up with Mum in the kitchen. Emily was a pianist and had a gig playing at a restaurant on Friday nights, so she wasn't there. Boyd had produced a couple of beers. It was warm out, and the cool amber nectar was perfect.

"You popping the question tomorrow night, then?" I asked my younger brother, cognisant of my elder brother asking Bridget to marry him at the gala five years ago.

"Nah. I mean, we're going to get married. That's a given. We don't need an engagement. We'll just tell you when to turn up for the wedding." Boyd shrugged, a wistful look in his eyes. I envied the love he'd found so young.

"If you'd thought about it, you should have just arranged the wedding for tomorrow night. I mean, we'll all be there, and I suspect most of your friends will be, too."

He shrugged. "We don't want big and flashy. We're not in any hurry, anyway. What about you? Seeing anyone?"

"A married douche tried to chat up Val and me on the plane. I seem to attract guys who either aren't available or aren't out, or just don't want a relationship. I haven't had sex this year," I admitted, playing with the label on the beer bottle I'd taken a swig from.

"What, like six weeks?" he gasped dramatically. "Shit, dude. Is it broken?"

I scoffed. "It works."

Six weeks. More like six months. Sure, I joked about my hand getting a workout, but my desire had also waned. Oh, to be twenty, like Val, again.

Perhaps I'd hit my sexual peak and was on the downhill slide.

As I lay in bed later, I doubted this. I could hear my parents hard at it from two bedrooms away. I hoped Millie was a heavy sleeper. No wonder Giles and Bridget slept downstairs in the guest room with Mia in a portable cot. Mum claimed she loved getting up for the girls, but Millie rarely woke overnight. It was me lying awake tonight. I'd never had trouble sleeping before this year. Now I lay in bed stressing about work, worried I had to choose a path that would determine the rest of my career.

Giles always knew he wanted to be a cardiologist. Bridget did too at first until she had a child of her own, then obstetrics and gynaecology won out. Boyd has always dreamt of being a paediatrician, and Emily was convinced she wanted to be a general practitioner. I thought back to my rotations last year. I enjoyed working with the geriatrician, but dealing with dementia and aging all day every day didn't sound like fun. Emergency medicine had been a lot of fun, but I was that bit more reserved, plus the idea of constantly being in a fast-paced environment didn't really excite me. Orthopaedics had been alright, but should, perhaps, have told me I wasn't cut out for surgery. There was always general medicine. I was scheduled to do a term in endocrinology later in the year, and that might be interesting.

Perhaps I wasn't cut out for medicine at all. Maybe I needed to do something else entirely.

I must have drifted off to sleep at some stage, because I was woken with a little face in mine, a finger poking my cheek. "Hammy, I did a wee."

"Did you wet the bed, Mills?" I asked my young niece.

"No!" She was indignant. "I went to the toilet like a big girl. Can we play?"

It was too early. "We can play pretending to sleep in Hammy's bed if you like."

It appeared the three-year-old did like this. I had no idea what the time was, but the sun wasn't yet up. Millie's small fingers stroked my cheek. She smelt of baby shampoo and lavender. I knew her mother sprinkled her pillow with lavender oil each night. Perhaps that was what I needed.

When I woke again, it was to giggles and the artificial sound of a camera shuttering, courtesy of Giles's phone.

"I hope you're wearing jocks at least, Uncle Hammy." Giles laughed from the doorway.

I was and wasn't even sprouting morning wood. Perhaps I was broken.

"Mills did a wee," I muttered, yearning for more sleep.

"Did you wet the bed, little miss?" Giles asked as Millie ran to her dad for a hug.

"No, silly. I used the toilet like a big girl."

"You didn't need to disturb Uncle Hammy."

"But I love Uncle Hammy."

My heart skipped a beat at Millie's declaration. It was nice to realise that someone loved me, even if she was three years old.

SPENDING the day with my nieces was lovely. Mum, Bridget, Emily, and Val spent the afternoon at the hairdresser. Val had forgotten her shoes for the gala, so an emergency trip into town was required. At the last one, Val had worn Doc Martens, but she was now that bit more grown up and wanted strappy sandals. I would have gone with her, as I love shopping, but the lure of a tea party with Millie won out. Giles had already shared the photo he had snapped of the two of us in bed with every family member he could think of.

"Grampy, come and have tea with Hammy, please." Millie dragged Dad from his seat where he was reading the newspaper.

I was glad Giles wasn't around, as Millie had us perched on the tiniest chairs, our knees around our ears. This would have seen more photographic evidence being shared. She poured water from the plastic teapot and pretended to cut cake for us to eat.

"Are you joining us, sunshine?" Dad asked his eldest granddaughter.

"No, silly. I'm the waitress. Can I get you anything else?"

"I'll have an Old Fashioned and a few more hours sleep please," I mused.

"I can only do tea and cake, Uncle Hammy." Millie placed her hands on her hips and shook her head as she went towards the kitchen.

"Do we need to see what she's up to?" I asked Dad.

"No. She'll be fine. She's a great kid. Reminds me of you a little. You used to hold tea parties. You poured water into Boyd's mouth when he was six weeks old!"

I hadn't remembered this story. "So, it was clear from an early age that I was gay, then." I laughed.

"There's more to you than your sexuality, son. Boyd loved playing tea parties, too." Even Dad's tone spoke of love. I'd always valued Dad's wisdom, so I figured I could pick his brain about work.

"How did you choose cardiology, or was it because it was what your dad had done?"

"It fascinated me. How's surgery?"

"I hate it." I knew I could be candid with Dad.

Dad's lips rose in a sardonic smile. "Never would have guessed that."

"Really?"

"You're not slimy enough. No, that's not right. Not all surgeons are slimy buggers, but they seem to think they know it all. Then again, I think we all think we know it all in our own disciplines and forget that we trained in many disciplines before we specialised."

"I'm not sure I'm cut out for medicine." I hung my head as I grasped the small cup Millie had poured for me.

"Medicine as in being a doctor? I think you're an amazing doctor, but you would also be amazing at anything you put your mind to." I loved how judgement free Dad could be.

"That's the thing. I love it, well, I did, but I haven't found my niche." I wished Millie had served us alcohol.

"What rotations are yet to come this year?"

"Fucking gastro next, then intensive care. They've mentioned endocrinology, but I'll probably be general med or surg at the end and work nights and weekends."

"Don't write off anything."

"Yeah, right." I tried not to scoff, but I felt as though I was writing off all I had studied for.

"I'm serious." Dad paused as he obviously thought about what to say next. "You seem down, son. There's no harm in seeking help."

Fuck. If my father, the cardiologist, could see I was down, then I most definitely was. I didn't really have a general practitioner in Brisbane. I went to the student medical centre a few times when I had tonsillitis, but I hadn't needed a doctor in years.

"Yeah, maybe. I'm not suicidal or anything, so don't stress about that. I'm, well, I'm lonely. Christian's no longer around, and as much as I love Val, she's hardly ever at home."

"Perhaps Brisbane isn't for you, and you need to head home here?"

That sounded more like Mum than Dad. I knew she wanted nothing more than for all of us to move back to Cassowary Point. Maybe one day, but what was here for me, apart from my brother and his family and my parents?

FIVE YEARS AGO, Mum and Dad hosted their first Valentine's gala. Being in Brisbane studying, I'd missed most of Mum's flaps when things hadn't gone as planned. I mean, hosting a gala in a marquee on a lawn in the wet season is bound to cause some problems, but try to explain that to my mother.

The weather gods had been on our side again this year, despite the rain the day before. The marquee looked amazing, and Mum and Bridget had spent Friday hanging fairy lights and ensuring things were arranged just as they wanted. Five years ago, silver accessories had decorated the space, but these had made way for a stylised pearl, signifying their thirtieth wedding anniversary.

I envied my parents and their love. To see my elder brother and his wife together over the last five years, emulating the love my parents have always embodied, has added to my depressed state. As much as I could desire love, I couldn't force anyone to fall in love with me. Hell, I've thought I've been in love over and over, and believed in love at first sight, but nothing has ever lasted.

As I glanced in the mirror and tied my black silk bow tie, I thought back to my conversation with Dad. Not good enough. As in, I wasn't. I may look handsome as fuck, even if I said so myself, but looks weren't everything. Work might be easier if I had someone at home to care for, to look out for. Someone who could look out for me. It wasn't that I felt I needed to be in a relationship to be happy, but I wanted what my brothers and parents had.

Giles has suggested I look out for Val tonight, concerned she's going to embarrass the family. He'd obviously forgotten what he was like at her age. Heck, even at my twenty-first, he hooked up with someone who helped with the catering. Fuck's sake, bro. Leave her alone. Val was more than capable of handling herself.

"Hey, Uncle Hammy, you ready?" Val knocked at my open door. She looked amazing in a black silk number with pearl earrings.

"Yeah. Not feeling it tonight, but fake it 'til you make it, hey?" I replied, a smile crossing my lips but not meeting my eyes.

"You look spunky as. I'm guessing Prince Charming is waiting out there for you. Em texted. She and Boyd are downstairs, waiting. Mum wants some photos."

Mum always wanted photos. "What about you? Think your Prince Charming might be there tonight?"

"Fuck that. No way. I'm not marrying a doctor. Anything but a doctor."

"Famous last words, Val. Famous last words."

I loved my family, and I loved being around them. I missed my parents and their constant presence, even though it had been over seven years since I lived at home. Perhaps that was what it was—I was experiencing the seven-year itch, except it was me wanting to be closer to my parents. Freud would have a field day with this.

I didn't have to lie, complimenting the women of my family on how amazing they looked. My parents and brothers were definitely loved up. I wanted to look at someone the way Dad gazed at Mum and have someone look at me the way Bridget eyed Giles.

"That's it, bro. I've had enough of this loved up shit. As the two single kids in the family, we owe it to our siblings to mingle and show how awesome single life can be." Val grabbed me by the arm and led me to the marquee.

Some people had arrived via the buses that transported folks to my parents' home from various pickup points in town. I recognised a few people as friends and colleagues of my parents. I'd been gone long enough that many people had no idea who I was. I quite liked this anonymity.

Val had bumped into an old school friend and was busy reacquainting herself with local gossip from the last few years. I made my way to the bar and grabbed a beer. Champagne was flowing, but I didn't feel like celebrating.

"No. Fucking. Way!" There was a scream from the other side of the marquee, which made me look. "Hen?"

"Billie, I didn't know you were up here."

I'd studied with Billie and loved the way she could make anyone at ease in any situation. I'd done a placement with her and learnt so much about interpersonal relationships and how to speak to patients, even though she was a medical student like me.

"Hen, this is Ken, my housemate. Hen and I were at uni together in Brissy."

I may have told myself merely hours ago that I no longer believed in love at first sight, but the tall, dark, and incredibly handsome specimen of a man with Billie had my mouth dry and my hands clammy.

There was no magic signal that we gays used to determine if others share our orientation. Sure, there was perhaps a gaydar, but mine often failed me. Nothing was working with this man. We held eye contact for a little more than normal, but he quickly looked away as if he'd been caught. In my head, I had to assume he was straight. Fuck, did Billie introduce him as the guy she lived with or as a flatmate? For all I knew, he was her partner.

I couldn't stop looking at this man. "Has anyone ever told you, I mean, those eyes..." I was screwing this up.

"Okay, you two. Behave. Or not." She giggled. "I've just seen..." And Billie was off, leaving me alone with Ken.

Ken was divine. I'd taken a course once in mindfulness where you trained yourself to scan your body from head to toe and take in how you were feeling in each part. Right now, my whole body was zapping with electricity. My heart raced, and my eyes simply wanted to stare at this amazing specimen in front of me.

The way his dark, milk chocolate-coloured hair sat on top of his head in waves that looked as though they were inviting my fingers to thread through them was one thing, but it had been his eyes that captivated me. At first glance, they appeared to be a deep ebony, but there were flecks of topaz around the iris. Framed by the longest lashes I had ever seen on a man. I was glad for my dry mouth, as it meant I wasn't drooling.

"Drink?" Ken asked, clearing his throat. I wondered if he was as nervous as I was.

"We are standing at a bar, I suppose." Fuck. I was blowing this. "I mean, yes, a drink sounds amazing."

A bartender handed us both a bottle of beer, and I took it as an opportunity to let my eyes rake over him again. The white of Ken's shirt cuffs highlighted the deep caramel of his skin. Seeing his long fingers grip the neck of the beer bottle had my mind in overdrive, wanting to feel those fingers caress my neck. Shit, where had that thought come from? I didn't usually think like this, but my cock was enjoying the imagery and let me know it was on board with getting to know this man better. His suit jacket sleeves were an inch or so too short, but it fit perfectly across his shoulders. They weren't broad, but they suited him perfectly.

"You, um, work at the hospital?" I asked, my beer suddenly empty, but I didn't remember drinking a drop.

"Yeah." Ken may have looked as though he came from a subcontinental heritage, but his accent was as Australian as mine. Well, from what I could tell from the few words he'd spoken.

Ken had also finished his beer. We'd made our way to a small table near the bar. The marquee had filled and was abuzz with laughter and excitement. I was abuzz with, well, something. Fuck, for all I knew, Ken was a straight dude who was being polite by hanging around me. The band started up, and people started hitting the dance floor.

My inner dialogue was going a mile a minute. I told myself that Ken wasn't a colleague. Heck, I had no idea what he did at the hospital, and knowing Billie, she would have befriended a cleaner or orderly. She said she'd studied with him. Did that mean medicine? This was an opportunity to put myself out there. I didn't get the impression Ken would be violent if I made a pass and he was offended, but, then again, it wouldn't be the first time I'd dodged a fist in a straight venue. I was always too eager and my gaydar often let me down.

"I love this song," I announced. The band had started the John-Paul Young classic 'Love is in the Air'. "Do you, like, want to dance?"

I looked for the fist to rise, or even a palm telling me I had the wrong idea, but I was greeted by a smile that made me wonder how I'd missed Ken's lips before now.

"Yeah. I think I'd like that."

I was no *Fred Astaire*, but I knew more moves than the step-tap or slow sway a lot of men seemed to rely on. Ken also knew how to move his body to the music. Several songs later, we were still out there, our moves becoming more adventurous and several touches happening with no hints they weren't wanted on either side.

We paused for speeches, my father being overly soppy towards my mother, and my mother reminding people we were there to raise money for the cardiac department at the hospital. A few hours ago, their words of love and connection would have seen me roll my eyes, but simply dancing with Ken had seen a lightness overcome me that hadn't been there for months.

Once again, the band started up. They were talented musicians who seemed to know exactly what to play when it was needed. I tried to not get ahead of myself when I mouthed the words to the INXS classic 'Need You Tonight' to Ken, and later on laughed at Ken's interpretation of riding horses way up in the sky.

"Hey, folks." The lead singer removed the microphone from the holder, flicking the cord away from the stand. "We're Medically Induced, and if you see us around the halls of the hospital, give us a wave. The auction is almost here, but beforehand, this one's for Dr Hills, a fucking MILF, if ever I saw one."

I scrunched my face in disgust that anyone would think about my mother like that. Ken threw his arm around my shoulder, laughing. The crowd quietened as the singer crooned out the opening lines of the Hunters and Collectors classic 'Throw Your Arms Around Me'. This had always been one of Mum's favourites and often played around the house.

Glancing around the dance floor, I saw Mum and Dad in each other's arms, Mum seemingly having taken no offence at the lead singer's declaration. Her eyes locked with my father's. Bridget and Giles were nearby with Boyd and Emily, all three couples swaying to the music.

Ken's arm moved from around my shoulders to around my neck as our bodies moved together. I discovered his lean frame was still muscular as I wrapped my hands around his waist, and our chests touched.

There was no way I could tell where my parents or siblings danced. I could hardly hear the music. My eyes found Ken's and were greeted with a look of desire. Licking my lips, I wanted to close the distance between our faces, but instead, I bit my bottom lip between my teeth.

Ever so slowly, our heads moved closer. I could feel the heat between us. My hands wandered up Ken's back, eliciting a smile from his eyes. I assume it would have crossed his mouth too, however, our lips had brushed together in the slightest of touches. We both pressed our lips forward and captured a small, tender kiss before our mouths crashed together.

Ken's lips looked soft and pillowy, but there was a firmness behind them that made me ache for more. I have no idea whose mouth opened first, but soon, tongues lashed together, and Ken's arms around my neck drew me to him.

My eyes were closed, savouring this experience. If I'd ever been kissed like this, I'd forgotten about it. Who was this man, and why was I so lucky to meet him tonight? His hand cradled the back of my head as our bodies pressed together, our hard lengths digging into each other. A cheer came up from the crowd as the auctioneer took the stage, and our moment was broken. Pressing my forehead into Ken's, I longed to drag him to the pool house, or even into my bedroom in my parents' home.

I yearned to know more about him, who he was, and what he did. I wanted to get to know him. If one kiss had seen my heart melt, then what could more do? My eyes were still closed as the auctioneer started the bidding on a signed football. Feeling Ken's hand move from the back of my head, I slowly opened my eyes, expecting to see the same awe and joy on his face as was on mine. Instead, I saw the back of his head as he turned away and ran from the marquee.

Chapter 4

Ken

As much as I'd complained about going to the gala with Billie, I was glad when we boarded the bus that would take us to the venue. There was a buzz of excitement, and it was great seeing people all dressed up.

My suit could have fitted better, but it would do. My gangly arms often had trouble with shirts and jackets. This time, I'd found a shirt with long enough sleeves, but I could have done with an extra inch or two on the jacket. Having shiny shoes made up for it, though. Even Micky had commented on them, and, seeing he was wearing black running shoes, I doubted my ill-fitting suit would be noticed that much, anyway. I'd just stand with my arms behind my back.

Billie knew everyone. Whereas I recognised faces, she knew names and little things about people. She knew that Nadir, one of the cleaners on the ward, had a five-year-old daughter who just started school, and Bob, one of the wardies who helped transport patients, whose daughter had recently become engaged. It shouldn't have surprised me when she entered the marquee and started introducing me to people.

I was awestruck by how beautiful the interior was. Thousands of fairy lights provided a warm glow, and strands of what I assumed were fake pearls swooped around the perimeter and were interspersed with the floral arrangements on the tables.

It wasn't a sit-down affair, but there was seating for those who didn't want to dance. I loved dancing. In year ten at school, we took dance classes with the year nine girls from a neighbouring school. I would have done almost anything to dance with Sean Carmody, but it would never have been allowed, and I doubted Sean would have been up for it, anyway.

"Hen!" Billie shrieked across the marquee. I may never have been with a man before, but I knew how to appreciate and recognise a good-looking one. My breath hitched as Billie drew me towards this hunk of a specimen.

A few inches taller than me, his hazel eyes captivated me. His lean physique looked phenomenal in the well-cut suit he wore. It was a toss-up between stroking the satin lapels of his jacket or the short beard that covered his chin, but I kept my hands by my side and resisted the temptation. There was a length to the top of his hair, pushed back on his head by fingers running through it, lighter highlights hinting at time in the sun.

Billie must have known he was into guys to introduce us, but I had no way of making sure. I felt like an imposter. Flirting had never been my strong suit, and here was a guy I was heavily attracted to. My cock was rising from its slumber at the thought of being touched by him.

In the end, flirting didn't matter. Cutting up the dance floor together was where it was at. Hen was a great dancer. He laughed at my stupid moves and way-out arm movements and even twirled me in and out from him a few times. When our hands touched, it felt like a jolt of electricity went straight from my fingers to my heart.

When the slow song came on and Hen moved closer, it was a given I would wrap my arms around his neck and draw him close. My fingers toyed with the back of his hair, short at the nape and soft and silky. The sensation of having him run his hands up and down my back was exquisite.

The kiss didn't take me by surprise. We'd been building up to it. Sure, I'd kissed women before, but it wasn't like kissing Hen. His lips were firm, and his beard scratched at my chin. My mind ran away with me, wondering what it would be like to have this mouth on my cock, or my mouth on his.

There was still another voice in my head, though. Here I was on the other side of the country, and yet my father was chastising me for bringing shame on the family. The euphoria of the kiss was replaced with fear. Hen had his eyes closed as he touched his forehead to mine and took his bottom lip between his teeth.

"I... I... Um... Sorry." And I ran.

Even in my beautiful shiny shoes, I ran from the marquee and down the street. Unclipping my tie and pulling buttons off my shirt as I tried to undo the neck and get some air, my feet kept moving. Billie knew Hen, and no doubt he worked at the hospital. At some stage, our paths would cross, and he'd shake his head and shame me for running.

Family bonds and my father's voice were stronger than any physical attraction I felt for him, and I knew I had to get out of there, hating that here I was, almost thirty, and still being controlled by my parents. Tears streaked my cheeks as I found a playground at the end of a street and perched myself on a swing.

As a kid, I couldn't wait to grow up, but now, I yearned for the carefree innocence of childhood. Of being able to play with my mates and not have to worry about relationships beyond friendships. Even though my parents controlled who I played with, insisting on either other Sri Lankan children or ones from our church, I'd had fun. As I'd matured, playing outdoors morphed into cricket club and study.

My parents were grateful for the opportunities living in Australia offered us, but, like many children of migrants, they had issues with the largely progressive society. Despite my sheltered childhood, I recognised it was different to their childhoods and upbringing. They'd been moulded by their parents, who had come here for a better life, and yet still seemed to be stuck in the past.

I could still taste Hen on my lips. Parts of the kiss came back to me as if I was experiencing it again for the first time. His lips had been softer than I would have expected. The sound that came from his throat as our tongues tangled for the first time went straight to my core. Memories of the groan set my cock on edge again.

Summoning a ride from the app on my phone, I headed home and tried to forget that this evening had even happened. Sure, there may be an attraction towards Hen, whoever-he-was, but nothing good could come of it. I'd focus on medicine and leave dreams of relationships and happily ever afters to others. There was no way they were for me.

IN MY DREAM, soft lips sucked my cock, and a beard scratched against my thighs. Despite his mouth being full, I could hear dream Hen telling me about all the things he wanted to do to my body. During our kiss, I'd felt his cock pressing against my stomach, and I knew it was sizable. What would it feel like to take it deep inside me? With enough lube and preparation, I could probably do it. Would Hen like that, or would he prefer me to be penetrating him?

Sliding into his mouth in my dream was enough, but just when I was about to come, my father's voice appeared, telling me I needed to rid my mind of these impure thoughts and spend time with people who would help me pray away my depravities and remind me that men lying with men was unnatural. I woke with a start when a bucket of ice-cold water was tossed on me by my dream father. Or perhaps it should be nightmare father. My heart raced, and I was surprised to find I wasn't drenched. My cock had receded though, putting even more distance between my memories and reality. I was disappointed in myself that I was still so controlled by my parents.

The apartment was quiet. Billie was starting nights, so I knew she'd be sleeping, which was good, as I didn't want to see anyone or do anything. Sleep wasn't an option, as I worried the dreams would return. I picked up the cricket biography my sister had given me for my birthday.

Despite my parents' fundamentalist Christianity views, they still had a statue of Shiva on the mantelpiece at home. Over the years, I'd tried to reconcile the kind and progressive Jesus of the stories I'd learnt about at Sunday school and Bible classes to the judgemental God my father threatened me with. I didn't want to judge their faith or their religion, but I knew it made little sense. It may have given their lives meaning, but to me, their values were screwed. Knowing this didn't make their judgement any easier.

I'd come here to escape them, and yet their voices, especially my father's, filled my brain. I knew being gay wasn't wrong. To be honest, I didn't believe in hell, or even heaven really, so the thought of burning for eternity didn't worry me. Deep down, though, I wanted the blessing of my family. I wanted them to see me for who I was and be proud of my achievements and my relationships.

At one stage in my early teen years, I thought I could become a professional cricketer. I was a bit of an all-rounder bowling medium pace, and being quite handy with the bat, I thought that would make my parents proud. When I brought home the letter stating I'd been selected to take part in an under fourteens cricket camp, my excitement had been palpable. Until my father said no, stating that we didn't know what type of boys would be there. If we'd been in Sri Lanka, I'm not sure I would have had the same opportunities I'd had here, but I also felt like I was in-between both cultures. I was never Sri Lankan having been born here, and I'd never embraced being Australian, seeing as my parents preferred to socialise with other Sri Lankan people.

I'd made the move to Cassowary Point, though. I'd chosen to live across the country. Weekly phone calls with my parents, who still believed that phone calls were expensive, talked about inconsequential things like the weather or cricket scores. Perhaps I needed to admit to myself that making the move physically had not helped me make a mental move.

No matter how hard I tried not to think about it, the kiss was never far from my mind. I could still feel the texture of his silk-like hair in my fingers. There was no doubt I was sexually attracted to this man. I'd have to buy more lube and tissues after I'd gone through plenty of both, stroking myself to orgasm several times over the Sunday. And not because of the book I'd tried to read.

As much as I wanted to mope, I knew cooking would help me escape my thoughts and memories of the gala, and, well, that kiss. The combination of cardamom, cloves, and cinnamon took me straight back to my mother's kitchen. Perhaps I should have thought about this before I started. Being back with my family was not what I needed right now.

"Oh, yum. Chicken or fish?" Billie appeared behind me as I stirred the spices in the oil.

"Chicken."

"Smells divine as usual. Did you enjoy the ball? I lost you. Hope it means you picked up and had a night of passionate sex."

"It was fine."

"Okay. So, you don't want to talk, I get that. I'm going for a run. But first, how was Hen?"

"I don't want to talk about it." My shoulders tensed, and I stirred the pan furiously.

"I'm sorry. I thought the two of you—"

"I said I don't want to talk about it," I bit back.

I hated being short with Billie. She knew Hen, and I was embarrassed that I'd run off on him. I'd have to prepare myself to bump into him around the hospital. I could simply apologise and ask him out for a drink. Billie said she'd studied with him, plus his air gave off strong doctor vibes. He didn't seem to have the arrogance of a surgeon, but who knew where he worked?

THREE WEEKS PASSED, and I hadn't bumped into Hen at the hospital. Fortunately, Billie hadn't pushed again and didn't talk about him, but that didn't mean I'd stopped thinking about him. Recurrent dreams of our kiss and my father voicing his anger haunted me. Perhaps I needed to move on and kiss someone else to have something else to focus on.

"Hey, Kandiah, you're not working Friday night, are you?" Bridget, my registrar, had cornered me in the lunchroom.

"No, but I could pick up a shift if needed."

"No, I was wondering if you were going to Prof Gibson's retirement drinks?"

I hadn't planned to. Prof Gibson had been the head of obstetrics and gynaecology for years and was well liked around the department. I'd had very little to do with him, but he seemed nice enough.

"Come on. It will be fun. You've been extra mopey the last few weeks."

I hadn't realised she'd noticed. Bridget was a strange one. She was very black and white and could be short-tempered, but she had a softer side that she sometimes showed. I hadn't taken the time to get to know her very well, but she seemed nice enough.

THE DRINKS WERE HELD at an old warehouse on the waterfront that had been converted into a brewery. Timber pillars held up the corrugated iron roof, and the concrete floor had been polished to within an inch of its life. The area was open and spacious, but somehow not too noisy. We'd been placed in an area in front of the large tanks that brewed the beer.

Billie and Micky were already there, and both held a schooner of beer.

"Kandiah," Bridget cried as she grabbed my elbow, as I was making my way towards my housemate and her partner. "Have you met Giles, my husband?"

"Ken," I introduced myself as I shook the man's hand. He was tall and solid, with dark, curly hair.

"Do you prefer Ken or Kandiah? Bridget hates shortening names."

"Either's fine." I felt my Adam's apple bob as I swallowed the saliva that had pooled in my mouth.

"I was about to grab a beer. Can I grab you something?" Bridget asked as she trailed a hand down her husband's arm.

"Um, an IPA, or something pale, if they have it," I said, trying to fish my wallet from my pants.

Bridget simply waved my hand away and left me with her husband.

"Are you enjoying your gynae rotation?" Giles asked.

"Not really. I'm not really into vaginas." My reply saw an enormous smile cross his face.

"You sound just like my younger brother." He laughed.

36

"What about you? What do you do?" I had to place a hand in my pocket to stop fiddling.

"Cardiology reg. Will you be rotating to us this year?"

"I don't think so. Currently, I've got psych, surgery, and emergency, but we all know things can change."

Bridget returned with our drinks, but she stepped aside to take a call. The IPA was fruity, just how I liked it.

"The gala ball seemed to be a success." I didn't know what to say to my registrar's husband.

"Yeah. Still waiting on the final figures, but it was lots of fun. Mum and Dad were thrilled. I mean, anything to show their love." Giles shook his head as he smiled and squeezed his wife around her waist as she returned from her quick call.

"So, you're a Hartman?" I was still trying to work out who was who in this family.

"Yeah. Mum and Dad have almost adopted Bridget, though, as if she's always been one of theirs. Same with my youngest brother's girlfriend. Family is family, regardless of blood, and all that. Are your family close?" Giles took a swig of his beer, licking the foam off his lip. I did not know why, but his lips reminded me of the kiss at the ball.

"I've moved here to escape my parents. They're a little old-fashioned."

"There you are. Hi, Giles, can I steal Ken please?" Billie had appeared and was dragging me away. "You need to meet Vlad. He's hot."

Vlad might have been hot, but he wasn't Hen from the ball. He was a nerd, and I didn't really understand computers, let alone play video games. I tried to carry on a conversation, but Vlad gave up after a while, saying he had to leave, as he was meeting friends online to shoot some zombies.

I sighed as I left the pub. Another night that had been a flop. Perhaps I did just need to download the app I'd heard so much about and start hooking up with randoms. Although I shuddered at the thought, but the alternative of being alone was looking less and less attractive as well.

Chapter 5

Henry

"**H**artman. Why the fuck did you change the rate of the heparin infusion on Bed 6?" My registrar was on me again.

Despite explaining that I'd followed the protocol, and it had been checked by a colleague, he insisted I was wrong and wouldn't listen to me when I refused to sign off on his incorrect calculations. I wanted to keep arguing with him, but there was no point. He would never listen. Instead, I found the nurse looking after the patient and asked her to double-check the new rates he'd determined.

This wasn't me. I cared about my patients, and this error could have catastrophic consequences. I only had a week left on this rotation. It had been three long months since the ball and that kiss, and still, I thought about it so frequently, I wondered how much was real and how much was fantasy.

I still hadn't forgotten about Ken turning and running away. Trust me to find another someone embarrassed about being with me.

"Henry?" The charge nurse for the shift knocked on the door to the small office I'd hidden away in to write some notes. "The calculations for this heparin infusion are all wrong."

Thank fuck the nurses knew their arse from their elbow. "I know. I asked one of the nurses to double-check them." I ran my hands through my hair before pinching the bridge of my nose. "He won't listen to me."

"Have you spoken to Mr Coltrane?" she asked. My laugh answered her question. "Well, I will then."

The last thing I wanted was Mr Coltrane screaming at a nurse, even though I knew this one could take it. Instead, I lifted my phone and pressed the speed dial I usually avoided.

"Mr Coltrane, it's Henry Hartman. I'm concerned about the calculations for the heparin infusion on Bed 6 and... No, sir, I understand. No, I have spoken to him. The nurses are also questioning it... Yes... No, I understand. However, he's wrong." My voice was raised by this stage. The bloody consultant had tried to cut me off several times and told me to trust the registrar.

Eventually, another registrar fixed the issue once mine had run off to theatre. It had all been unnecessary and showed me why I hated this rotation so much. It shouldn't have surprised me when my evaluation came through the following week, saying I needed improvement, and they would not be recommending a permanent place in surgery for me.

I could have fought the assessment, but I couldn't be bothered. It was a black mark against my name. In the past, I would have gone out and picked up at a bar, but I wasn't feeling it. Instead, I swung by the bottle shop and took the bar home with me. Val wouldn't be home for a while, and she was probably going out tonight, anyway. Me and my old mate, Jack Daniels, would have a date as I tried to block out how much I hated my job. At least I was starting in gastroenterology on Monday.

GASTRO WAS SLIGHTLY BETTER than general surgery had been, but only just. The team was friendly enough, but my heart wasn't in it. After a month, I was pulled aside and asked what I really planned to do with my life. I knew what this was code for. They didn't want me either.

"How was uni?" I slurred as Val came in the door. Over the last few weeks, Jack and I had become firm friends.

"Yeah, good. Got 98 percent on my last assignment. Won't ask how work was. Was that bottle full?"

"It might have been. But I might have bought it like this. See, is the bottle half full or half empty? That seems like a lawyer question, not a fucking doctor question."

"Drink this." Val passed me a glass of water as she sat next to me on the couch.

"I hate it. Medicine, I mean. Like, perhaps I need to be a lawyer." I looked at my sister as she laughed.

"I've ordered pizza." Val placed her phone on the arm of the couch.

"No pineapple. Pineapple does not go on pizza."

"Shut up. I'm buying, so you get what you're given."

"You sound like a bloody doctor telling me what to do."

"Have you spoken to Giles? Or Boyd?" Val sounded concerned, but I wasn't convinced.

No. I was speaking to Jack. "They'd want me to move home."

"Then why don't you? I'm big enough to look after myself, and then I can have loud sex all over the place," she declared jokingly.

"You wouldn't." I chuckled.

"No, I wouldn't, because I know not to bring men home because it's too dangerous. I think you need to bring a man home though. You haven't had anyone here for months and haven't spent the night anywhere else either."

"Don't remind me." My head fell back against the sofa. "I met someone, and I fell in love at first sight, and he kissed me, and I saw fireworks, and it was perfect, and we were going to get married and have babies and live happily ever after, and he just turned his back on me." I knew I was drunk, but still, tears flowed down my face.

"Oh, Hammy. You've got no idea about love. You found a guy who made your cock throb, and you think it's love. Even I know that's bullshit."

Whatever. Perhaps Val was right, but I'd rather she wasn't. I liked the fantasy of uncomplicated love and happily ever afters, and I had to believe it was bound to happen to me. But until it did, the idea of moving home was appealing. I'd be able to get support from my family and spend time with my nieces. The thought of leaving Val, though, was hard.

After pizza and falling asleep during the action movie Val put on for us to watch, I headed for bed. I needed to think more once I was sober. There was no point making decisions when drunk, even though Val had hidden my mate, Jack, anyway.

My head pounded when I woke up to my phone ringing. I'd taken to having a couple of shots when I finished a shift, and on nights where I had a day off, I was drinking more. It wasn't a problem. I knew I could stop at any time, plus I knew many of my colleagues had a beer or three after work each night. It was how we wound down. This wasn't winding down though. I was miserable, and I wasn't going to get solace from a bottle.

"Hey, Dad." Dad had waited until eleven to call me. I needed painkillers and water, not a lecture from my old man.

"Morning, Henry. Val called me."

"That's nice. Did she want medical advice?" I shuffled through my bedside drawer, trying to find something for the pain.

"She's worried about you." I could picture Dad sitting in his chair in his home office, the crossword nearby, no doubt with a cup of tea.

"There's nothing to worry about. I'm going through a rough patch, that's all."

"I'm worried about you, son." Dad had pulled out the son card. This would not end well. "What are you up to today?"

"Sleep. I've got a date with Jack later."

"Val told me about your relationship with alcohol." Fucking snitch.

"Look, Dad, I'm fine." I sighed, rubbing the bridge of my nose.

"I thought I'd surprise your mum with a trip to Brisbane next weekend. Now that Millie and Mia are up here, we seem to have stopped visiting as much, and although we said it was to visit the girls, it was also lovely catching up with our other children."

"I'm on call next Saturday."

"We can do brunch on Sunday then." Dad's voice was gentle. I knew he cared, and he would not take no for an answer. Val was at work, which was lucky for her, as I wanted to call her out on her tattling to our parents.

Despite my head thumping, fresh air and caffeine would help, so I threw on some clothes and walked down to grab a coffee at a local café.

I knew my family was worried about me. Giles's mate had killed himself when they were at uni, but I wasn't suicidal. Sure, I had some impure thoughts about what I'd do to some of the more senior doctors at the hospital. Who were they to say I wasn't good enough?

It wasn't that I was a poor doctor. I knew my stuff. My grades had been great throughout my degree, and three hospitals begged me to do my junior doctor years with them. I went with the Royal because it had a great reputation. Perhaps I should have gone somewhere else. Giles and Bridget had both worked at the Royal and liked it. Things had probably changed.

I sometimes thought I was treated differently because of my sexuality, like noticing when some colleagues got a hug from a man and I was given a nod as if they'd 'catch the gay' if they embraced me. I was often mistaken as straight based on the number of women who tried to pick me up. Even this week, a nurse had hinted we should grab a drink sometime.

No, I was drinking alone.

"Henry Hartman. Well, I never." Fuck. What was this guy's name again? We'd studied together, I thought. Or maybe we'd had a placement together somewhere? He'd stopped me right next to the place I bought my coffee. So close, yet so far away, and my head still thumped like an African drum circle was practicing inside it.

"Mate," I exclaimed. "How's it going? Where are you these days?" I knew my smile didn't extend from my lips.

"St Swithin's. I'm on the oncology training program there. Geez. So much has happened since I saw you last. I met and married my wife, and she's expecting our first. She's a doctor at St Swithin's too, but in infectious diseases. How about you?" It was hard to tell if he was really interested in my response, but I offered it anyway.

"I'm at the Royal. I'm doing another house doctor year because I still haven't decided what to specialise in."

"I thought you'd do cardiology like your family. Is Giles still down here? Geez, I still can't believe he settled down." The number of people I studied with who looked up to Giles because of his playboy reputation during his first few years of medicine still amused me.

"No, he and Bridget and their girls moved back to Cassowary Point before Christmas."

"Courageous leaving the city. They'll be stuck up there if they aren't careful."

I saw nothing wrong with that. People in rural and regional areas were just as entitled to healthcare as those in the big cities. "Anyway, I'm meeting someone." I pointed to the coffee shop.

"Sure, sure. Great to catch up. We should do dinner sometime."

"Sounds good."

Wanker. I couldn't even remember his name, and I doubted I had contact details for him. He might have been a Mike, Matt, or Mark. Maybe Jake? Hell. It didn't matter.

When I stepped inside, the noise in the coffee shop was loud, so I grabbed a takeaway and headed home, wishing I'd just had something delivered.

Mum and Dad were staging an intervention the following weekend. I loved my family and always felt completely accepted. But I hadn't gotten that bad, had I?

I tried texting Christian, but he was on a mine site and probably had little reception. I hadn't seen him in months. He'd been my best friend throughout high school and into our university days. Christian loved that I was gay; he told me it meant more women for him.

Flicking through the telly, I couldn't find anything to catch my attention. Dozens of channels, from cartoons to romances, and nothing appealed. There was sport in the afternoon, but even that I found uninspiring.

Everything was uninspiring. Work bored me to tears. It wasn't just the attitudes of senior staff, but also the never-ending tasks that made little sense. My cock was definitely uninspired. It had been months since it had taken notice of a cute guy. Not since the Valentine's gala.

I picked up my phone and texted my sister-in-law.

> Did you enjoy your intern year?

BRIDGET:

> It had its moments. I had a goal though by this stage, and I knew what I wanted to do. Plus, Gee and I were in it together. That helped.

> Yeah. Perhaps I need to talk to my colleagues more.

BRIDGET:

> No boyfriends at present?

> Hardly. I'm broken. I'm drinking too much and not really enjoying life.

I waited for Bridget to text back, but there were no dots on the screen. She'd seen the message, but not replied. I was about to grab a shot of bourbon when my phone rang.

"Hey, Bridget. You didn't need to call."

"Henry Alexander Dominic Hartman. Listen to me!" she yelled down the phone. "Be pleased I've moved outside. How much are you drinking?"

"Last night was too much." I winced, as I felt like I'd been called to the principal's office.

"You know that my progenitor was an alcoholic!" Bridget was still yelling.

"I'm not an alcoholic. Alcoholics go to meetings." I chuckled, hoping to calm Bridget down.

Bridget sighed. "*He* never went to meetings. So, tell me what's really wrong."

"I met a guy, and he seemed to be amazing. Like, drop-dead gorgeous, and he had the most beautiful eyes, and his lips. Oh my god. His lips were like the most perfect things ever to touch mine. But he's not available. Story of my life."

"So, it wasn't meant to be. Move on!" Bridget was back to yelling. I could picture her waving her arm around.

"I hate work."

"Move on!"

"How?" I whined.

"Quit. Go back to selling suits or whatever. Get a job doing something you love." Bridget blew out a breath that I could hear down the phone.

"But I like medicine. It's just all the grunt work. I hate having to tick so many boxes."

"Oh, Hammy. Everyone has to start at the bottom and do the grunt work. When you sold suits, did you start doing all the measuring and pairing ties and socks or whatever it was you did?"

I hadn't. I'd bitched about being on the steamer preparing shirts for months, even though I studied out the back of the store. "That was different, though."

"Bullshit. Go for a run or something. You're obviously not on call, like some of us."

"Sorry. I didn't realise you were working."

"All good. I stood back and watched as the midwives delivered an almost five-kilogram baby. Or as the parents keep saying to everyone, ten pounds, fourteen ounces. Midwife thought she might get stuck, but the mum was a trooper and pushed her out in under ten minutes." It was clear she'd found her niche.

"Ew! That vagina will never be the same." I winced.

"You'd be surprised. Giles said you're doing gastro. How's it going?" Bridget had calmed down.

"It's better than surgery, but only just. I think I need to move hospitals. I'm not enjoying the Royal. One of the consultants studied with Mum. I think they had a thing for a while, but it made me sick thinking about it."

"I'll let you in on a secret, Hammy: your mum had a sex life before she met your father." I didn't need to think about this. "But hey, I rang to talk about you. When was the last time you exercised?"

It had been a while. Throughout uni, I'd kept up a routine of running and hitting the gym. I didn't aim to be too muscular, but I liked the feeling of strength from pumping iron. There was a gym in the apartment complex we lived in. I knew the basics of keeping myself mentally fit and that it started with physical fitness, but knowing and doing were different things.

Bridget's work phone rang, so I knew she had to go to catch another baby. I missed my nieces something fierce. I'd spent my last years at uni giving my brother and sister-in-law date nights and covering when they were both on call.

I knew it would never be impossible to be a father, considering I never planned on being with a woman, but it would be difficult. Bridget had often commented that her original plans were to do it all alone, and I knew that would be possible, but working as a single dad and a doctor, especially one in training, would be a challenge.

Getting myself in order was a necessity before I even considered taking on the responsibility of raising a child. The coffee had eased my headache somewhat, and I decided that a trip to the gym in our apartment complex would not be the worst idea in the world.

I didn't look flabby in my gym shorts and singlet, but I could do with some definition. Our complex was quiet as I rode the lift to the basement and entered the small exercise area. The air-conditioning was on and the speakers set for me to pair my phone and blast out some tunes, but I couldn't listen to anything. The usual songs about love I listened to reminded me of Ken, and my head still felt fuzzy. Plus, I was wary of listening to my playlists in public or with other people. It wasn't that I was embarrassed about what I listened to, but living on a diet of romance and heartbreak was bound to deter guys. I'd do that with my personality instead.

Fortunately, there was no one else present, and I sat on the rowing machine and tortured myself to the sound of the chain rolling in and out of the mechanism as I propelled myself down a mystery river. The inertia of moving and yet staying in the same place was an apt description of my life. I was going through the paces, but I was going nowhere. This needed to change.

Chapter 6

Ken

I never expected to enjoy my time in gynaecology and obstetrics. Sure, I didn't get to experience many births, but I enjoyed being with new mums and dads and women who had issues with their reproductive organs.

Bridget had been amazing to work with, as had Dr Rodriguez, our consultant. Bridget even brought a cake she said her mother-in-law had baked on my last day.

Surviving my first rotation seemed like a milestone. Sure, it had involved a lot of grunt work, but I'd been able to solidify a lot of what I'd learnt studying. It wasn't just our team that was lovely, the nurses and midwives I worked with had my back when I made mistakes.

It hadn't surprised me when my rotations were changed. I was annoyed I wasn't heading to psych, but I'd been promised a rotation there later in the year. The emergency department was desperate for more staff, and they stole from the other departments, claiming they'd create a backlog if people couldn't be cleared from the department in some strict time frame.

If gynae had been the frying pan, the emergency department was the fire. It was so fast-paced, and a lot of the time, I did not know what was going on. I'd been told I needed to be faster with my assessments, but I was sure I'd miss something.

"Day off tomorrow, Ken?" Micky asked as he assisted me in stitching up a head wound on Mrs Carmichael, a dear old lady who had banged it against a kitchen cabinet. Fortunately, the tear to her skin was the only casualty, and she showed no signs of concussion.

"Yeah. I was going to do up a batch of beef curry and maybe even see what the fish is like at the market. Are you working?"

Micky had officially moved in with us recently when his lease ran out. It made my rent cheaper, which I didn't complain about.

"Yeah, no rest for the wicked. Have you met Armon? He's one of the physiotherapists around here."

"Don't you start with your matchmaking." I shook my head as I tied off a stitch. Mrs Carmichael smiled.

"I don't think his wife would like me matchmaking. I just know he's involved with the local cricket club, that's all, and I thought you might like to check it out."

Billie had all but stopped with her efforts of finding me a man. I was glad for the reprieve but felt guilty, as I knew she wanted to help. The problem was, I still had the hottie with the satin lapels and the soft lips in my head. There'd been something about him, something I'd been unable to shake in the months since that eventful evening.

He was in my dreams at night, and I woke hard as a rock, begging for release. I imagined our cocks rubbing together as our lips devoured each other. I wanted to nip at his earlobes and suck on his nipples. I knew it was simply a physical reaction, but it was a reaction I'd never really had before.

I'd looked out for him around the hospital, but I'd never seen him. I thought of asking Billie, but I could never bring myself to. A man that hot was sure to have a bevy of suitors lined up for him.

"Ken?" I'd paused for a cup of tea in the break room, as Mrs Carmichael was on her way back home.

"Yes?" I turned and saw the polo shirt the man wore, putting two and two together. "You must be Armon. Micky told me to seek you out."

"Yep. Micky was saying you're a medium quick bowler."

"I think he's overselling me. I haven't played in a year or two."

"We play through the cooler months here. There's training tomorrow night. We're super casual, really. I mean, a lot of our team are medical people, and we work shifts, so we play with who we can, when we can. You'd be welcome to join us."

I liked this idea. Armon seemed friendly enough, and meeting people outside of work seemed like a great plan. I worked longer shifts in emergency, meaning I had more days off. Sure, it would change when I hit my next rotation, but even if I trained every week or so and met someone I could hit the gym with, then it would be something.

WE WERE GOING AROUND in a circle introducing ourselves at cricket training. I recognised a few people from work. It was a good setup with nets near the clubhouse and a ground that was surrounded by large tropical trees. I'd always imagined Cassowary Point would be covered in palm trees, and whilst there were plenty of them around, there were also tropical rainforest trees with large canopies and big leaves that provided shade from the tropical heat.

"Hi, I'm Ken, and I, like it seems a lot of you here, work at the hospital. I haven't played in, well, a while, so I'll be pretty rusty, but it will be good to get the body moving again." I wasn't usually this nervous meeting new people.

There was a range of ages present, from a father with his teenage son to two retired men who told everyone they were the water boys.

"Now, guys." Armon clapped his hands to draw our attention. "As most of you are aware, the women's comp has taken off up here, and they've said that if you want to train with them at all, you are welcome, so perhaps we should also offer the same courtesy to them. Thoughts?"

"Are they hot?" One guy grinned, high-fiving the man next to him.

"I hear their opening batter's a stunner, but she's married to some knobhead." One bloke laughed as his mates pretended to push him.

Armon turned to me. "His wife's the opening batter."

"I thought most of them were bloody dykes," one young guy sneered.

"Macca," Armon snapped. "That's it. You're out."

"My dad played for Australia. You can't do this." Macca jabbed his finger in the air.

"He can, mate. We do this for fun, and it's never that much fun when you're around. How about we take a vote? All in favour of kicking Macca out?" Armon was swift in his reply.

Everyone raised their arms. I stood back, not knowing what to do. Uncomfortable was one word that sprang to mind, but it was more than that. Billie had joked to me that Cassowary Point had a reputation of being a little redneck, but I'd never found that until now. And yet, the other people here seemed to cut down his tiny outburst. I wasn't really sure about how my sexuality would be perceived.

Macca didn't leave quietly, yelling that he was going to tell his dad and contact the local newspaper. Armon simply shook his head and dismissed us into groups. We did some fielding drills, and I rolled my shoulder over a few times, sending down some balls in the nets.

I was a stranger to these people, and yet, they tried to include me in their group. I had hoped I wouldn't be the only new person here, but it seemed I was out of luck. Armon assured me there were a couple of other people who'd expressed interest, but no one else had shown up.

"Hey, Ken, you joining us for a beer?" A lanky fast bowler asked me as we packed away the stumps and kit. I think his name was Fletch.

"Um, sure," I offered.

"Sorry about Macca before. I didn't think he'd show." Fletch held the door open as we entered the clubhouse.

It reminded me of every other clubhouse I'd been in. Brown vinyl covered the chairs, with tufts of foam poking through. Laminate tables held glass salt and pepper shakers, with table numbers printed on plastic squares wedged into wire holders, most of which looked like they were as old as the clubhouse itself. A long bar stretched along the far end with an enormous television screen that showed a sports channel. The wooden barstools were also cushioned with foam and brown vinyl, and mats advertising a popular beer hid who knew what on the bench top.

"He's got a history, I assume?" I pulled out my wallet to buy a beer, but Fletch insisted on shouting me, seeing I was new.

"Yeah. Last year, we had a bloke playing with us who got engaged to another man, and Macca couldn't cope."

"You trying to explain Macca, Fletch?" Armon joined us, beer in hand, opening a bag of chips for us to share.

"Yeah. I was saying how he couldn't cope with Rick announcing his engagement. No matter how much we told him that a, it wasn't likely he'd catch 'the gay' like he was worried about, or b, Rick was deliriously happy with his partner and wouldn't be looking to seduce Macca, Macca was threatened."

"Did he scare Rick away?" I asked, taking a swig of my beer and wiping the foam off my top lip.

"Rick got transferred down south. He was good about putting up with Macca and ignored him," Fletch explained.

"I told him to pull his head in," Armon added. "He got personal with me. My sister's bi, and Macca couldn't stand that either. I'd like to think we were more tolerant. What he said tonight was pretty tame, but he'd been warned that any repeat of his homophobia wouldn't be tolerated. I'm sorry that's what you were greeted with on your first night."

I wanted to open my mouth and say that I was gay, but I couldn't bring myself to come out to these people. I hardly knew them, for one, and also, I hadn't come out to anyone really, so why choose a random group of new acquaintances on a Tuesday evening? Sure, I was scared. Macca had been open about his homophobia, and yet there were probably more amongst us who hid theirs behind silence.

Although we didn't discuss heritage, almost a third of the team was subcontinental, and I had no idea if others on the team held the same views as my parents. Sure, Armon had opened up about his sister, but that could have been the exception, like me.

It was times like this that I hated myself. I'd been born in Australia, but I didn't look Australian. It was my preschool teacher who'd called me Ken. She'd said it was too hard for the other children to say Kandiah. They were all able to say Siobhan, and Zachariah had been the one to insist he was called Zach. At that time, my identity was Sri Lankan. Now

I liked being called Ken. I knew it upset my parents, particularly my father, but it made me feel more Australian.

I turned my attention back to the room where conversation flowed about Australia's tour of England and how the weather was deciding more matches than the skills of the players.

Something inside me softened as we chatted. I felt safe and respected. I'd felt this a little at work, but I'd spent years being conditioned by my parents and their unsupportive environment.

"We're going to invite the women's team to training, yeah?" Fletch drained the last of his beer, placing the empty glass on the cardboard coaster in front of him.

"I honestly can't see why not," Armon replied. "I mean, we're a bloody social team after all, and I'm sure some guys wouldn't mind socialising with women who enjoy the same sport we do."

"Well..." Fletch looked at his phone. "I'm heading off to snuggle with my baby girl. She'll be going crazy after being locked up all day."

"He's talking about his bloody Dobermann." Armon laughed when I looked confused. "I hope tonight hasn't put you off, Ken. We're a weird lot, but we tend to get along. So, what do you do outside of work and cricket, Ken? Girlfriend, boyfriend?"

Even though I could feel my pulse race at Armon's seemingly innocuous question, I paused perhaps a moment too long.

"There's no one at the moment," I said to Armon. "I'm, well, I'm gay, so I really appreciate the inclusive space you've created here."

The surrounding men made no comment. They weren't shocked. Lightning didn't bolt from the sky, and God definitely didn't smite me down.

WHEN I ARRIVED HOME, my coming out hit me. It was nothing like I had ever planned. I mean, sure, some people knew I was gay. Billie definitely knew as I'd told her, but I'd never told virtual strangers. This had been different. This had been me telling the world. Well, a small cricket club anyway, and at that, only a few of them who'd been sitting around the table with me.

Was it a relief? Yes and no. I was glad it was out there. Perhaps now other gay men on the team mightn't be afraid to approach me, not that I'd noticed anyone avoid me. I could spend time getting to know someone else who liked cricket and shared similar interests to me. Maybe I'd even find someone who could take the memories of the kiss at the ball away.

I jumped in the shower, and my mind immediately drifted to Hen, the man from the ball. After all these months, why was I still reliving that kiss? Sure, it had been my first with a man, but it had set all my synapses on fire. There was something about him that called me. It wasn't just that I thought it would be cute to be Hen and Ken, but I wanted to walk around and hold this man's hand. I wanted to steal kisses with him in a dark movie theatre, and I wanted to stroke his thigh under a table at a restaurant in town. I wanted to take him to cricket training and show him off as my partner. He probably hated cricket. He was probably into the arts and theatre and stuff. We probably had nothing in common.

As always, when I thought of Hen, my cock stirred. It was never a gradual stirring, either. I was always instantly hard and yearned for release. Propping my forearm against the shower wall, I laid my forehead on it as I teased the head of my cock. As much as I wanted to come, I wanted the sensation to drag out too. I bit my lip as I moaned, imagining Hen's mouth licking the tip. That short beard... I wanted to feel it rub against my thighs. I wanted to feel it trail kisses from my cock to my neck and let me taste myself on his tongue after I'd come in his mouth.

My cock ached as I gripped it tightly, slowly easing my hand up and down. My mouth hung open, breaths coming hard and fast as I imagined Hen engulfing my length with his mouth, swallowing down as much of me as he could. Would he gag as he inched more and more of me inside him? I imagined him humming, the added sensation drawing me closer to my release.

I didn't care if anyone was home. My forehead was still against my arm as the water sluiced down my back. Grunts and moans reverberated around the bathroom. As much as I wanted to stay in the blow job fantasy I was imagining, it was the memory of the kiss again that threw me over the edge.

Sure, I could imagine Hen's beard against my thighs or chest, but I could remember the feeling of it against my clean-shaven face, the friction and sensation as we devoured each other's mouths. Ropes of cum exploded from my cock, spraying everywhere from my hand to the tiles, some even hitting my chin.

Trying to calm my breaths, the euphoria of coming was replaced with a sadness. I'd been the one to run away. It had been me who escaped the situation I kept remembering and fantasising about. I hadn't seen my mystery man for months. He probably wasn't even a doctor, not that it mattered. Billie had said they'd studied together, hadn't she? Did she mean they'd studied medicine together? Perhaps he wasn't even medical. He could have been anything.

I had to put him behind me. I'd come out, and I needed to look for someone who would help me forget this mystery man.

After my shower, I downloaded a gay dating app. I lay on my bed and scrolled through the profiles. Nothing really caught my attention. Most men had photos of their chests or their tightly covered crotches. There were no photos of faces, save for a few chins that crept into chest shots.

I found a photo Billie had taken before the ball and cropped it so you saw my throat above my black tie and suit. It wasn't at all revealing. It could have been anyone.

The questions for the profile were hard for me to answer, as I had no idea what I was looking for, so I left it vague and hit publish.

Within a few minutes, I had messages piling into my inbox. Most were sexually explicit, telling me I looked fuckable. How they knew from the shot I'd posted I'll never know. I didn't reply to any of them. I flicked through some of the profiles and scrunched up my face. Most were men looking for hookups. Perhaps I'd chosen the wrong app, because I wanted more than a casual one-off. I wanted romance and to get to know my partner.

I wanted more than a kiss on the side of a dance floor at a ball that I still couldn't stop thinking about. Yes, my mind had gone back there. It was pretty clear. I still wanted my mystery Hen.

Chapter 7

Henry

My work week had been a little better. My registrar was on nights, so we had a reliever. He enjoyed showing us juniors a few different things. My favourite nurses were working too, which helped. When the nurses had your back, you knew things were going okay.

Gastro was more than colonoscopies. We had several patients on the ward with chronic conditions that impacted their lives. I often found I was dealing with the emotional side of their illnesses, and that excited me, which came as a shock. Our reliever was amazing at the counselling side of things, and I learned a lot from him. He was never scared of silence and gave the patients time to gather their thoughts and speak or ask questions. I'd been trying this out myself when talking with patients and had found one young man in particular open up to me when given space.

He wanted to break up with his girlfriend, convinced he was heading for a colostomy bag and she would find it gross. My advice had been to talk to her about it and ask her what she really wanted. They seemed like a lovely couple, and she was often on the ward, visiting. I'd hate to see love derailed because of a false thought by one party.

In turn, he became more open about asking questions about his condition and wanted to learn more from the medical team treating him, rather than simply Dr Google.

Our registrar had seen this as a win and even praised me, and for the first time in a long time, I felt like I'd gotten something right. I'd made a difference and actually done some good. It carried over to the grunt work. If insulin orders were completed each day and the nurses didn't have to chase you, things were brighter on the ward. If I noticed medications needed recharting before someone had to remind me, it also brought a sense of calm. It was the calm I enjoyed. Perhaps simply reframing the menial jobs as things that brought calm was all I needed to do.

In the evenings, I stayed away from Jack. My liver was thankful, I'm sure, and my head seemed a lot clearer. Whereas I'd been staying back for an hour or two to chase my tail, I found myself doing minor tasks as they appeared instead of writing notes to complete them later. I was getting away on time and, in doing so, found time to hit the gym.

Even though we had a small gym in our apartment block, I had a membership at a local fitness centre. On Wednesday, I called in after work, having packed a gym bag that morning. It was busy. After rowing for ten minutes, I hit the weights room. The guy on the leg press next to me had it loaded up with what looked like all the plates that would fit. I had considerably less weight on mine, but it was still a challenge.

It was never meant to be a competition, but I tried to outdo my neighbour. It wasn't an even contest, as he was so much bigger than me, plus, he was pressing much more weight, but if he did twenty reps, I aimed for twenty-five. I doubt he even noticed me, but he pushed me in ways he never knew. Not that I wanted to look like him, but I wanted to achieve something.

I realised both my time at the gym and at work saw me wanting to achieve something, and that had been missing from my life for months. Indulging in alcohol after work wasn't achieving anything. Bridget's lecture about her father and alcoholism came back to me, and I thought about all she and Giles had achieved. They both were closer to being consultants and had an amazing marriage with two beautiful children. They didn't do it all at once. Perhaps I needed to start small.

The man on the other machine finished after two sets, and when I was undertaking a third, he removed the weights from the machine like they were rolls of toilet paper. My legs wobbled like jelly as I stood, and I had to pause to catch my breath. I wiped down the machine before removing the weights and was glad when someone approached me, keen to use the machine with my weights already on there.

Several people exercised in pairs, spotting each other while chatting, but most of us were there by ourselves. Christian and I used to exercise together when we were flatmates. When Millie was a baby, Bridget convinced me to get Giles out of the house, and we also hit the gym together. Giles was a lot bulkier than me, but spending time together exercising had been good.

I thought back to a conversation I'd had with Giles when we'd been at uni. He'd asked me what I did for myself. I'd told him I shopped, which was still true, but exercise was something else, even if I preferred to do it with someone else.

Life as a junior doctor meant you moved frequently around the hospital and never really got to set down roots in any one area. I knew plenty of my colleagues, but I couldn't say I was overly friendly with any of them. The Royal was a large hospital and easy to get lost in. It was time for me to admit that, yes, I was lonely.

"Hey, stinky." I greeted my sister as I threw the keys onto the kitchen bench and my gym bag towards the washing machine. She was lying across the couch, her laptop on her chest as she typed away. It looked pretty uncomfortable.

"You call me stinky, yet look at you." Val pinched her nose. "You could have showered at the gym."

"Too busy there, plus, I didn't want the guys to get jealous when they eyed my wonder cock." I peeled a banana and took a large bite, walking towards the couch to look over Val's shoulder. "Whatcha working on?"

"Family law assignment. I'm really loving this subject and can see it as an area I'll move into." Val barely looked up from her keyboard.

I moved to the bathroom and stripped off my still sweaty clothes. It took forever for the water to heat.

I'd caught sight of a man at the gym who'd reminded me of Ken from the ball. He had the same caramel complexion, but his hair had been darker. He was also exercising with a woman. Just why had Ken run away from me? I didn't think I was a terrible kisser, and for me, the kiss had been amazing. It was probably the same old thing—he was straight or perhaps bi-curious, and I'd been an experiment. He was probably at a gym at Cassowary Point exercising with a woman as I showered down here.

I hadn't thought about Ken in several days. Well, not consciously, anyway. I'd dreamt about him, his long, slender fingers running through my hair, his tongue duelling with mine. I'd felt his cock rub against mine through our suits, and I wanted to be skin to skin with him, creating a friction that saw us both come.

My hand wrapped around my cock and stroked as I thought about my mystery man. Even though I knew in reality, he probably wanted to fuck me and run, like so many other guys over the years, I wanted more. I wanted to stroke him and kiss him all over. I wanted to explore his body and ways of bringing each other to climax that weren't simply Part A in Slot B.

With my back against the shower wall, I beat my cock as water sluiced over it.

My mind went into overdrive as I imagined all kinds of scenarios. I'd always wanted to try docking and had been practicing with a dildo, but so far, the guys I'd been with recently just wanted a blow job or to fuck my arse. I wondered if Ken had a foreskin. It didn't worry me one way or the other. Size had never worried me either. I'd taken cocks that were larger and smaller than mine, and mine was larger than average. A few guys had balked at the idea of me going anywhere near their arses, and some had kept a firm grip around most of my cock as they blew me so they wouldn't take too much of it.

It was to thoughts of Ken that I saw my cum flow down the drain. It had been far too long since I'd seen any action apart from my hand. A quick wank wasn't enough. I wanted, no, I needed more. I thought of hitting up a gay bar but remembered Mum and Dad were heading down this weekend. Perhaps I could hit up an app and find someone to help relieve my blue balls, but even then, I'd probably be stuck in the same pattern I was trying to avoid: simply being there as an orifice for someone to use.

After stepping out of the shower and drying off, I threw on some sweatpants and went to cook dinner for Val and myself. I was gutted to notice that it was too late to FaceTime with our nieces. I couldn't believe how much I missed them. Perhaps I'd need to book some time off and head up to Cassowary Point to spend time with them. Val could spare me for a few days, surely.

"Come and give us a hug." Mum rose from the couch where she'd been knitting when I arrived home from work on Friday. I'd skipped the gym, wanting to see them, but now I was second-guessing my decision.

"Hey, Mum. How was your flight? Where's Dad?" I hadn't even taken my satchel off my shoulder when Mum enveloped me. I instantly relaxed into her. She gave the best hugs, and I'd missed them.

"Your father's on the balcony doing the crossword. We used our points to upgrade to business class, so you can imagine how good the flight was."

"Hammy, my boy." Dad slid the screen door closed behind him as he stepped inside. The breeze was lovely as it flowed through our apartment. "I thought I heard you. How was work?"

"Yeah, not too bad." I sighed a sigh of both contentment and sadness as Dad also hugged me. Having my parents here showing me how much they loved me was one thing, but it would be all too brief. Dad was a couple of inches shorter than me, but he still commanded a presence to which I looked up to. I loved he was my dad and couldn't have asked for a better one.

"Enough work talk." Mum pretended to sound angry, but her smile gave her away. "Your sister finishes work in half an hour. We're meeting her at the bookshop, and I've booked a table at a Moroccan restaurant that had rave reviews online. Oh, and Boyd and Emily say thank you for the notes, but please don't tell Bridget that you also gave them notes. She thinks she's getting them through fifth year. She's got Emily meditating and Boyd running with her every morning."

It was rather sweet to hear this. Bridget had a sort-of breakdown in fifth year and almost let her study get on top of her. Fortunately, Giles was there to help her, and they are now living their happily ever after.

Val had forgotten about dinner and was surprised when we all walked into the bookshop she worked at part time. I swear, she'd forget her head some days if it wasn't screwed on.

Even though it was just the four of us at dinner, it reminded me how much family meant to me. Of course, it would have been better with Giles, Bridget, and the girls and Boyd and Emily present too, but spending time with Mum, Dad, and Val was special, even though Mum annoyed the bejesus out of me at times.

"So, how's your love life, Hammy? Tracked down Miles Burnham yet?" Mum scraped some dip onto a piece of bread before placing it in her mouth and licking her fingers.

Miles was an English actor Mum had fancied for years. He'd married a sound engineer last year, and they seemed happy enough. I had to give it to Mum, though, and admit he was hot.

"He's started back at the gym," Val said ever so matter-of-factly as she reached across the table for some more couscous. "He'll probably meet some hulk of a guy there and make me listen to it all night."

For fuck's sake. I clenched my palms under the table and counted to ten in my head.

"Remember, honey, it's your place too, and if he parades too many men through, you can tell him." Comments like this were why the women in my family annoyed me at times.

"Nah, Hammy's cool. He hasn't brought back anyone when I've been there, and I'm not there all the time." Val was carefree talking about this, which still surprised me. When I'd taunted her the first morning she returned home from being out all night claiming she was doing the walk of shame, she informed me she was doing the stride of pride. "I think he's fixated on that kiss at the ball."

My eyebrows raised. I didn't know Val knew I'd kissed Ken. I'd almost forgotten we were on the dancefloor and not in a dark corner. In my mind, it had been a private moment. That she'd seen and realised I was still fixated on it meant I really wasn't hiding it well.

"I didn't want to talk work." Dad took a sip of his red wine after placing the knife and fork together on his plate, possibly eager to change the subject. "But they are awfully short of junior doctors at Cassowary Point Hospital this year. There's definitely a job there, and you could slot in there in a matter of weeks if you wanted."

"All my boys at home. How amazing would that be?" Mum's smile saw tears appear on the edges of her eyes.

"Yeah, well, I wouldn't live with you. You talk about Val having to listen to me have sex, but you two hornbags never stop." Mum and Dad gazed at each other. Longingly, with no sign of embarrassment. I folded my serviette and stood to head to the bathroom, needing a break from them all while I thought about my options.

Could I move up north and work up there, and would I bump into Ken? Would he be interested, or was he just another man looking to investigate his curiosity?

I knew there were more gay and bi men in Brisbane than in Cassowary Point. But here I was again, yearning for a relationship, something I'd never been able to achieve.

Giles had been totally anti-relationship until he met Bridget. It was like he transformed overnight from this love them and leave them character to worshipping the ground Bridget walked on. Boyd was the opposite. He declared his undying love for Emily at his eighteenth birthday party, and they've always been together. They've only ever had each other. It wasn't a matter of if they got married, but when.

I was in the middle. I wanted to do relationships, but I usually came on too strong. It meant sex happened pretty quickly, something I never complained about, but I then pushed too hard and scared them away. I'd never dumped someone, instead, I was always the one being dumped. Perhaps I should realise that when guys tell me it's not me, it's them, it really was me pushing too hard.

"Ah, Hartman." Our consultant was on the ward first thing Monday morning. "There's been a flu outbreak on the surgical wards, and most of the interns are off sick. I said I could spare you seeing you've had experience there. Should be just a week. Make sure you wear a mask." He was short and to the point, and his words reminded me that I was simply a cog in a machine.

Just what I needed. I'd had a week thinking I could do this and having my confidence boosted, only to have to head back to the surg ward to have it knocked back down again.

When I arrived on the ward, it was bedlam. Over half the patients on the large ward had come down with influenza, with several more being tested. We were lectured again about the basics, making sure we washed our hands, not touching our masks, how to get into and out of our gowns and gloves so we didn't add to the spread. I think they forgot we'd been to medical school.

Being sent here almost made me forget I'd had a day off. Sunday had been spent browsing the markets with Mum and Dad. There was no more mention of jobs at home, but there were hints of how different the lifestyle was. Pointing out how much cooler it was in Brisbane this time of year, how crowded the markets were and how things were mass produced, how noisy everywhere was.

Cassowary Point wasn't a backwater town. It had a sizable population and a decent hospital. Due to its location, there was a large focus on tropical medicine. This would be different, but it would also be something new. Sure, it only had one gay bar, but there were plenty of other bars that promoted inclusivity.

I didn't get home from work until after 8 p.m. There was no time for a gym session. Val was on the phone with Emily, and I knew they'd talk for hours. Emily was two years older than Val and two years younger than Boyd. She and Val had shared a babysitter when they were preschoolers, and Emily had always been around. If anything, Val and Emily were more like sisters, even though that made things with Boyd seem that much ickier.

My thoughts returned to the weekend with my parents. Brisbane wasn't home. It never would be, even if Val was here. Home was Cassowary Point. I always believed I'd head back there, but I also planned to do it as a consultant. There aren't many specialties that don't require at least six months in a metropolitan hospital. If I headed back now, I'd possibly have to turn around and head back down here for a bit, anyway. General practice had never excited me, but it meant I'd be able to stay up north. Psych was another, but that was low on my list of choices.

Val was more than capable of looking after herself. None of us had been overly protective brothers towards her. I mean, she's seven years younger than me and I would never have imagined her wanting to chase any of my friends when I was younger, and now, well, I had no friends. Apart from Christian. He and Val got on okay, but I could never see the two of them hitting it off. Stranger things had happened, I suppose.

Deciding to at least investigate moving, I fired off an email to the recruitment department at Cassowary Point Hospital.

From: HADH
> To: Recruitment.CPH
> Subject: Junior doctor jobs
> Good evening,
> I was told that there might be positions for junior doctors at CPH. I grew up in the area before moving to Brisbane to study where I wanted to gain experience, away from people who associate me with others because of my surname.
> I would need to give four weeks' notice at my current position, but I think it's time to head home.
> Please let me know if this might be a possibility.
> Regards,
> H

As soon as I'd sent it, I realised I should have sent it from my hospital email that had me listed as Henry Hartman and not simply my initials that I used on my personal account. And I'd signed it from H, my usual practice. At least I'd attached my CV, so they knew who I was. Perhaps not the most professional of starts.

TUESDAY on the surg ward wasn't much better. We'd had no fresh cases, but two patients had been shipped off to intensive care and were ventilated, and a seventy-year-old who'd come in for a hernia repair didn't look like he would survive. There was no time for breaks or lunch. One kind nurse shoved a protein bar at me as I charted some pain relief, for which I was grateful.

It had been another busy day, but it differed from when I'd been there before. I had a different registrar, which made heaps of difference. The nurses knew me and were looking out for me. We were all stretched.

I was exhausted as I grabbed a burrito from a drive-through on my way home. Walking in the door, I simply dropped my satchel by the couch and flopped onto it. Val wasn't home. I took a bite of my dinner and groaned as the spice from the chipotle sauce hit my tastebuds. At least I wasn't on nights, but it wouldn't surprise me if I had to work overtime this weekend.

Flicking open my emails on my phone that I'd not had a chance to check all day, I saw a reply from Cassowary Point Hospital.

From: Recruitment.CPH
    To: HADH
    Subject: Junior doctor jobs

Henry,

I'd been expecting an email from you. I worked in cardiology clinics for a while and know your parents. And yes, I understand the thing with surnames—my mum's been an admin officer here for over forty years, and I was glad to get married and be rid of her surname.

Your father's correct, and we have over a dozen vacancies for junior doctors. If you could be here to start in five weeks, I know mental health is desperate. It might be a six-week slot, as new rotations start after that, unless you like it, of course. Possibly rotations for the next term include cardiology (not sure of your preferences), obs/gynae, general surg, or mental health. Possibly a general medical too.

Let me know if you're still interested, and we can get the paperwork rolling.

Regards,

Jenny Diaz
(Used to be Jenny O'Donnell!)

I had no idea who Jenny was, but she obviously knew of me. Thank fuck she said she was married or else I might have thought she was coming onto me.

"Hey, Bridget, it's me. I thought I called Gilbo." I was so tired, I could have called anyone.

"No, you did. Mia's being clingy, and he's upstairs, trying to get her down again."

It amazed me that my brother was the dad he was. I knew it shouldn't have, as we had amazing role models as parents, but he went above and beyond. After joking for many years that he would never have children, Giles was into everything his daughters wanted him to do.

"How's the new house?" I asked.

"It's wonderful," Bridget moaned. "Don't get me wrong, I adore Hills and Charlie, but having our own space is pretty special. Plus, the shower off our bedroom has an amazing ledge in it, and—"

"Bee, honey." I heard Giles in the background, sounding as if he didn't want Bridget to continue. Our whole family had heard the story of Bridget slipping over in the shower as they had sex early in their relationship.

"What? It's just Hammy." Bridget huffed. "I'll put you on speaker. You still there, Hammy?"

"Hey, Gilbo. Is Mia okay?" I laughed. I really missed the four of them.

"She's fine. She doesn't have a temperature. I think she's overtired, that's all." Bridget squealed, and I decided not to ask what her husband was doing to her. "So, why the call?"

"There's a job. At the hospital." I knew I sounded uncertain. I pinched the bridge of my nose as I talked.

"What, the Royal?" Bridget asked.

"No, Cassowary Point." There was silence for a few seconds before I heard Giles laugh. "What?" I asked, trying to interpret my brother's amusement.

"Nothing, it's just." Giles paused, and I could sense genuine happiness in his voice. "It would be great to have you up here. What does stinky think?"

Val had been called stinky since she was a baby. I felt guilty for leaving her alone in Brisbane, but I needed to focus on myself. Val was a big girl now, a grown woman, in fact.

I heard the keys turn in the door before two voices interrupted my call. "Hammy?" Val yelled. Our apartment wasn't large. The door opened into the kitchen living area, but Val couldn't see me slouched on the couch.

"Hey, stinky!" Giles yelled down the phone.

"Gilbo!" Val shrieked as I stood up. "Sorry, Hammy, this is Janet. She's a friend from uni, and she's going to stay for a bit because she's just broken up with her girlfriend."

"Is that alright?" Janet asked. She was tall with long dark hair, which she flicked behind her ear and then over her shoulder.

"It's perfect." Giles was laughing again down the phone. "Hammy just called to tell us he's moving home. It's perfect timing."

"I—" I tried to talk, but everyone was talking over me.

"Oh, are you?" Val clenched her hands in front of her and bit her lip between her teeth. "That's awesome. You'll be able to chase kissy boy. Oh, Gilbo, ever since the ball, he's been miserable. I think this one might be the one, you know."

"Who's kissy boy?" Bridget asked in her typical flat tone.

"No one," I replied, my voice louder than it needed to be. "And, anyway, I haven't decided if I'll take the job."

"Yes, you have." Giles sounded smug, as always. "Now I assume you don't want to stay with Mum and Dad. We don't have room here. Rental market is really tight, but there are usually notices around the staff cafeteria, so we'll be on the lookout and let you know. Sorry, Janet. Welcome to our family chaos, oh, and Hammy." Giles sounded full of glee. "I want to hear more about kissy boy, too."

I went to reply, but Giles hung up. My family was lovely, but they could be a lot. I'd called to talk through things, but Giles sounded genuinely happy that I would move home. Val had brought home a friend who needed somewhere to live, so perhaps this might work. We'd have to just wait and see.

Chapter 8

Ken

When I woke up, I had sixty-eight notifications on that damn app I'd downloaded. My inner twelve-year-old boy sniggered at being almost to the magical sexual number, but I took it as a sign that the app wasn't for me. Sure, it was nice to be popular, but I figured I was fresh meat rather than anything special. In the end, I deleted it, not even bothering to close my account.

I glanced at my phone to check the time. I didn't start work until the afternoon, but it wasn't an overnight shift. I'd be home after midnight and back to do the same shift tomorrow.

There was time to get some more sleep, but I was wide awake, my brain focussing still on cricket training the night before. I checked my schedule and was glad I'd probably be able to make it to training next week, too. I'd come out of the closet my parents had ensured I'd been stuck in for so many years. I never planned on keeping it a secret, but my parents were so hung up on their church that they would have disowned me. I needed to live with them whilst I was at uni, and I was at uni for much longer than my peers because I'd started studying something I hated.

Respect was huge in the Dissanayake family. As Tamil people, we didn't have a surname, but had our father's name as our first name, and our name as our second name. When my father's parents came to Australia, they took my grandfather's name as their surname. My father then became Baadal Dissanayake instead of the other way around.

My father, being such a traditionalist, insisted that I had a middle name, thus keeping his given name alive. Not that I'll ever have children, but I can't imagine hoisting Kandiah on them. I never used my middle name on anything. It wasn't on my testamur when I graduated, and, despite having to provide a copy of my driver's licence when I applied to work at Cassowary Point, I avoided having Baadal listed as my middle name on my work email or my electronic signature on the notes in our medical records program.

Amongst the dating app notifications, my mother had been texting me again. She'd never been au fait with technology really and insisted on typing in caps.

AM'MĀ:

KANDIAH. CALL NOW. PLEASE.

AM'MĀ:

KANDIAH. WE MISS YOU.

And then half an hour later:

AM'MĀ:

KANDIAH. THERE'S A GIRL WE WANT YOU TO MEET.

There was always a girl. Mostly, they were members of my parents' church, and usually, they were subcontinental, like me. Perth was a couple of hours behind us, time wise, and I figured my father should have left for work. I threw on some sweatpants and headed downstairs, calling home to get it over and done with.

"Am'mā, it's me. Sorry. Your messages were late last night."

"Kandiah. My boy. I miss you so much. When are you coming home? There are some fine hospitals here, and I'm sure you could get a job. Have you found a faith community yet?" I could picture my mother in the kitchen as she spoke. My parents still had a landline, and the phone could stretch to the stove. I'd bought a cordless phone for them for Christmas one year, but they never used it.

"Work's great." I tried to ignore her questions as I brewed a cup of tea. "I'm really settling in. Billie and Micky are great housemates."

"Are they"—I could hear my mother take in a breath—"boys?"

"Billie wants to be an obstetrician. She's hoping to start training soon. Micky is her partner, and he's a nurse in the emergency department."

"A nurse." I could hear the shock in my mother's voice and imagined her eyes shooting wide. "What do his parents think? Is there shame on the family?"

That's what it boiled down to. Shame.

"How are Abha and Dipti?" I knew my mother loved talking about my sisters and their families.

She prattled on for several minutes, telling me about my sisters' husbands and how successful they were. Abha has two sons, and Dipti has a son and a daughter. Abha and her family are part of my parents' congregation, with Dipti worshipping elsewhere. Both married Sri Lankan men with conservative values. I get along alright with my brothers-in-law, but we've never been close.

"... And he's so smart," I heard my mother continue, not sure which of my nephews she was talking about. "And he says he wants to become an accountant, like your father. Isn't that just wonderful." It wasn't a question.

"I have to get to work, Am'mā, but I'll try to call you next week."

It took my mother a few minutes to finish the call. Yes, I was eating well, and yes, I was exercising. She seemed somewhat happy that I was playing cricket. Naturally, she ended the call telling me they were all praying for me.

I didn't not believe in a higher being, but I wasn't convinced of an all-judging God, either. It baffled me that the Gospels could be so firm on Jesus talking about love and its importance, and yet, my parents and their church didn't believe the love I felt was appropriate.

Not that I'd ever been in love. I knew I was attracted to men from a young age, and no amount of pretending otherwise was going to make me happy. It hurt that I'd probably end up keeping my private life a secret from my parents. If I ever found someone and fell in love, that was.

I was conscious that both Billie and Micky were on nights and sleeping upstairs, and I hoped my call hadn't woken them. Our unit was more of a townhouse, with bedrooms upstairs and a kitchen and dining area downstairs. I knew that the lounge area was directly under their bedroom and tried to be quiet. I was a few pages into the latest biography I was reading when I heard Billie scream a shriek of delight, followed by Micky laughing and yelling at how proud he was of her. Soon, there were heavy thuds on the stairs as the pair of them came down.

"Oh, Kenny. It's a miracle." Billie had tears in her eyes and a smile as wide as her face. "I've got a place in the gynae program at St Bede's in Brisbane," she cried. "They want me to start in a month."

"That's wonderful." There was no way my smile reached my eyes as I tried to sound happy for my friend.

"It is, isn't it? I mean, I know you'll need to find a new flatmate, but there are so many people looking for accommodation. You know Jan?" I knew of Jan, I thought. "He put up a notice and had seven applications in an hour from people around the hospital looking for a new room and housemate."

It was all so sudden. I really enjoyed living with Billie and Micky.

"I can help you do up a poster, Kenny." I suspect Micky noticed my shock at the situation.

"Nah," I sighed, running my hands through my hair. "You two need sleep if you're going to work tonight."

As much as I tried to stay quiet downstairs, the rhythmic squeaking of Billie's bed showed sleep was the last thing on their minds.

ARRIVING AT WORK EARLY, I grabbed a piece of paper from a printer and a thick marker and simply wrote: 'Housemate wanted. Modern townhouse near hospital', and included my email address. I figured if they could spell my name, it would be a good start. I made my way to the staff cafeteria and surveyed the board.

"But I want strawberry milk!" I turned as I heard a young girl scream.

"That tone is unacceptable, Millicent Grace. We're coming in to fill your water bottles. Oh, Kandiah, hello." Bridget Hartman looked frazzled. She had a young girl gripping her hand and another on her hip.

"Dr—" Her eyebrows shot up reminding me that she'd told me time and time again not to call her Dr Hartman. "Good afternoon, Bridget."

"Kandiah. Sorry, this is Millie and Mia, my daughters. They usually stay with Mrs McIntyre during the day, but her mum's just had a turn, and she has to head to Sailor's Bend to check on her. Giles is in the middle of a procedure, and his parents are at a conference. Are you looking for somewhere new to live?"

"Uncle Hammy's moving home." Millie jumped up and down as she turned in a circle, the strawberry milk long forgotten.

"That's right, Mills, but he needs somewhere to live."

"He can sleep on the roll-out in my room."

"Not really, sweetheart. Uncle Hammy needs a room of his own." Bridget smoothed her daughter's hair down.

"Well, that's why I'm here," I offered. I liked my rotation with Bridget and had met her husband a few times. Whoever this Uncle Hammy was, he was probably an alright person if they were anything to go by. Well, I hoped, anyway. "Billie's moving to Brisbane, and I need a new housemate."

I handed the sign I'd made to Bridget, who folded it and placed it in her bag.

"You, my dear Kandiah"—Bridget smiled as she repositioned the child on her hip—"are probably a lifesaver. I'll have him email you. Now, come on, girls. We need to fill these bottles and wait for Daddy."

It wasn't a busy ED shift. I stitched up a few lacerations and took some medical histories for the registrars. The nursing staff changed over a few hours before my shift ended. Micky looked like he'd had no sleep.

"You look like shit," I told him as he handed me the chart of a lady who'd come in from a nursing home.

"Worth it." He grinned. "I'm so bloody proud of her, and, hey, I'm looking forward to moving to Brisbane, too. But I know we're leaving you in a bit of a pickle, and I'm sorry for that."

"Nah, it's cool. I bumped into Bridget Hartman when I went to put up the notice I'd drawn up, and her brother or something is moving up here and needs a room."

"Nice one." Micky was finishing labelling some bloods he'd drawn from our patient. "I think she's the one who got Billie the job. Well, I know she put in a good word for her, so you'd think her brother is a good person."

I hoped so. I'd try to suss him out via email. The last thing I wanted was to give my parents an excuse to have me move back to Perth. Sure, I could afford the rent by myself for a few months, but sharing expenses would be preferable so I could pay back my student loans faster.

The apartment was quiet when I got home. Micky and Billie were both still working. I was tired, but not tired enough to wind down and sleep.

I checked my phone, but there were no emails from this Uncle Hammy. Hammy wasn't a name I'd come across before, but then again, I'd led a sheltered life with few contacts outside of my family and faith community.

Almost a week later, I still had no email from the mysterious Hammy. I was ready to put a new sign up to see if someone else might want the room. I was working an early shift in the ED when I saw Bridget in the department.

"Um, Dr— Sorry, Bridget." I could feel the blush creeping up my cheeks, as once again, I forgot how Bridget preferred to be addressed. "I still haven't heard from this Hammy. Do I need to find someone else?"

"Leave it with me, okay?" Bridget shook her head. I was unsure if she was upset with me or him.

A few minutes later, as I was typing up some notes, Bridget reappeared. "He's emailing you now. Bloody stubborn... Sorry. Now I have to see the woman with the heavy vaginal bleeding. Is she one of yours?"

"No. Check with Samella. She's running the show today."

Bridget tucked her phone into her pocket before leaving me with my notes.

I knew other people were waiting on notes, and I should be focusing on them, but all I wanted to do was check my emails. Before I could even get my phone out, I was interrupted by nurses wanting more pain relief for their patients, other doctors wanting to talk through presentations, and even Armon, who sought me out to check if I was coming to training that evening.

And then it turned busy. An emergency case came in, and even though I wasn't on the trauma team this shift, it meant that I needed to cover my colleagues who were. We had patients on stretchers in corridors, and the waiting room was full to overflowing.

"Ken." My registrar gripped my shoulder as I typed up more notes, knowing there was so much still to do. "You need a break, mate. Grab a coffee or something and take half an hour. You'll work better then."

Rubbing my eyes, I knew he was right. I trudged down the hallway towards our break room past patients on ambulance stretchers. It had been a while since it had been this busy.

It was subdued in the break room. Usually, people laughed and joked. The TV was muted, with no one wanting to watch the daytime talk show.

I was usually a tea snob. I liked nothing more than preparing a pot by heating it, measuring in the tea leaves, following by water at the right temperature, and letting it steep for the right amount of time. It must have been in my blood, as my great-grandparents ran a tea plantation in Sri Lanka, the same plantation my grandparents left to come to Australia for a new life. Today, though, a tea bag would have to do, and the variety I liked the least. It was all the health service could afford. I kept meaning to throw some decent tea bags into my locker, but I always forgot. Bridget had always provided Earl Grey tea bags on my first rotation, which I appreciated.

Thinking of Bridget brought me back to remembering to check my emails. There was one from someone I didn't recognise.

From: HADH
    To: Kandiah Dissanayake

Subject: Room to rent

Hi, Kandiah,

Bridget mentioned you have a room available. Sorry it's taken me a few days to get to you—I hadn't decided to move up really until Bridget told me how much it would mean to my nieces. She's good at using blackmail like that. Never get on her wrong side—she's the smartest person I've ever met.

Anyway, I'll be working at the hospital. I don't have a start date yet, but I'll let you know. When is the room free? How much is rent? Is it furnished? I kind of hope not, because I bought the most comfortable bed down here, and I want to transport it up.

I can promise I'll be an okay housemate. I'm not into loud parties and will abide any rules you have. My family tease me, but I'm really into cricket. I used to play at school, but now I prefer to watch it. If you don't have a sports subscription on your TV, I'll be happy to provide it.

Talk soon,

H

I wasn't much into English and grammar, and I found it hard to see how you could get Hammy from HADH, but there was probably some convention I didn't know about that saw a D and an H produce an M sound. Hammy sounded alright. Nothing screamed red flags. But then again, I probably wouldn't know what to look for.

I took a sip of my tea, but it wasn't cutting it, so I headed to the vending machine and grabbed an energy drink and a chocolate bar. So what if it made me crash in an hour or so? I sat back down at the communal table in the break room and typed a reply to this mysterious H.

From: Kandiah Dissanayake

To: HADH

Subject: Re: Room to rent

Hi, H,

Your niece seemed very excited that you were moving here last week when I bumped into Bridget. I think Bridget seems excited too. You must be close.

The townhouse isn't large. There's a carport attached, but I don't have a car, so you can use that. Inside the front door is a toilet. There's an open-plan kitchen/living area. The stools at the breakfast bar came with the place, and that's where I usually eat if I'm not plopped in front of the telly. At the moment, it's a little cluttered. My housemate's boyfriend moved in a couple of months back and brought an extra couch and TV. They're both arguing about which couch they want to take with them. I've offered to buy the one they choose not to take and to buy one of the televisions.

Upstairs are two bedrooms and a shared bathroom between them. Billie's always had the larger room, but I was planning on taking that when they move out. Perhaps having the larger room will make up for you getting the carport, assuming you have a car?

Sorry, my break's over, but I'll reply more tonight.

Regards,

K

If he could use initials, then so could I. My break over, I headed back to the coal mine that was the emergency department. I had a good feeling about this Hammy person. He appeared friendly enough. Things didn't need to be complicated. Perhaps this would work out perfectly. I just had to wait and see. Whatever happened, it was one less thing to stress about.

Chapter 9

Henry

I'd spent a week hemming and hawing over whether to move home. Val was encouraging. She and Janet were thick as thieves, and I think Janet was a good influence. She'd worked Val out just fine and knew she needed reminders about everything.

Having Millie call me over FaceTime, her large blue eyes pleading with me to come over for a tea party, probably sealed the deal. But I still hadn't reached out to this Kandiah Bridget had found who had a room to rent.

Bridget told me he was an intern who had impressed her with his work ethic and manner. To impress Bridget was a feat, as she didn't suffer fools. I'd heard stories of her ripping colleagues to shreds in her forthright manner. Giles had tempered her somewhat, but she still lost it from time to time.

The fact she'd called me in the morning as I was finishing notes from a disastrous round told me it was meant to be. I fired off my notice to move districts and emailed Kandiah. He'd replied straight away, which had surprised me. He'd only given me a description of the place, though, and not answered any of my questions.

Not that I didn't trust Bridget, but she'd never really rented before. She lived in Halls until she moved in with my brother to the apartment my parents bought for us to live in. Giles had lived in a shit-hole before then. That Kandiah was an intern didn't mean he lived in a nice place.

From: HADH
To: Kandiah Dissanayake
Subject: Re: Room to rent
Hi, Kandiah,
The place sounds nice. I suppose as long as it's well maintained, and the shower has a decent pressure, I'll be alright. Is it modern? I know some places in the area are a little run-down. Not to want to sound like a snob, but, well...
Let me know the rent and lease situation.
Cheers,
H

I might have gone overboard with my reply. My online searches had shown there was nothing I could rent by myself without losing most of my pay packet each week. I needed a roommate, and Bridget had vouched for this person.

There was another reply later in the evening.

From: Kandiah Dissanayake
To: HADH
Subject: Re: Room to rent
Hi again,
Sorry. I had a crap day at work. Yes, the place is modern, complete with a kitchen with granite tops and a modern stove and oven. There's even a dishwasher. Did I mention there's a laundry in the bathroom upstairs? I've attached the lease, which runs until mid-January next year. I'm happy to split the rent if that's alright with you? The landlord uses an agent and there's been no issues having things fixed. Oh, and the shower has great water pressure.
Another cricket tragic—I'm glad. I've just started with a local

men's team for fun. I played in Perth growing up, but I haven't turned the arm over for a few years now, what with uni and all.

I hear you regarding your bed. The first thing I purchased when I moved here in January was a decent bed. The thought of dismantling it to move it across the passageway is the only thing that makes me question my desire for Billie's room!

I'm not a big party animal either. I'd much rather sit around a table with friends drinking good wine with soft music playing, rather than head out to clubs and bars.

Billie and Micky leave on the twenty-seventh after their furniture is packed into a container for transport. They say they'll pay rent until the middle of next month, but I can't expect them to do that, really.

Bridget was an amazing teacher in my first rotation. I was gutted when they gave me O&G, partially because I'm not really into vaginas, but Bridget made it a lot of fun. Being so close to Bridget, I assume you know Giles, too. I haven't had a lot to do with him, but he seems like a nice enough bloke.

Anyway, I've got to get to training.

K

This email made me take notice. One reason I'd agreed to move home was I wanted to find this mysterious Ken, the man from the ball. One kiss had sealed it for me, or so I'd thought. Now this man I was probably going to share a townhouse with was giving off all sorts of vibes.

He didn't do vaginas? Was he gay like me? I wasn't sure what Bridget had told him about me, but he obviously did not know I was Giles' brother. And being into cricket? That was something I could get behind.

Over the next couple of weeks, we sent brief emails back and forth. The Royal had been good and allowed me to only work two weeks of my notice and take two weeks of annual leave between finishing there and starting at Cassowary Point. I had little stuff I wanted to transport up there, but I really loved my bed. It was so comfortable, and I needed that after a hard day or night at work. I'd bought matching bedroom furniture and had a bookcase full of textbooks.

"Hammy, sweetheart." Mum was ecstatic I was moving back. "You know you can stay here. Your bedroom is still the same, and your father and I would love to have your company."

"Thanks, Mum." I sighed. Mum's call had caught me at a weak time, and I should have let it go to voicemail. I ran my hands through my hair and slumped further into the couch. I would love to have taken this couch with me to Cassowary Point. It was soft and enveloped you like a hug. "Bridget and Giles have found a place for me to rent with another doctor. I told you this."

"I know, sweetheart, but the offer is still there if it doesn't work out or anything."

Mum prattled on about how proud she was of me and how she thought I'd do wonderfully well in psych. I still wasn't convinced. I'd done a bit of reading and bumped into a friend from medical school who'd recently started the path towards becoming a psychiatrist. He'd told me how rewarding he found it.

"If I get there early, I'll bunk with you and Dad for a bit, okay?" I tried to appease her. I'd planned on taking four days to drive from Brisbane to Cassowary Point. Sure, I could do it in two days, but it was going to take at least five to get my furniture up there by truck or container, or whatever I'd arranged with the removalists.

"Of course, Hammy, of course." I could hear the love in my mother's tone. I'd never doubted the love she and Dad showed every day. Sure, they were crazy about Valentine's and all, but to them, love really was a verb.

One day, I wanted the love they had and to share it with the world.

THE MOVE DIDN'T GO to plan. My pride and joy is my black Jeep Wrangler. I bought it secondhand when I was in medical school. The week I was supposed to leave, I took it in for a service and discovered it needed new tyres and something was faulty with the brakes or something. Now the removalists were running late, but I needed to pick up my car today if I wanted to get away before Monday.

I had a few boxes of things by the door that I wanted to take with me, but the rest was packed in my room.

"Don't worry, Hammy, I'll sort it. You go get your car." Val practically shoved me out the door.

I did worry, though. With having to pay extras on my car, I couldn't stay at the opulent resorts I'd planned on up the coast. I had two options: stay in backpacker dives, or head home early and stay with Mum and Dad.

Giles and Bridget's new place only had the three bedrooms. I thought they might have another child, so it seemed tiny, but they were happy with it. Millie had reminded me I could sleep on the trundle in her room, which was sweet, but I also knew it would mean she would climb into bed with me each night.

There was still no sign of the removalists when I returned home. I was getting frantic. They assured me they'd be there. Not liking the idea of staying in backpacker resorts, I'd channelled my inner extrovert and reached out to a couple of people I'd studied with who were posted up the coast. As I was checking my phone for the hundredth time that hour, I noticed a message from Jon, a friend from uni.

JON:

Henry Hartman! Long time no speak. Sorry it's taken me a few days. Yes, stay. I need you to meet Sasha, my girlfriend. She's a paramedic up here. We've got a spare room. Stay as long as you need.

You sure? Things have changed a bit, so I might have to take you up on that.

JON:

Positive. You got me through fifth year exams, and I owe you!

Jon was exaggerating. I remember finding him in the library hyper-ventilating a week before our finals. He knew the stuff, he was just convinced he didn't. We had a placement together in sixth year too, which was lots of fun. He'd moved back to Rockhampton after graduating. It would be good to catch up.

> You working this weekend?

JON:

Nope. Here's my address.

Jon pinged a map of his address. At least I now had a Plan B. One terse phone call with the removal company when the office was about to close showed me that no, they wouldn't be able to pick up my things until Monday, but they assured me they'd get it to Cassowary Point by the following Friday. I doubted it. I was furious. My hands were clenched into fists as I hung up. If they weren't, and I hadn't flung my phone onto the couch, I would have left a crappy review for them online.

"You need to get laid." Val came out from her room dressed for a night on the town. She still exhibited the tomboy streak that we'd all known and loved whilst she was growing up, but she was definitely a woman now.

"I need to be on the road," I muttered through clenched teeth. "And I'm not dressed for going out."

Val looked me up and down. "You'll be fine. We're just going to The G Spot."

The G Spot was the bar Giles had worked at throughout uni and at which Janet now worked. It was a typical student bar with sticky tables and cheap beer. Perhaps one or two drinks wouldn't hurt.

Janet was behind the bar when we arrived, twirling her hips to the rhythm of the music blaring from the speakers. I forgot students either started early and went all night or started late and went all night. The place was pretty packed for six on a Friday night.

The wine list at The G Spot was nonexistent, and they had wine that came from taps. I couldn't think of anything worse. The beer was cheap and nasty, too. I settled on a rum and coke. A few women came and tried to grab my attention. I wasn't sure what part of "Sorry, hon, I'm not interested" they didn't understand.

I sipped at my drink. There was no way I wanted to be hungover for the drive tomorrow. I'd be sleeping on the couch tonight anyway, as I'd packed up my bed, and it would be too much effort to rearrange boxes to lay my mattress on the floor. As much as I would miss Val, I'd miss the couch more. When Christian and I had moved out of Halls into our shared apartment, the couch had looked great, but it was as uncomfortable as a concrete slab. Giles had tried to get the couch from our current apartment up to Cassowary Point when he and Bridget moved home late last year, but Mum and Dad insisted it stay put. At the time, I'd been thrilled, but now, I was regretting it.

Val dragged me to the dance floor, and we got our groove on. There were plenty of guys hitting on her. I knew my sister well enough to know she could handle herself. I grabbed a water from Janet, who was still bopping behind the bar.

"She won't be home tonight!" Janet yelled over the loud music, a huge grin on her face. "You can take her bed."

I shook my head and laughed. A guy sat beside me. He seemed a little young for me, probably still a teenager, but he kept eyeing me up and down. "Well, hello, Daddy." He cupped my chin as he whispered in my ear.

He was cute, but he was young. I'd been with older men myself over the years and been the one approaching them in bars like this. I grabbed his hand and dragged him towards the bathrooms.

As soon as the door closed behind us, the noise from the bar was muffled.

"Hey," I said in what I hoped was my kindest tone. "I've been in your position before. You come onto any guy in the bar hoping they'll pay attention. But..." I paused, so I could gather my thoughts. "It's not worth it. You're worth more than that. Fuck, you're sexy as hell, and there are hundreds of guys out there who want to fuck you into next week, but remember, be safe, and only do it if it's really what you want."

The guy started crying. Shit. I'd gone too far. I pulled him in for a hug and let him get it out. After several minutes, he calmed a bit. "Thank you. Thank you so much. I broke up with my boyfriend last week, and he's moved on, and I just, well, I don't know what I want."

"He sounds like an idiot. Are you at Brisbane Uni?" The guy

nodded. "Join the Pride Tribe. I was always too busy to get to their events, but they're good people."

If I had any regrets about my time at uni, it was that I spent too much time studying and working and hadn't made time for groups like the Pride Tribe.

The guy gave me one last hug before telling me he was heading home and thanking me for my advice.

After taking a slash, I made my way back out to the bar to find Val sucking face with some guy.

"Hey." She paused when she saw me, the guy still nipping at her neck. "We're heading out. If I don't see you tomorrow, drive safe, and we'll FaceTime, okay?"

She didn't wait for an answer, dragging her victim out by his hand, not that he was complaining.

Not in the mood to party, I made my way back home, well, my home for the last night.

In the cab on the way home, I thought how easy it would have been to hook up with the guy at the bar. He was cute, and I'm sure we could have had fun together, even though he was younger than me. But he wasn't Ken. I'd felt almost guilty even emailing Kandiah back and forth over the last few weeks. It wasn't flirting as such, and the emails were usually short and to the point, but I sensed there was something there too.

Jesus. Perhaps it was true, and I just needed someone else to get my mind off that damn kiss.

It was fun staying with Jon and catching up on what we'd been up to. When he was at work, I did a few hikes on clearly marked trails, something I'd not done in ages. Perhaps I'd be able to do some at home, too.

Jon was getting into general practice and made it sound appealing. He'd recently completed a psych rotation and told me about the fun he'd had and how he'd really gotten on with the clients. It was a relief, because I never would have thought someone like Jon would have liked psych.

The removal company collected my things first thing on Monday. I'd sent so many reminders to Val, and I had to trust she'd got my things into the container. They called me Thursday to say there'd been a slight hiccup, and they wouldn't be able to deliver things until Saturday morning. They'd taken 10 percent off the quote they'd given me, so that was at least something.

I emailed Kandiah to apologise, and he said it worked better for him, as he was working early on Friday and had the weekend off. Relenting, I arranged to spend Friday night at my parents' house. Giles was working, but Bridget, the girls, Boyd, and Emily joined us for dinner. Poor Boyd and Emily were harangued about their upcoming exams by Bridget and me. They'd both be fine, but it made me laugh Bridget was already pulling out the 'When I was at medical school...' phrase, something we'd all sworn we'd never do when we were actually at medical school.

Millie convinced her grandparents to let her have a sleepover, and sometime overnight, she'd climbed into bed with me. Having her stroke my hair out of my eyes with her little fingers and tell me how much she loved me showed me I'd made the right decision to be here. Hearing my parents' bed squeak and the giggles coming from my mother in the morning also reminded me I'd made the right decision to not move in with them.

The removal company texted me soon after 8 a.m., telling me they were half an hour away. I wish I had Kandiah's number to text him, but I flicked him a quick email. I jumped in my jeep and headed down the road to my new place. The weather was perfect. It was cooling down, and I couldn't wait to take the roof off my car and feel the breeze through my hair. Kandiah had given me the combination to open the gate and told me he had a remote control for me. I found the townhouse and parked my car.

Pushing my sunglasses on top of my head, I found my way to the door and knocked. My back to the door, I looked at the mountains in the distance. Everything was close in Cassowary Point. I'd loved growing up here, and, despite enjoying my time in Brisbane, it felt right to be home.

The door opened, and I turned, only to let out a gasp as my jaw dropped and my eyes bulged.

"Ken?"

Chapter 10

Ken

I shut the door and opened it straight away again. It couldn't be. After all these months, the guy from that kiss had found me. I was expecting my new housemate. Our email correspondence had given me good vibes, and I was excited to meet him. To discover he was one and the same did something strange to my insides. There was probably a medical term, but it was gone in the moment as I focused on trying to breathe and talk through my suddenly dry mouth.

"Sorry. I, um..." My mouth wouldn't work after all. It was too busy gaping open looking at the guy I'd fantasised about standing in front of me. He looked amazing in a tux, but in jeans and a plain black tee, he looked delectable.

"Wait." Hen ran his hand through his short beard, making me focus on his gorgeous lips—the same lips that had brought me undone those few months ago. He almost-whispered, "Kandiah?"

"No, you're Hammy?" My brain was still slow.

Henry laughed.

What were the chances? I knew Cassowary Point was small, but not that small. Perhaps the hospital was smaller.

"Can we start over?" Henry now ran his hand through his hair, drawing me to his eyes. The same hazel-coloured eyes I'd dreamt of. In the daylight, they looked like they had flecks of gold floating near the irises. Man, I was fucked. "Hi, I'm Henry Hartman."

"Ka— Ken," I stuttered. "Kandiah Dissanayake. But I usually go by Ken."

"Don't tell me, Bridget?" Hen was still laughing.

"Bridget what?" I asked, still confused by the situation.

"She doesn't like shortening your name. You've never called her Bridge, have you?" Hen looked at my furrowed brow. "Her daughters are the only ones she shortens, and sometimes my mum gets Hills instead of Hillary."

"But you're... you're Hammy?" I asked.

"My youngest brother, Boyd, could never say Henry and always called me Hemmy. When Milly was a toddler, she changed that to Hammy. It's, like, changed over the generations, I suppose."

"I just..." I was still trying not to stutter, my mouth still incredibly dry. "I just never realised it was you." It was my turn to run my hand through my hair. To an outsider looking in, seeing us mirror each other might have been amusing, but being in this moment filled me with feelings of both possibility and dread. I'd thought about this guy for months, and now here he was.

I'd been the prick to run away from him. Looking at him now, I had no idea how I could have done such a thing. He was gorgeous. "You're not Bridget's brother."

"No," he laughed. "Giles. You really didn't know?"

"How could I? I was the idiot who ran away from the best kiss of my life."

Before he had a chance to reply, there was a loud honk from a truck that broke our reunion.

"Delivery for Hartman?" A gruff-looking man in a navy singlet and shorts that sat under the apron of his belly jumped down from the cab. "I think it's boxes and a few bits of furniture."

I directed Hen where to park his car and watched as the removalists manoeuvred their truck onto our driveway.

I let my mind spiral, trying to make sense of what was happening.

Hen was real, and he was here. I was like a kid who had been shown that there was indeed a Santa, and he could do magic.

It struck me that Hen hadn't run away or told the removalists there had been a mistake. He really was here, and it looked like he was hanging around. I felt my heart race at the thought of sharing a home with this man. Suddenly, it seemed much smaller than it had when Billie and Micky lived here.

While the truck was being unloaded, we took a quick walkthrough of the townhouse. I mean, it wasn't overly large, and I left Henry to deal with the removalists. Needing to centre myself, I made my way to the kitchen and switched on the kettle.

Perhaps the only thing I had in common with my parents was a love of tea. I found the process relaxing, and I needed to calm down. My breathing was slowing, but I could feel sweat pooling on my brow. Even removing my hoodie didn't help. Had I manifested this man here?

I was second-guessing everything. I should have kept my old room and not moved across the hallway. Sure, I'd taken the slightly larger room now, but perhaps Hen needed more room? I was a tidy person, and I hated clutter. The few days since Billie and Micky had moved out had been bliss. I'd done a deep clean on my day off. I hoped Hen wasn't a slob. Fuck. What if we hated each other and couldn't get along? What if it was just that kiss holding us together? What if he wanted more?

Stuck in my own thoughts, I missed the commotion Hen was creating with the removalists.

"No, there's a mattress somewhere. There has to be," he hollered as he followed them out of the front door.

I scurried after them.

"Sorry, mate. As you can see, a piano, some chairs, and a table. Just cartons at the back. And we have to deliver these to our next place before lunch." Henry had jumped into the open container, as if he would find what I assumed was a missing mattress.

"I'm going to kill her." Henry had climbed back out and was pacing up and down the driveway. Grabbing his phone from his pocket, he had to type in the pin, as his face was not recognised by the camera. "Valerie Hillary Charlotte Hartman, where the fuck is my mattress? Answer this message or else I'm going to... fuck. I don't know. Did you fucking forget to load my mattress with the removalists? Huh? Shit. Call me."

The guy in charge shoved a clipboard in front of Henry, and he scribbled something that might have been a signature across the page. He was still pacing up and down as the truck pulled away, his face red and his arms pumping at the side of him.

"Um, tea? Coffee? Er, water?" I asked sheepishly, realising I was simply staring and not really doing anything.

"Don't tell me," Henry huffed. "Cheap tea bags and instant coffee?"

"Er, no. I've got a filter and some Ethiopian beans if you want a coffee and loose-leaf Darjeeling, Russian Caravan, French Earl Grey, or a breakfast blend if you want me to brew a pot of tea."

This got his attention. "Wow, um..." His tone softened, and he stopped pacing. "What were you going to have?"

"I think a smoky Russian Caravan sounds good, to be honest. I've only got full-fat cow's milk though, none of those nut blends or anything."

"I may be a tea and coffee snob, but I'm not that hipster as to demand plant-based milks." Hen followed me into the kitchen, a smile on his face. "This is nice," he offered, leaning up against the breakfast bar as I poured fresh water into the kettle.

"Yeah, it's not bad. I was hoping you'd be able to help me pick up a table and some chairs I've ordered from a local place. I'm sick of sitting here to eat and wanted a dining table. Not that this room could fit a big table, but I found a circular glass one that should sit nicely in the corner." Henry looked at me as I pointed where I thought the table could go. "I played my cards wrong with Billie and Micky," I tried to explain. "They had two couches, and I much preferred Micky's. It was a three seater and super comfortable. Just the right length for me to lie on. I knew Billie preferred her couch, as she and Micky argued over it so many times, so I told them I'd prefer Billie's, as it was smaller for the space. They believed me and took the couch I wanted. That one is too short." I spooned tea leaves into the warmed pot, conscious I was babbling.

"I wondered why you had a rose-coloured couch." Henry walked towards it and ran his hand down the velour back.

"The colour doesn't bother me, and it will allow a table in this space, I suppose. It's been nice putting my touches on things and, well, you know."

I hoped he did. I forced myself to shut up. There might have been room for a table and chairs now, but the elephant that also inhabited the room was taking up a lot of space. I wanted to tell him why I'd run, why I'd escaped the best kiss of my life, but I couldn't. He'd think I was coming on to him. Hen was going to be my housemate, and things would get messy if any form of relationship, let alone feelings, developed.

"So, there's an issue with your things, then?" I asked gently as I poured two cups of tea.

"Yeah." Henry huffed again, shaking his head. "My damn sister forgot to make sure they brought my mattress. The frame's there—and the chest of drawers and the bookcase and all the boxes I'd packed—but no mattress."

"She forgot?" I scrunched my nose, wondering how you could forget something like a mattress.

"It's what she'll claim. She forgets everything that's not important to her. Don't get me wrong, I love her to bits, but she's infuriating at times." Henry clenched his hands into fists, his words full of anger.

"You lived together?" I took a sip of my tea, leaning up against the kitchen side of the breakfast bar. Henry had taken a seat on one of the stools.

"Yeah. Mum and Dad bought an apartment in Brissy when Giles was at uni. He and Bridget lived there until they moved back up here. Val, my sister, she decided she didn't want to live in Halls, so she moved in with them when she came to Brisbane for uni."

"So, she's younger than you, obviously." I loved the way Henry's fingers curved around his cup. Perhaps if I focussed on them, I could ignore how good looking he was.

"Yeah. She's nineteen and in second year of law."

"Not medicine?" I asked, still imagining Hen's fingers snaking through my hair like they did at the ball.

"No." He laughed. "It's a sore spot with Giles mainly, but she was never going to be a doctor."

"So, there's an age gap between you and your sister?"

"Yeah. Seven years. Boyd's three years younger than me, and Giles is two years older."

"So, there's four of you? Is Boyd a doctor too?"

"Fifth year medicine at the uni up here." Henry took a sip of his tea. "His girlfriend—maybe fiancée, but I haven't heard yet—is close to her mum and didn't want to study in Brissy. She's also studying medicine."

"I can sense a pattern. So, your partner is a doctor, too?" As soon as I'd said this, I wished I hadn't.

"I'm single." Henry curved his lips a little, not a true smile, though. "Anyway. Did you want to pick up this table?"

WE DROVE in a deafening silence to the furniture store. I wasn't sure how to broach the kiss. He'd recognised me and looked like he'd been as shocked as I was. I didn't think Bridget would be one to arrange such a clandestine arrangement as having the two of us living together. I mean, how would she have known? Billie, yes, but she'd been too preoccupied with arranging the move, and too excited to be heading back to Brisbane to start a training program.

I wondered if we'd need a couple of trips, but the chairs and table were flat packed, and we managed to fit them into the back of the Jeep. Henry had his phone hooked up to it, but he switched off the sound system when the car started. I'd caught the first few bars of 'Plans' by Birds of Tokyo. My parents hated that I listened to pop music, thinking it was laced with messages from the Devil, but I had headphones and used them accordingly. I doubt they even realised I wasn't listening to their approved playlists.

My parents never bought flat-packed furniture. They argued it was for 'poor people'. As far as I was concerned, we weren't well off. We never had fancy holidays, and, sure, I was sent to a small Christian school, but it wasn't one that charged exorbitant fees. I'd amazed myself that I'd managed to disassemble then reassemble my bed frame when I moved it earlier in the week. When it first arrived, I paid someone to put it all together.

"I must say..." Henry was walking backwards as we carried the box containing the table into the living area. "I love putting together flat packs."

"Really?" The surprise in my voice made Henry laugh. I didn't want to accuse his family of being well off. Heck, I didn't really know them, but their home where we'd had the ball looked like it was bigger than the home I'd grown up in.

"Yeah. When Christian and I moved in together, it was all flat packed. Except for our bloody couch. That thing was as hard as concrete." I loved how expressive Hen was, his hatred of the couch shining through.

So, Hen had someone. Perhaps he wasn't in his life at the moment, but there was no doubt in my mind Hen thought highly of this Christian dude from the way he smiled when he spoke about him. I couldn't help but feel disappointed, but I wasn't surprised. Someone as amazing as Henry deserved to have people who made him feel the way I felt about him.

I was crazy to think someone as sexy and experienced as Henry would want anything with me. I'd watched some porn, but only since I left home. Mum and Dad would have had a fit if they knew what my eyes had seen. So, yeah, I knew gay guys seemed to like it when someone took their cock all the way down their throat, and they liked to pump it in and out of a guy's arse. I just doubted Henry would want to do this to me.

I offered for Hen to hook his phone up to the speaker downstairs to play music whilst we assembled the furniture, but he said he was fine and suggested I put a playlist on. I didn't really have anything. Sometimes, I listened to the radio, but the whole music culture had escaped me. Another result of my parents' fundamentalism. Henry was no doubt used to guys who knew their music and probably listened to a huge variety of genres. It wasn't that I wasn't from his world, but I'd lived in a different orbit. My mind was duelling. On one side, it wanted Henry, and I would do almost anything to make him notice me. On the other, I didn't rank high enough to be noticed.

After opening my music app, I scrolled a little before finding the *Mamma Mia!* soundtrack. This was one film I'd watched repeatedly, but never in my parents' presence. I hated that I was almost thirty years old, and I'd experienced nothing. I'd been sheltered well into my twenties, long after my friends and colleagues. At uni, there were others who were socially awkward, so I never stood out this much. Billie had laughed at my awkwardness to begin with, but she had also accepted me as me.

Last week, she told me she was proud of me finding a new housemate so quickly. She thought I'd actually end up paying the whole rent myself. It had been tempting until I examined my finances. The first few years of an accounting degree came in handy, after all.

I wasn't sure Hen would cope with my idiosyncrasies.

He had the table out of the box and parts in piles before I could even open one of the chairs. The instructions were simply pictures with no text. I couldn't work out which bits went where, but Hen had the table assembled as I'd finally worked out which way the seat went on the chair. And I hadn't even put any screws in.

"Want some help?" I was sitting on the floor. Hen was on his knees as he almost crawled towards me. I hoped he didn't notice my breathing quicken.

"I'm hopeless at this." I shook my head and hoped he thought my embarrassment came from my lack of skills with an Allen key instead of from being so close to him that I could smell his scent of sandalwood and citrus.

"Practice. That's all you need. If we do these together, next time, you'll be quicker." Hen's smile was captivating. I knew what his lips tasted like, and I wanted to taste them again. I realised I had no idea what I was doing, and not just with the furniture assembly.

Hen hadn't brought up the ball. I wanted to. My swift exit after our kiss was hanging over us like a stench in the room. Neither of us wanted to mention it, and yet, it was there.

"I, um, I, well, I didn't..." I started as Hen turned a hex nut with the Allen key, putting the third chair together. It was going quicker now, and we were in a rhythm after assembling two already. His phone rang, and he held up a finger as he answered it, as if telling me to hold that thought.

"Valerie Hillary Charlotte Hartman. Where the fuck is my

mattress?" Henry had placed his phone on the glass table and hit the speaker button, meaning I was listening in to their conversation.

"What's with the full names, Henry Alexander Dominic Hartman?" So, that was where the HADH had come from. It wasn't a weird combination of letters that sounded like an M.

"My mattress, Val. Where is it?" Henry stopped tightening the screw he had been working on and sat back on his haunches.

"Yeah, well, about that." Val drew out the last two words, as if she was trying to plan what she was going to say. "See, you always told me how luxurious it was, so I decided to test it out. And I might have put it on my bed on Saturday after you left and forgotten about it. Sorry!"

"Valerie!" Henry yelled as he stood up and picked up his phone. "How could you?"

"You're right." Val didn't sound at all repentant. "It's a bloody comfortable mattress. How about I buy you a new one?"

"You can't afford it," Henry huffed. "It's not one of those out of the box numbers. It cost thousands."

"Well, more fool you for spending money on something so frivolous." Val was giving back as good as she got.

"When you work twelve-hour night shifts, I'll let you call sleep frivolous. I can't even with you at the moment." Henry pressed the button to end the call without a farewell and tossed his phone on the table. "Shit. Sorry. I hope I didn't scratch the table."

"It's all good. I totally get the nice mattress, though. It was the first thing I splashed out on, too." Well, apart from the black suit and the clothes I'd bought leading up to the ball.

"She doesn't do it to be selfish, either." Henry had sat back down as we worked on the last chair together. "She literally has a mind like a sieve."

"Perhaps she needs better sleep, and she'll get that on your mattress?" I offered.

"Look at you and your positive reframing. You'll be following me to psych next." Hen laughed as he tightened another screw as I held the chair in place.

I didn't tell him it was the area I wanted to end up in and that I was so infatuated with him, I'd probably follow him anywhere. I was as screwed as the bolts that held my new table and chairs together.

Chapter 11

Henry

I still couldn't believe it. Somehow, I'd managed to rent a room and share a place with the man who had given me the best kiss of my life. For months, I'd dreamt of Ken. I knew that deep down, one reason I'd returned home was to see if I could find him. It had been stupid to think that anything would come of it. After all, he was the one who ran from me. He probably hated the kiss and didn't know how to tell me.

Assembling furniture had been fun, but neither of us had addressed what happened at the ball. I sensed Ken was about to when Val finally returned my call. I had no idea what to do about my mattress. It would cost an arm and a leg to get it up here. With the car repairs and the move, I had little spare cash floating around to buy a new one.

Pretending I needed to get some groceries in town, I made myself scarce as soon as the furniture was finished. Ken had explained he enjoyed cooking and promised me a curry for dinner that night. I'd already arranged to have dinner with Giles and his family on Sunday and wondered if I should invite Ken.

Part of me wanted to, but I also didn't want my brother to see how I was around Ken. I knew I was infatuated. I knew I wanted to stare at him for hours. This was how I was when I met a new guy. In my head, I was planning our wedding—as the sun set on the beach with all our family and friends present, followed by cocktails and canapés at a resort and dancing until dawn. Then Ken and I would jet off for a week or two of a honeymoon in a secluded place where we could just be together.

I wasn't sure why I wanted a beach wedding. I hated going to the beach and getting sand between my toes, but, somehow, it seemed so romantic. We wouldn't be too formal, linen probably. I could imagine white linen would look stunning against Ken's skin.

Shit. I had to stop this. There was no way I could develop a relationship with Ken, because in a few weeks, he'd be sick of my clinginess, and I'd be looking for somewhere else to live. Overhearing my parents having sex this morning had been enough. I didn't want to have to experience that regularly by moving back in with them. Last night, I'd tried to argue that I could sleep downstairs, in what had been Giles and Bridget's room when they were living there, but Mum said my room was sitting there with my things in it.

I wandered around the shops looking at shoes and ties. No one wore ties in Cassowary Point. At uni, I'd displayed them on a wall in my room by draping them over a piece of thick dowel that I'd attached to the wall with black silk ribbon. I now had a couple of pieces of art to display and nowhere to really display my tie collection.

The department store was the main place in town to sell nice ties. The ones in the local menswear stores were mainly polyester and had garish prints. Nothing caught my eye. I tried on some shoes, not that I needed any, but they were another one of my vices.

Walking past a shop, I saw some rose-coloured placemats in the window. They were an almost perfect match for the couch, so I bought four to go on Ken's new table. The sales assistant even talked me into purchasing matching serviettes. She tried to get me to buy candles, too, but I figured that would give Ken the wrong message.

The trouble was, I wasn't sure what the right message was. Well, my head did. It knew that thoughts of candlelight dinners and romance were a hell no, even if my heart disagreed.

So, yes, I ignored the candles and walked past the flowers in the supermarket, even though they would look great in the living area. I grabbed a bottle of wine, figuring I could argue it was something I wanted to drink. Ken had drunk beer from memory at the ball. Who was I kidding? I could still picture him bringing the bottle to his lips, wishing its opening was my lips.

As I drove home, I wondered if I should have bought beer instead. I mean, Ken said he was cooking curry, and beer went with curry. Was he Indian? Fuck. I didn't even know. Probably. I was second-guessing myself, as if I was going on a date. Taking a few deep breaths, I reminded myself that this definitely wasn't a date. It was two housemates sitting down to a meal together. Come Monday, we'd probably have different rosters and end up hardly seeing each other. I just had to get through this weekend.

I didn't have any plans for Sunday, other than dinner with my brother, but I knew I could drop in on my parents or visit Boyd. Boyd and Emily were probably studying, but I could help, couldn't I? No, I'd turn up at Giles' early and offer to babysit Millie and Mia and let my brother and his wife have an afternoon at the movies or something. Whatever I did, I had to make sure it didn't involve spending the day with the man I was lusting after.

The smells that permeated downstairs as I walked in the door made my mouth water. A mix of spices that I couldn't put my finger on, combined with the smell of coconut and ginger.

"Wow! That smells amazing." I walked into the kitchen and placed the wine on the bench before leaning around Ken's shoulder for a look. "Have you made enough for an army?"

"It's always better the next day, and I like to take some to work for lunch during the week. I tried not to make it too spicy. I hope it's okay." Ken seemed concerned he might offend me. There was little chance of that happening.

"I'm sure it's fine. I love spicy food, so don't worry about me." Pouring a glass of water from the tap, I went to sit at the breakfast bar.

"Tea?" Ken offered.

"Water's fine. I grabbed a bottle of wine, which I'll open in a bit. Oh." I dug into the bags I'd put on the table. "And I saw these and thought they'd look good on the new table."

I handed the placemats and serviettes to Ken, who stroked them as if they were made of silk instead of raw cotton. "Thanks." He smiled. "I... That's really thoughtful. Did you get a new mattress?"

"I'll sleep on the couch tonight." I hadn't even thought of looking. On Monday, I'd check how much transport would be, but I figured it would probably be cheaper to hire a truck and bring it myself, not that I had a week to take off work to arrange this. Bloody Val.

Ken asked me to set the table, which I was happy to do. I arranged it so we sat next to each other instead of opposite where we could stare at each other. This was probably some form of self-preservation and not that I wanted to be close to him.

The curry was sublime. I moaned as I forked mouthfuls in and had a whole-body experience where I had to put the fork down, as my shoulders relaxed and lowered.

"I'm glad you like it." Ken smiled, as if satisfied with my reaction.

"Where did you say it was from?"

"Sri Lanka. My grandparents came to Australia as newlyweds, so I'm, what, third generation."

"Where are your parents now?" I asked, trying to concentrate on the flavours of the spices. I definitely detected cumin and coriander, but was that fennel seeds too?

"Perth." Ken cut some chicken with a knife, the force suggesting he didn't want to talk further. "I..." Ken cleared his throat, "I, well, I, um, I'm sorry I ran away. At the ball."

Finally, we were addressing the subject I wanted answers to, but I wondered if Ken's explanation would be like opening Pandora's box. Would I be better off not knowing and simply lusting after my new housemate, believing he ran because he wasn't into me? I almost willed my heart rate to slow—which didn't help, of course—and took a steadying breath.

"I'd thought it was a pretty wonderful kiss." I tried to remain upbeat and hoped my smirk and raised eyebrows conveyed this, despite fearing what Ken was going to tell me next.

"Oh, no." Ken played with his serviette, and I suspected the sweat on his brow wasn't from the curry. "It was magical. It was just..."

I wanted to give him time to gather his thoughts and say what he wanted to, but I also wanted to put him out of his misery.

"Don't worry. I seem to be a testing subject for guys working out their sexuality. I get it. You're not gay, and that's okay. Most guys figure that out once they've fucked me. It's why I don't bottom anymore."

"No." Ken looked at me with sad eyes before he placed a hand on my wrist, and I wondered if I would have been better sitting opposite him. "I'm gay. I just..."

Ken's hand on me sent volts of electricity through my veins. My heart was definitely beating faster. In the part of my brain that tried to deny the kiss had been as magical as my memory portrayed, I rationalised that I'd overthought how amazing Ken's touch was. It was lovely to realise my memories were indeed correct.

"My parents." Ken let out a huge breath. "They're ultra conservative and involved in a church that is more like a cult. It's so fundamentalist. They want me to marry a nice Sri Lankan girl, have one or two children, and take over my father's accountancy firm."

"But you're a doctor, aren't you?" Had I missed something in the emails we'd traded?

"I did a few years of an accountancy degree before I realised how much I hated it, and then I had to do a bridging course before I started medicine. I did my first couple of years part time too, so it's taken me ages to finish. My parents let me live at home, but they don't support my decision to become a doctor."

"I'm sorry." Ken removed his hand, and I wanted to reach out and touch him and maintain this intimacy and connection that felt so right, but I didn't want him to get the wrong idea. Well, the right idea maybe that... Fuck, who knew what the wrong or right idea was in this situation? "And they don't approve of you being gay?"

"Not exactly." Ken chuckled, once again playing with the serviette on his lap. "I tried to tell them when I was about fifteen, but then I backtracked and told them I was joking when they threatened to send me to a conversion camp."

"At least they're trying to stamp it out here." I'd heard of such atrocities overseas, but not here. Perhaps it shouldn't have surprised me.

"So, yeah." Ken went back to eating. "I have no experience with men, which was why I ran. I thought you'd want to, I don't know, take me behind the marquee and just, well, fuck me, and I got scared."

"Oh my god. No," I exclaimed, this time unable to stop myself grabbing Ken's wrist. "Sure, I've blown guys and been blown in bathrooms at clubs before, but unless a guy begged me, I wouldn't go from kissing them to fucking them without, like, a conversation at least."

It was hard to break away from touching Ken, but I managed to. We both finished our meals in silence, our eyes meeting frequently. I wanted to eat as slow as possible to prolong this silent moment, but soon, my plate was empty.

"Well, now you understand why," Ken said eventually as he stood and gathered our empty plates. "And now we're housemates..."

"Exactly. And I don't want to stuff that up, so, well, how about I do the dishes, and..." I swallowed the saliva that pooled in my mouth. "And I'll unpack some things and find my doona, which is in one of the boxes upstairs, and I'll sleep on this stunning rose-coloured couch tonight. Deal?"

"Deal." Ken tried to smile, but his eyes were round instead of tilted upwards like his lips were, hinting he was scared.

My bed frame slotted together, and whilst it would have helped to have someone to assist, I needed time away from Ken. Sitting next to him at dinner had been torture. His deep-brown eyes were so expressive, and as he explained about his family and their reaction to him coming out, he looked as though he was seconds from bursting into tears.

My mum could be a lot at times. She meant it in a good way though and was always so apologetic when she realised she'd upset someone. I couldn't imagine my parents not accepting my sexuality. It had taken me a while to tell them I was gay, but they'd suspected it.

I was seventeen when I first had my heart broken. Jesse had been a year older than me and in his final year of school. We caught up after school to study. Study sessions turned into make-out sessions, which turned into blow jobs. I assumed he was as gay as me. He'd pass me in the corridors at school and smile at me. My heart fluttered with every bit of attention. One weekend, he told me his parents would be away and suggested I come over to study.

We didn't get a great deal done, well, not the chemistry that awaited in our textbooks. Neither of us knew what we were doing, but after kissing for a shorter time than usual, he led me to his room where he had me climb onto his bed, placed me on my hands and knees, smothered lube on his cock and around my hole, and pressed inside.

There'd been no prep, and it had hurt like hell. Fortunately, Jesse came quickly, but I was soft by this stage. There'd been no talk of me reciprocating the experience. Jesse climbed out of his bed and went back to playing the video game he was obsessed with. Even though I felt used and more than a little sore, I wondered if this was what teenage relationships were about. The guys in the locker room at school talked about getting their rocks off and fucking girls, but it was always about them, and never about their partners. I vowed to be different if I got to fuck him and at least try and make it pleasurable for him.

Later that evening, I suggested I try fucking him. He thought we needed to try him fucking me again to see if he could last longer. He praised my tight hole, telling me he'd never come so quickly before, and perhaps that should have shot up some red flags.

Another red flag should have been that Jesse never wanted to talk about our future. His senior formal was approaching, and I assumed he'd invite me. When I broached the subject, he'd simply smile before leaning in and kissing me.

A week before the formal, he told me he was taking Evangeline Miller. Evangeline was the school captain and a really lovely girl. She was kind to everyone and the type of person you couldn't help but like. I was still jealous though. Ignoring how hurt I was, I went over to help Jesse get ready. We made out, and I blew him. I can still remember the stroke of his fingers down my cheek when he told me he wished he could take me instead.

I tried to be happy for my new friend, my boyfriend. When I saw photos afterwards, Jesse and Evangeline were a gorgeous couple. He looked attentive, and she looked at him as if she couldn't believe she was there with him. She had the same hearts in her eyes as I did.

No one expected Evangeline to run from class six weeks later to hurl in a waste paper bin. Jesse and I were studying one afternoon when Evangeline came around in tears to tell Jesse she was pregnant. I can still hear him yelling at her to get rid of it as he threw his arms in the air. This was a side of Jesse I'd never seen before.

Even after all these years, I can still picture the lounge room at Jesse's house we were sitting in, its brown leather couches and the vase of silk orchids that sat on the side table. After she'd gone, I was simply sitting there in shock, lying on a cushion on the floor, contemplating that Jesse had been screwing someone behind my back. I thought back to the times Jesse had screwed me. We'd never used a condom, and I'd never asked. Had he used one with Evangeline? Had he used one with anyone else? Was there a chance I was infected with something?

I asked him what he thought we were.

"Bro, we're buddies. I'm not gay or anything."

I could still feel the metaphorical punch to my gut and was glad Jesse's mum had those horrid silk flowers I could stare at. Fortunately, I tested not-positive afterwards and had always ensured me and my partners were wrapped up well after that.

I'd not thought of Jesse in years. I didn't know where he was, but I assumed he was with a woman and that he was the type of guy who'd picked guys like me up in bars for a night of fun.

I hardly met his parents, but I never got the impression they would care if Jesse was into guys. There didn't seem to be any reason for him to have to deny his sexuality, but he'd still chosen to do it.

Coming out hadn't been a big song and dance. I assumed that if I went to formal with Jesse, then that would have been indication enough. In the end, I told my family around the dinner table one Friday night, and they were cool with things. Dad asked me to pass the salt, and Mum reminded me there were condoms in the bathroom drawer.

It angered me that Ken's parents were so judgemental, and the fact they had threatened him with conversion therapy shocked me. No wonder he'd run from the kiss. Shaking off my memories and thoughts about Ken, I gathered my doona and pillows and headed downstairs. It was quiet, and I assumed Ken had escaped to his room. It sounded different in Cassowary Point. There wasn't the same level of traffic, and the insects and frogs created a symphony of sound outside the open glass door that led to our courtyard.

As much as I liked the breeze, the sound was annoying. It wasn't late. I didn't want to watch television. I let out a breath and reached for my phone.

"Y-yes?" Giles answered in a breathless voice. "This had better be important."

I could hear Bridget moaning in the background and telling Giles to hang up the phone.

"It's nothing." I sighed. Giles simply hung up on me and no doubt went back to what he was doing, which was his wife.

Putting my headphones on, I reached for my favourite playlist. I wanted the love that was talked about in these songs. I wanted an all-consuming heat that burned for another person, one that was reciprocated. I wanted to be truly, madly, deeply in love.

I tried to get comfortable on the couch. It was difficult. It wasn't meant for my six-three frame, and it wasn't meant for lying on. Checking the time, I figured it wasn't too late to call my younger brother. Boyd didn't answer, messaging me fifteen minutes later, telling me he'd been balls deep in Emily, but if it was urgent... I wanted to leave him to his postcoital bliss, but I needed to make plans for getting away from Ken in the morning.

Need help studying tomorrow?

BOYO:

Nah, thanks, bro. All good.

I needed to be out of this place. I couldn't stand another day around Ken, what with his smouldering glances and the way my skin prickled in the best way when he touched me. Perhaps I just needed to bite the bullet and move home to Mum and Dad's until I could work out the mattress situation. I could probably even borrow one from them if I wanted, but I wanted *my* mattress. Damn you, Val.

"Ha, Hammy." At Mum's breathlessness, I could feel my cock and balls shrivel. "Is this urgent?"

"No, Mum." I let out a breath and rubbed my forehead with my fingers. "Get back to Dad. It had better be Dad there with you."

"Is it urgent, blossom?" I heard Dad in the background.

"Talk tomorrow, Hammy." Mum must have dropped her phone, and I hung up before I could hear any more.

There was no way I was going home. I couldn't believe how sexed up my parents were after thirty years of marriage. I wasn't sure if I should be proud or disgusted. It wouldn't have surprised me if Val was out getting some too. Every single member of my family was getting down with their partners. I was the odd one out, alone and lonely.

I wanted to talk to someone, but I wasn't sure what about. I thought of Ken in bed above me and wondered if he was thinking of me in the same way I was thinking of him. Did his yearning match mine, and did he feel the same way from the touches we'd shared over dinner? In the end, I texted Christian.

Christian was the first person I told I was attracted to boys. I'd tell him about the bums I'd noticed, and he'd tell me about the breasts he'd been obsessed with that week. There was never any sexual tension between us. We accepted each other as friends, and that was it. Christian had been there when so many of my short-lived romances ended. He tried to suggest I ease back a bit, but he also knew I threw myself all in at any hint of a relationship.

He and I talked one-night stands and how I even entered into them thinking they might go further, usually disappointed when they didn't. Christian had had a few girlfriends at uni and dated the same girl for several months in his last year. But he went to the mines, and they broke it off.

> Hey. You out west or in the big smoke?

CHRISTIAN:

> Hey! I'm in Brissy. How's CP?

> Arrived yesterday. Moved into the shared place today. You'll never guess, but my housemate is the guy I kissed at the ball.

CHRISTIAN:

The one who ran?

> Yeah. He's got some baggage, I think. Anyway, I'm determined that we will be housemates and nothing more. I will not get romantically attached, and there will be no happily ever after.

CHRISTIAN:

You tell yourself that, buddy! I'm heading up next weekend. You working?

> Don't think so. Wait, you've got more than one weekend off?

CHRISTIAN:

Yeah. Taking some leave. Checking out CP Uni. Hey. I'm out tonight but talk tomorrow.

> Balls deep, I assume.

CHRISTIAN:

Not yet, but the night is young!

It would be good to see my best friend again. We could head out and see if we could both hook up. It would help me get my mind off Ken. One week until I saw him. One week to keep things purely as housemates. Surely I could do that.

Chapter 12

Ken

Henry had insisted he help with the dishes, but I'd all but shooed him out of the kitchen. I couldn't be near him any longer and not leap into his arms. When he touched me, I thought my skin might melt. If that was his hand on my arm, I couldn't help but imagine our naked chests pressed together or even the feel of his penis against mine. Thinking of his cock had mine swelling.

As soon as I finished at the sink, I headed to my room and shut the door. Why was God punishing me like this? Were my parents correct, and this was temptation? If things carried on as they were, I'd need to be delivered from evil.

Except, my attraction to men wasn't evil. I'd tried to justify Jesus' message of love and that we should love both God and our neighbour as ourself so many times. Love wasn't cutting off family because they were programmed differently to what had been the accepted for eons. Sure, there were depictions of homosexuality throughout history, but it had never been accepted as well as it had over the last couple of decades. Why couldn't they accept me?

I needed to acknowledge that my parents were wrong. Heck, I didn't believe in that God anymore, but old habits die hard and all.

Henry was downstairs. Well, I assumed he was. His bedroom door was open with the lights off when I used the bathroom. The couch was mighty uncomfortable to lie on. Henry was an inch or so taller than me, so it would be worse for him than when I'd tried it in the past.

I couldn't stop thinking about his body draped over the sofa. He was so close and yet so far away. He'd been clear that we were housemates, and that was it. That was the sensible thing to do. I'd always done the sensible thing, always taken the approved path. The least sensible thing I'd done was kiss him at the ball. That kiss, though. My lips tingled when I remembered it. It hadn't been my first kiss ever, but the first time I'd kissed a man. The feelings it evoked in me, not just lust, but acceptance and belonging. A sense of finally doing the right thing for me and not the *sensible* thing.

Kayla had been my first anything. She wasn't Sri Lankan, but her parents were members of the same congregation as my parents. Kayla was studying to be a teacher and busy with her classes. We had dinner together as families once a week as part of home fellowship, and sometimes, we'd go to approved movies or out to dinner. I never told her I was gay. Her friendship was nice. She was as confused about her parents' faith as I was but went along to keep the peace.

We were leaders at a youth camp one summer when we first kissed. The last ones around the fire at night. It was romantic, I suppose, and she leant in. There was no spark or passion, but her smile showed she seemed to like it. Don't get me wrong, Kayla's a gorgeous woman, but she did nothing for me. A month or so after the camp, she told me her parents were away for the weekend, and she wanted to have sex.

Her bluntness surprised me. One of the reasons I'd gone out with her was because I figured she wouldn't expect intimacy because of the teachings of our parents' church. She told me she trusted me and wanted me to be her first. We'd talked about our faiths and how I was growing more and more apart from my parents, and she thought that meant I wanted to have sex, too.

Some may call it experimentation, even though I was twenty-three. I forced myself to close my eyes and picture the men on the fragrance ads that graced the bus stops near the uni. I tried to imagine Kayla was a man, but she was too soft and gentle. She didn't come, but she told me it was enjoyable. I'd closed my eyes and envisaged a fantasy man in order to fill the condom with my spunk.

So, yeah, it wasn't the best experience for either of us, really. We tried again another time, with similar results. A little later, Kayla told me she'd met a teacher at her school, and she really liked him. They're married now, and I hope the sex for her has improved.

It was more than craving a hard body underneath or on top of me, though. I want to be close to someone, to sit and watch telly together, to touch them and be in someone's presence. My parents have no great love story. Their marriage was all but arranged. They've never been ones for public shows of affection or stolen kisses in front of my sisters or me, but despite what I saw growing up, that's what I dream about having.

At midnight, when I still couldn't sleep, I crept downstairs, concerned Henry would be awake on the couch. A streetlight shone in from below the blinds on the glass doors to the courtyard, ensuring the room wasn't in complete darkness. Henry's chest rose and fell in a rhythmic pattern. He looked so uncomfortable folded around his makeshift bed. One arm was wedged against an arm of the couch, the other across his stomach. A foot was on the ground, the other draped over the end. The couch was hardly long enough for his tall body, but he slept. His doona threatened to hit the floor, so I grabbed it and tucked it around him.

I wanted to kiss his cheek but settled for gazing at his closed eyes. His lashes were long and touched his cheeks. Every so often, his nose twitched, and he mumbled something I couldn't understand.

Heading back to my bed, I wished the couch was wider so I could have laid next to my new housemate. I'd never spent a night with anyone. My parents would have questioned my absence if I'd ever tried. The thought of curling up with Henry made my chest warm and my cock swell. It was probably better we weren't sharing a bed, after all.

THE SOUND of the shower woke me soon after 6 a.m. Immediately, my thoughts turned to a naked Henry in my home. I'd felt his body through his suit that night. I knew he was firm, and there was hardly a skerrick of fat on his lean frame. Had he woken up with a cock as hard as mine? Was he in the shower stroking and playing with himself, bringing himself to orgasm? Did he have the same urgency to come as I did, or was he so experienced that I wasn't even a blip on his radar?

As soon as he finished, I took his place, avoiding him whilst he was getting dressed in his room. I imagined showering with him, soaping him up, and washing all of him. I wanted to touch and play with his cock, feel its weight in my hands, and perhaps even drop to my knees to take him in my mouth.

The man I'd craved for months was in my home, and I was standing naked in the same place he'd stood minutes before. My cock twitched without me touching it, yearning for release. I could hardly hold myself up at the thought of a naked Henry. I braced myself, one fist curling against the tile, the other grasping my cock and squeezing, trying to both chase the release I desperately needed and make this feeling continue for as long as possible. My breaths heaved as my hand imagined it was Henry touching me, and it didn't take long to come, ropes of ejaculate mingling with the water before washing their way down the drain. Would they join with Henry's down there? For all I knew, he hadn't made himself come in the shower. He probably hadn't even thought of me as he performed his morning ablutions.

There was a cricket game that afternoon, and I wanted to invite Henry along. I usually went to the market on Saturday or Sunday morning and grabbed items for the week ahead. Billie and I had pooled food money. She loved my creations, and I loved cooking, so it seemed to be a win-win. Micky had helped when he moved in, but more often than not, I was the one in the kitchen. I tried to ensure there were always leftovers in the fridge.

"Morning." I bounced off the bottom step into the kitchen. Henry was sitting at the breakfast bar, a mug of tea in his hands.

"Hey. I just made a pot of tea. Hope you don't mind." He winced as he sat upright.

"You okay?" I poured a cup for myself and added some milk before grabbing ingredients for an omelette.

"Yeah. Stiff back, that's all." Again, Henry shut his eyes tightly as he rubbed his lower back. "You were right about the couch not being comfortable."

He looked peaceful when I came down and ogled him overnight. "So, mattress shopping today, then?" I started chopping bacon and tomatoes. "I hope you don't mind, but I'm cooking omelettes."

"You don't need to cook for me, but thanks." Henry smiled, still with his hand on his lower back.

Pulling open drawers, I searched for the heat pack I thought I'd seen somewhere, hoping Billie hadn't taken it with her. I found it and threw it in the microwave for the required time.

"Here." I wrapped it in a tea towel and walked around to press it against Henry's back.

"Thanks." Henry's voice was soft, and our eyes lingered on each other for slightly longer than was normal.

"I, um, Billie and me used to pool grocery money, and I'd shop and cook most of the time. Not sure what you want to do." I went back to chopping vegetables and sipping my tea.

"You sure? I mean, that curry was delicious."

"Yeah. I'm sure. Is there anything you don't eat? I usually head to the market on a Saturday or Sunday morning. You could join me?" I swallowed, hoping I didn't sound too eager.

"You just want my car." Henry laughed.

"No." I hoped he didn't think I was using him. "I usually walk down there, and if I grab too much, I catch a cab or something home."

"Sounds good. I haven't been to the Point Markets in years."

Henry seemed to enjoy breakfast, and I let him help with loading the dishwasher. He told me the heat pack had done wonders for his back, but he still stretched it out by twisting at his waist. I wished I was adept at giving massages, but then again, I didn't think I could trust my hands on his body.

We made the trip to the market in silence. Henry again turned off the music that started when he connected his phone to the charger in the car.

It seemed almost domestic to be at the markets with him. I had the people I usually saw for my things and a route I tried to stick to. Henry simply followed, his dark glasses covering his eyes.

"Dr Ken." Tam, a delightful woman who spoke Vietnamese with her family and was always on the lookout for exotic ingredients for me, waved me over as soon as she saw me. "I got eggplant."

She held up some purple and white eggplant in a way that looked quite phallic.

"Looks great. I'll take six." Henry was giggling next to me.

"Eggplants look like penis. Don't stick them up poop hole." Tam placed the eggplant in one of my burlap bags as if her conversation was normal market talk. "This your boyfriend?" She nodded at Henry.

"My new housemate. Henry, this is Tam, Tam, Henry."

"He's a good doctor. He looked after my Lin when she had Kylie." I pointed at some other items as Tam added them to the bag whilst talking to us. She kept a running total of what I owed in her head. "You want fresh galangal?" She added some to my bags without a response.

I was handing over my cash when Tam grabbed my arm and started waving over my shoulder. "Dr Bridget! Dr Bridget!"

Henry and I were here as housemates and nothing more, so there was no reason this needed to be awkward. I felt uncomfortable, though, wondering if Bridget could see the desire I had for her brother-in-law.

"Mrs Tam. How are you?" Bridget asked as she picked up some parsley.

"Just Tam. Dr Ken introduced me to his new houseman. He's very sexy." The older woman giggled as if she was a teenager and Hen and I weren't there.

"Yes, Henry's my brother-in-law, Giles' brother," Bridget explained as she handed over some coins for her herbs.

Tam went on to her next customers as Bridget followed us. She was wearing a hat, which was a little unlike her. I thought it best not to ask.

"Where are the girls?" he asked his sister-in-law as we wandered.

"With their father. I'm on my way to the hairdresser. I was reading an article last night, and Milly came up behind me, and I wasn't listening to what she was saying, but apparently, she wanted to play hairdressers, and she's hacked half my hair off." Bridget was so matter of fact.

"No!" Henry gasped. "Giles must be heartbroken. He's always raved on about your hair."

"It's my bloody hair, and it's time for a change. You two seem to be getting along alright." Bridget paused to grab some mandarins from another stall.

"You're coming to dinner tonight too, aren't you, Kandiah?" The way Bridget spoke, it was more of a statement rather than a question.

I looked to Henry, who was examining bananas. Did he want me there? "Um, alright?" The inflection at the end turned my response into a question, but Bridget left it.

There was never a list when I shopped, but in my head, I was planning a menu for the week. I was on late shifts on Thursday and Friday, but I'd cook in the mornings. I had no idea what Henry's roster looked like. As soon as I bought something, Henry took the bag from me, insisting on carrying our purchases. And after we'd finished shopping, we loaded up the car and headed home.

"No, don't." I reached over and almost touched Hen's hand as he went to turn off the music again. "I like this song."

"You know Augie March?" Henry sounded surprised.

"Yeah. I went to a concert in Perth a few years back. 'One Crowded Hour' is one of my favourites." My parents hadn't known about the concert or my listening habits.

'Why Do I Keep You?' by Telenova was up next, and Henry tapped along on the steering wheel.

"There's cricket this afternoon," I mentioned as casually as I could as we unpacked the bags from Hen's Jeep.

"Yeah?" Henry's eyebrows shot towards his hairline, and he appeared to be interested.

"It's just a social thing, really, but I'm sure they'd love to see you."

"Lock it in, Eddie." Henry smiled, repeating the catchphrase from the quiz show on the telly.

I wasn't sure why I was doing this to myself, spending time with this man who was only going to be a housemate. His smiles went straight to my heart, and the sound of his voice reverberated from my head to my toes. There must be other men in Cassowary Point who I could form an attachment to. But then I'd be forced to see Henry parade his conquests through our place. My chest tightened at the thought. I didn't want Henry parading anyone but me. And that was out of the question. I was well and truly screwed.

I SHOULDN'T HAVE BEEN SURPRISED that Hen fitted in perfectly at cricket. He knew a few of the guys from growing up in Cassowary Point, and so many there knew his family. He was a handy left-handed bowler too, and it didn't show that he hadn't played for a while.

In many ways, it was easier being around him with others. I could watch him listen and focus on Armon talking about something his wife had achieved or one of the other guys talking about the enormous fish he'd caught the day before without getting caught staring.

"Do we need to grab a bottle of wine or some flowers?" I asked Henry as we left the cricket ground to head to his brother's home. I had been nervous the first time I headed to cricket training, but it had nothing on the thought of dinner with my former registrar and her family.

"Nah. It's just Giles." Hen tapped away at the steering wheel again, another boppy song floating through the speakers.

"I just feel awkward turning up empty-handed," I admitted.

"Could always grab some lollies for the girls, I suppose. That would really piss Gilbo off." Henry was smiling.

"Gilbo?"

"Giles. It's just a family nickname. He hates it, so make sure you use it."

I would do no such thing. I'd received an email telling me that my next rotation was probably going to be in cardiology, so I didn't want to say anything that would piss off a Hartman.

Giles and Bridget's home was gorgeous. An old Queenslander style house on stilts with a garage underneath. Its white weatherboards looked fresh and clean, and I could imagine listening to the rain pelt on the tin roof in one of the many summer storms that came through Cassowary Point.

"Uncle Hammy's here! Uncle Hammy's here!" Two little faces peered out of the picture window at the front of the house as we made our way up the path.

"Get away from the window." Giles sounded stern as he talked to the girls, appearing at the door with one on each hip as we climbed the stairs.

"Uncle Hammy." The older girl, Millie, swung from her father's shoulder into Hen's arms.

"Welcome, Kandiah." Giles shook my hand now that he had a free one. "Come in, come in."

"Ken is fine, sir." I hoped my voice didn't croak, but I cleared my throat just the same.

Polished floorboards were the first thing I noticed as we headed straight into the living area. The girls had a playroom off to the side of the space to which Mia, the younger daughter, ran when her father put her down. Millie wasn't leaving Hen's side. It looked like bedrooms were off the living area with a kitchen at the back.

Giles led us outside onto a large deck. Bridget was watering some plants in the spacious backyard. There was a large round table that looked like it could seat a dozen people, and an outdoor couch and chairs.

"Have a seat." Giles pointed to the chairs. Hen and Milly had taken the couch, and I was glad I didn't have to sit next to him.

Mia appeared, pushing a doll's pram with a plastic dinosaur and several books in it.

"Girls, you remember Kandiah from the hospital?" Bridget appeared up the back steps, wiping her hands on her jeans.

"Please, Ken is fine," I said. Mia shoved a book in my lap and proceeded to climb up onto my lap. "Nice hair." I nodded to Bridget, who sported a pixie cut as she removed her sun hat.

"It's going to take some getting used to, that's for sure. And no more hairdressers, Miss Millie." Bridget laughed.

"I get to pretend I'm sleeping with a different woman tonight." Giles grabbed his wife and drew her in for a kiss. "I'm just glad she smells the same, or else I might not be able to get it up." I could feel my cheeks redden at Giles' sexual talk. None of my sisters or their husbands talked like this.

As Giles and Bridget went inside and fussed in the kitchen, Hen and I entertained the girls. I read a story about a boy with two mummies, to which Millie piped up that she wished she had two mummies because her mummy was awesome. They were such lovely kids.

There was no way my parents would have entertained sharing a book with such subject matter with me or my sisters.

After dinner, Giles took the girls for their bath, and Hen and I helped Bridget with the dishes.

"I heard about the mattress." Bridget laughed, her hands in the sudsy water.

"Bloody Val." Hen shook his head as he wiped a large platter that wouldn't fit in the dishwasher.

"So, what are you doing? Did you get a new one this weekend?" Bridget had pulled the plug and was wiping around the sink.

"Not yet. I'm on the couch. Christian's got time off, and he's planning on coming up here. I thought I might offer him petrol money if he drives and brings the mattress in his ute." Henry folded the tea towel and draped it over the oven handle.

I hated hearing about this Christian dude. He was obviously close to Henry, and even if they weren't in a relationship now, they were probably friends with benefits or something, and I'd spend his time up here listening to Henry moan through the walls.

"Two clean children ready for bed." Giles again had his daughters on his hips, both in pyjamas with chickens on them. I had to admit, they were very cute.

"Story?" Mia looked at me with large blue eyes.

"Ken's read enough stories before dinner." Bridget scooped up her younger daughter. "Now say good night to Uncle Hammy and Ken."

"Good night, Uncle Hen, good night, Uncle Ken." Millie giggled. "See, they rhyme."

Bridget took her daughters towards the bedrooms.

"We should go." Henry looked at me as he spoke to Giles.

"Tea, coffee, another beer?" Giles offered.

"No. I've got orientation tomorrow." Henry drew his head backwards as if he was recoiling from the thought.

"You'll be fine." Giles slapped him on the shoulder. "Glad it's not me doing psych, though. I hated that rotation."

"Well, I've hated almost everything else so far. Surely something will agree with me?" Henry looked pained as he cast his eyes to the ground.

"You've got amazing emotional intelligence," I offered. "You were great with the people at cricket today."

"See." Giles nodded his head at me. "Someone who's known you all of a weekend can see that. You'll be fine."

Driving home, a soft song played through the stereo. I couldn't place it, but the melody was lovely.

"You really think I'll be fine?" Henry asked as he drove, his brow furrowed.

"Yeah," I said. "But not with a sore back and not without a good night's sleep. You're taking the bed tonight."

"No—" Henry started.

"I insist." I was adamant he was going to have a decent night's sleep before he started his new job.

"What size is your bed?" Henry asked, his bottom lip between his teeth.

"It's a king," I said, gazing out the window, not wanting to look at the man sitting next to me who made my cock take notice at the mention of beds.

"I only got a queen, but I'm regretting it already. I mean, we could..." Henry paused, and I looked at him as he studied the sun visor as we stopped at a traffic light. "We could share and like put pillows down the middle if you're concerned. I mean, I'd respect your boundaries and I don't mean, like, it wouldn't mean—"

"Okay," I said, my voice sounding so much calmer than I felt.

I'd just agreed to spending a night sharing a bed with a man I was so attracted to it wasn't funny. I mean, what could go wrong?

Chapter 13

Henry

There was no way I was letting Ken sleep on the couch downstairs. We both have important jobs, and we need our sleep. I mean, he's in ED, and that can be hectic. The thought of lying next to him all night, though... my cock thought all its birthdays and Christmases had come at once.

I hadn't planned on spending the day with Ken, let alone sharing a bed with him tonight.

At times, today had been torturous. He'd chatted easily amongst many of the store holders at the market, clearly having a set group he visited. I could almost see his brain ticking over as he picked up fresh produce, inspecting or smelling it before either placing it back or putting it in his bag. I had high hopes for dinners this week.

Cricket was a lot of fun. I never expected to play, but someone produced some cricket whites, and I was soon rolling my arm over. I even got a wicket. Seeing Ken running towards me as my teammates gathered around to celebrate and then feeling him pat me on the bum... not going to lie, I had to think about dissecting cadavers to calm the state of arousal that threatened to break through.

Then, seeing Ken with my nieces, happily reading a story to Mia, it was all too much. I was all but planning our wedding.

Sharing a bed will not help me slow things down.

Ken was in the bathroom as I contemplated what to wear to bed. Usually, I just wore my boxer briefs. I don't own pyjama pants. My gym shorts covered as much as my briefs, so I figured I'd be safer in them.

My breath quickened as Ken left the bathroom for me. I brushed my teeth and willed my heart rate to slow down as I contemplated heading to his room and climbing into his bed.

I willed myself to keep moving when I stepped into the room, wanting to simply stand and take in the wondrous sight before me. Ken was topless, his chest covered in dark curls. He was fit. I mean, I knew that from cricket, but his muscles were even more defined than mine. I'd brought my pillow with me, so I used it to cover my erection.

"I didn't know, what, do you, like, um, didn't, side, sleep?" Words came from Ken's mouth that made no sense.

"I'm just happy for a bed. Do you usually take the left or right?" I hoped I was making sense.

Ken didn't answer, so I simply climbed into the side that was free, the sheets feeling silky smooth against my skin.

"What time do you start, like, tomorrow? In the morning?" Ken cleared his throat as he spoke.

"Um, eight. You?"

"Same."

We both laid down on our sides, our backs to each other, and Ken switched off the light.

"Thanks for this." I hoped Ken could hear the gratitude in my voice.

"No problems." Ken cleared his throat again.

It took me forever to fall asleep, but I suspected it took Ken longer. I kept listening for his breathing to slow and even out, but it never came.

I woke before our alarms went off. It was light outside, and I could hear birds chirping away. I could feel a large erection in my hands, and I gave it a squeeze, only to realise in my half-awake state that it wasn't mine.

"Huh?" Ken let out a high pitched almost yelp as I woke him up.

"Oh, man. I'm so sorry. I thought it was... Never mind." Flying onto my back, I immediately regretted losing the warmth of being curled up against Ken.

"Well, that's a first," Ken mumbled. "I've never been woken up by someone squeezing my penis before."

"I'm so sorry. I'll take the couch again tonight." My forearm covered my eyes, my morning wood well and truly receded.

"I was in the middle of a really lovely dream, too." Ken laughed. He was taking this much better than I was.

"Yeah?" I all but squeaked.

"Yeah." Ken reached out and squeezed my hand before swinging his legs over the bed and heading for the bathroom.

Mortification remained in the room, and its name was Henry Hartman. If only there was a way I could get downstairs and out the door without having to speak to Ken.

As Ken showered, I ironed a shirt. We'd been told no scrubs in mental health, and I was okay with that. As I ran the iron over the pale-blue cotton, I imagined how striking this shirt would be against Ken's caramel-coloured skin.

"It's all yours," I heard from the bathroom as I switched off the iron.

When I entered, the room was steamy. Like a lovesick teenager, I used my finger to write my initials, a heart, and Ken's initials in the condensation on the mirror before rubbing it out.

Fuck. I needed to stop this obsession. It was easier when I thought Ken was a straight or bi-curious guy wanting to see what kissing a man was like and who then ran from the experience. Knowing now that he did it because of family indoctrination and that he was as gay as me, well, it made things different.

I turned on the shower and stood under the steaming water. Perhaps I needed to find somewhere else to live altogether. I'd stick out this week, but it would be easier on everyone if I found someone to take over my room here whilst I looked elsewhere.

"I'm so sorry." I sat at the breakfast bar as Ken plated up some mushrooms on toast. There was no way I could look him in the eye.

"No harm done." Ken poured a cup of tea and pushed it towards me before standing at the sink to eat.

There was distance between us, and it was good.

"I get all…" I started. "I mean…" What did I mean? I ate some more of the delicious breakfast Ken had cooked. "I get clingy and possessive, and I've ruined every relationship I've ever been in by coming on too strong and pushing hard for things too quickly. I can't do that to you."

Glancing up, I saw Ken moving mushrooms around his plate. "I wasn't going to talk before we both went to work, but…" I sighed as I gathered my thoughts. "You're so incredibly sexy and hot, and… Fuck. I don't want to ruin our housemate situation, and you don't need to be finding someone else who's new and all and—"

"Henry." I looked up at Ken, who'd placed his plate to the side. "It's okay. I get it."

I didn't think he did. I mean, I didn't get it as much as I wanted to. How could I be so attracted to a man and so scared at the same time? If we hadn't had the kiss at the ball, things might be different. I knew, however, how soft and pillowy Ken's lips were, and now I'd felt his girthy cock, I was desperately trying to stop thoughts of swallowing it down my throat.

It was lucky Ken had left by the time I came back downstairs. I had a new job to start, and I was going to enjoy it.

My orientation day went by in a whirl of faces and rules and regulations. There were new systems to learn and government legislation I needed to understand at a deeper level than my undergraduate knowledge provided.

I was amazed at how friendly my colleagues were. They seemed happy I was there. The consultant, Jack—just Jack, as he'd introduced himself—was laid back and an amazing teacher. He took me aside for an hour to chat and get to know each other better.

"So, why psych?" he asked as we sat in his office, gross health service tea in our stained mugs.

"To be honest," I replied, trying to formulate a response that was indeed honest and not too douchey, "I wanted to come home, and this was the only position available. That being said, though, I will admit, I haven't felt at home in any of my rotations so far, so I figured why not try something totally different?"

"It sounds like you're open to new things, then?"

"Yeah. I mean, the thing I liked most in gastro was talking to people with chronic conditions. I don't know if I did a decent enough job, but it was rewarding getting someone who's been told they have to make permanent lifestyle changes in order to manage their condition to admit that it sucked and to find solutions together."

Jack nodded as I spoke, a gentle smile on his face.

We talked more about expectations and the material he advised me to read. He explained that most people who were in the mental health ward were incredibly sick, not just experiencing mild anxiety or depression. We ran through his current clients, as he preferred to call them, on the wards and what had brought them in.

There were harrowing tales of childhood abuse and substance dependence. In the psychiatric intensive care unit, there were forensic clients, people who would otherwise have been in prison except for their mental state.

Jack voiced his frustrations about the situations in many cases. He was honest and admitted with a couple of the clients he wasn't sure what we could do.

I was sent home a little early, clearly brain drained from all the information. But I felt good about it all. Most other rotations didn't offer orientation or information like the psych department had. It was refreshing and appreciated.

The couch at home was comfortable enough to sit in to read. I brushed up on some papers that Jack suggested but kept looking at my watch to see when Ken might be home.

He was meant to finish at half past four, but five rolled around and then six. Perhaps he'd gone out? He was probably avoiding me.

At half past six, I figured I'd be cooking my own dinner tonight. I knew we had eggs, bacon, and cheese, and I found a packet of spaghetti in the cupboard. Carbonara it would be.

Mum is a massive Nigella fan. I remember sitting through her cooking programs as a child. In one episode, she talked about making carbonara in the middle of the night and taking it back to bed to share with a new lover. At the time, I simply focused on cooking in the middle of the night and taking it back to bed. It sounded so exotic.

When Mum cooked carbonara a few nights later, I asked if we were eating in bed, and she laughed. It was one of the few dishes I learnt to cook and one of my go-to comfort meals.

As I was dicing the bacon, the front door opened, and Ken appeared. "What a fucking shit show." He looked exhausted and sounded worse.

"I hope you don't mind, but I started dinner," I explained. "Wine?"

"I think I need a decent cuppa." Ken slumped onto a stool at the breakfast bar and laid his head on the bench. I yearned to hug him and tell him I'd look after him, but we weren't in a relationship.

After brewing a pot of tea, I listened as Ken debriefed about his day in the ED. A child who had broken their arm and looked like he was being abused at home, a couple experiencing a miscarriage after trying for eleven years to have a baby, a horror car crash that saw three people needing a lot of work before being transported to the operating room.

"Less than six weeks to go," I offered as I scooped some pasta into bowls for us.

Ken didn't move from his stool, so I stayed in the kitchen and leant against the sink as he had done over breakfast.

"This is great." Ken spoke with his mouth full, twirling more pasta onto his fork, ready for his next bite. "I didn't get lunch."

"It's quick and easy." I shrugged.

At least talking about food, we were ignoring the events of the morning.

"How was your day?" Ken asked as he scraped the last of the sauce from his bowl into his mouth.

"It was great," I replied, nodding. "I really enjoyed it. The team seems friendly, and I've already learnt so much."

"I'm so jealous." Ken chuckled as he shook his head. "I'd give anything for a psych rotation."

"Ask then," I suggested as I placed my bowl in the dishwasher and leant over to take Ken's from him.

"You think?" Reluctance shone through in his voice, and he bit the corner of his bottom lip.

"Yeah. Speak to someone. They're usually desperate for people in psych, and, as Jack told me today, they'd rather have people who wanted to be there. Go for it."

Ken nodded and stood from the stool. "I'm so sorry, but I'm going to grab a shower and fall into bed. Leave the dishes, and I'll do them in the morning."

Covering his yawn with his forearm, I shooed him upstairs. I wanted to talk about this morning, but he was clearly exhausted. I was tired too, so I figured I'd ignore Ken's instructions, do the dishes, and head to bed myself.

I came to the top step as Ken emerged from the bathroom, a white towel wrapped around his waist. "Don't even think about sleeping downstairs." Ken pointed a finger at me as he spoke.

"Sure thing, boss." I chuckled back at him.

I doubted Ken realised how much I'd enjoyed waking up spooning him, his cinnamon scent shining through and his body fitting so well with mine. As awkward as it had been, I didn't regret waking up spooning him, only what came later.

Ken wasn't asleep when I made my way to his room. His lamp was on, and he was reading a biography on a cricketer from the Caribbean.

"I feel like I need to put pillows down in the centre of the bed tonight." I moved one between us as I climbed into bed.

"There's no need, really." Ken smiled as he closed his book and placed it on the table next to his bed. "It wasn't unpleasant waking up like we did."

Although Ken didn't look at me, there was sincerity in his voice.

"I still think about our kiss at the ball," I almost-whispered as I lay next to him, both of us looking at the ceiling. "But I can't form a relationship with you, because I'd smother you like I do every other guy I've been with, and I enjoy living with you."

"I get that." Ken sighed. "Do you think...? No.

I lifted onto my elbow to face him, despite him still staring at the ceiling. "Do I think what?" I asked gently, forcing myself to not reach out and stroke away a strand of hair that had flopped to his forehead.

"Do you think..." Ken moved onto his elbow to mirror me, a redness in his cheeks. He didn't look into my eyes, but over my shoulder. "Perhaps, like, could you show me, like, some gay stuff, and, I mean, I know nothing, and perhaps it's only fair to any guy I go out with in the future that I, like, know things."

"What sort of things?" Ken's statement caught me off guard.

"You could be my tutor and show me what you like in bed and help me discover what I might like. In the future. With a real partner." Ken was now bright red, but he looked me in the eye.

"So we wouldn't be in a relationship, but..." I said slowly, trying to get my head around what Ken was proposing.

"Yeah. I mean, if I meet someone, I'll tell you. It's just, I've never been with a man, and I'm at an age when men expect me to know things. I don't want to disappoint anyone. Well, except for my parents, but that's a given."

I couldn't take it anymore and reached out and stroked my hand through his hair. He moaned, and his eyes fluttered closed.

"Fuck." His eyes shot open, and he sat up in bed. "Christian. He's going to be here this weekend, and you two will want to hook up. We can wait?"

"Huh?"

"Christian, the guy who's bringing your mattress. I assume he's..." Ken circled his hand in front of him as he scrunched his nose.

"Christian?" I asked again, utterly confused until I figured out what Ken was getting at. "No." I laughed, reaching out to grab Ken's arm. "He's as straight as an arrow and my best mate. We've never been there, not even as teens. He's been really supportive of me, though."

"Oh..." Ken laid back down.

Was he jealous? Surely not. I mean, he told me he wants a tutor. To be honest, it's been far too long since I've seen any sort of action that didn't involve my hand.

"I like your suggestion," I muttered as I swept my hand through Ken's hair again, loving how it felt between my fingers. "How about we sleep on it? Because you're exhausted."

"Good idea," Ken said as he turned off the bedside lamp. "But if you wake up holding me, don't suddenly break away from me."

Ken fell asleep almost straight away. I lay there contemplating his offer. It may just solve both of our problems. It would be no hardship exploring things with him, that was for sure.

Chapter 14

Ken

Sure, it had been a manic day at work, but it wasn't helped that my mind was elsewhere.

Waking up having Henry spoon me had felt right, even if it felt strange having my junk squeezed by someone else. It wasn't the type of strange that would have seen me break away, but a strange I wanted to experience more of.

As I'd carefully sutured a head laceration on an old dear who had taken a tumble at the bowls club, it came to me that perhaps Henry could show me the ropes, so to speak. He'd said he got possessive with relationships and tried to take things too quickly, but I realised that if I framed it as an almost teaching gig or something, that might be different.

The truth was, I wouldn't have complained if Henry had wanted a relationship, or if he had taken things too quickly. I was the one who ran away from him, and I needed to show him it wasn't because I was repulsed by him. In fact, it was the opposite. I wanted him more than I could even articulate.

In the shower when I got home later that evening, I tried to imagine what might have happened if Hen had continued to stroke my cock, just as I was doing as the water sluiced over my back. Henry had a gentle side to him, but I wanted him to be rough with me, to squeeze as he stroked, urging the cum from my balls. It didn't take long, and I'd drawn the cum out of my cock as it spurted over the walls of the shower. The relief wasn't enough. I needed more. Henry was so close, and we were sharing a bed.

Waking up the following morning, it had been me spooning Henry. His chest felt smooth under my hand. He was muscular, but not overly defined. I could feel his heart beat slowly as he still slept. Using my pointer finger, I drew tiny circles over his heart. My lips were pressed against his shoulder.

"Mmm..." Henry stretched before sinking back into me.

Even though I was nervous and hoped I was doing things properly, I took this as permission and increased the size of my circles, widening them to reach a nipple. His nipples were smaller than mine. There were a few stray hairs around them, but nowhere near as much as what covered my chest. Henry placed his hand over mine, and I froze.

"I didn't mean to stop you," he said as he rolled onto his back. "What a way to wake up. Beats any alarm clock."

"Sorry. I think I'm twenty minutes earlier than our alarms. Was it, was it okay?" I whispered.

"It was lovely." Henry swallowed as he looked at me through the early morning light that came around the edge of the blinds in the room. "I thought about your suggestion."

Was he going to let me down? I dropped my gaze to my chest. Henry used his long finger to tilt my chin so he could look into my eyes. "I like the idea. We'll be like, I don't know... housemates with benefits?"

We both laughed as Henry's finger moved from my chin to stroke up my jaw, the hairs on my arms and chest rising at this gentle touch, yearning to be caressed by the same finger.

"I was wondering," I spoke quietly, forcing myself to maintain eye contact with the man in bed with me. "Do you think the kiss at the ball was a fluke?"

"There's one way to find out." Henry smiled as he closed the distance between us.

It was both joyous and tortuous to discover it had indeed not been a fluke. Our mouths fit together just as perfectly as that night in February. This was no tender peck, but there was a possessiveness on both of our parts where we wanted to be showing the other how good it could be. Tongues entwined, Hen's beard rubbed against my face. Its roughness only added to the sensation of being kissed by this amazing man.

My eyes were closed, a hand still on Hen's chest. Hen used his spare hand to scratch down my back. His nails were short, so there was no chance of leaving a mark, but the sensation went straight to my already aching cock. Sliding his hand under the waistband of my underwear, he cupped my bum and squeezed.

The kiss intensified as I ran my hand down his stomach, and he moaned as I felt his cock over his shorts. As unsure as I was as to what to do with my hand, and whether I should place it inside Hen's briefs, he made the choice for me as he used his spare hand to drag his briefs down his leg. I did the same, only to feel more pressure from Hen's lips.

I'd only ever felt my cock before. Hen's was just as hot as mine but felt smoother. I traced a vein that ran up one side and was surprised to find foreskin. Although circumcision was uncommon in Sri Lanka, it had been popular when my father was born in Australia, and, wanting to fit in, my grandparents had decided to remove my father's foreskin as an infant. Although it was more uncommon when I was born, my parents decided it was an Australian thing to do. I'd seen men both cut and uncut during my studies and in my limited practice of medicine so far, but finding Henry and manipulating his foreskin was a turn-on.

Jesus, I needed to stop thinking about foreskins and get back to the penis in hand. Henry trailed the backs of his fingers up and down my cock. It felt better than any attention I'd ever given myself, and I was worried I was going to blow prematurely.

Henry groaned as I wrapped my hand around him and tugged gently. "Is this alright?" I panted as I broke the kiss. He simply nodded as our lips found each other again.

My brain was short-circuiting—Hen's hand on me, and my hand on him. There was so much sensation. I'd never been as turned on. Henry's hips jerked at my strokes, and I broke away from our kiss again to let out a breath when his hand finally engulfed my cock.

"This is..." A guttural sound came from my throat as Henry stroked. As much as I wanted to keep kissing him, something had to give or else I would have exploded on the spot.

"Hmmm..." Henry's eyes were still closed, our foreheads touching as we jerked each other off.

My speed on Henry increased, as I could feel my release building. "I'm..." Henry silenced me with another kiss as I erupted over his hand and onto both of our stomachs. A few seconds later, he also spurted, our cum combining on each other's bodies.

This was bigger than any satisfaction I'd received from wanking before. It felt monumental in that I'd crossed a line and actually taken what I wanted from another man, all whilst he pleased me. Henry talked of falling fast, but I was sure I was falling quicker than him, and all from a hand job, a wristy as I'd heard guys at the cricket club call it. It felt right; it felt amazing.

ALL DAY, the euphoria from the morning's orgasm carried with me. It wasn't just the physical feelings, though. When I saw Henry's lidded eyes and gentle smile after we came and his suggestion that we didn't shower together as we had to get to work, and he knew that if he saw my body all wet he would want to press me up against the shower wall... Yeah.

We'd been clear that this wasn't a relationship. Having never really been in a proper relationship, I had to assume that this was a friendship, and that was fine by me. I hadn't had many of those either. Rationally, I could compartmentalise this in my brain, however, I felt my heart telling me that Henry was indeed a special person in my life.

"That smells great." Armon plopped next to me on one of the couches in the break room.

"Yeah, Henry cooked it last night." My heart beat faster at the thought of Hen standing at the stove.

"Nice. You both coming to training?" Armon took a bite of his salad, looking at the news on the television.

I hadn't talked about it with Henry. "Let me check."

> Hey, there's cricket training tonight.

HENRY:

Cool. Want me to drive? Don't tell me you usually walk there.

> That would be great. Things are not as manic around here today, and I should get away on time.

HENRY:

I'll swing by after I finish and drag you away if need be!

There was something about that thought that made my cock stir and reminded me of our morning activities. I was too big for Henry to throw over his shoulder, but it was a visual that appealed to me.

"Yeah." I stood from the couch as Armon flicked the channel on the television to a basketball game. "We'll be there."

The thought of us being a 'we' really excited me, but I knew it wasn't what Henry wanted, and I had to respect him. If I was still on that stupid app, Henry was the type of guy who would tick all the boxes in someone I was looking for. Kind, caring, considerate, and hellishly sexy. I love the way his hair flops over his forehead too. He's always pushing it back with his hands. And that beard. It might be part jealousy that I can't grow one. I mean, I can, but it looks like a few stray pubes on my face. The irony that the rest of my body is rather hirsute is not lost on me either.

Henry's family is lovely, too. His parents are amazing people who appear to do so much good in the community. Their Valentine's ball raised thousands and thousands of dollars for the cardiac ward. Then there's Giles and Bridget. They are so different from each other but work so well together.

My thoughts were interrupted by my phone vibrating in my scrubs pocket. I opened the door to the break room and started wandering down the corridor back to the ward when I saw my mother was calling.

"I'm at work. Is this urgent, Am'mā?"

"That is not how you speak to your mother, Kandiah." My mother spoke forcefully. She was never this forceful with my father, only with her son.

"I have to work. Is this urgent?" I must have sounded clipped as I leant against the corridor and rubbed my forehead with my first two fingers.

"You could work here. But no, you have to adventure." I could almost see my mother waving her hands in the air, her melodramatic tone shining down the line. "It's your father. He is stressed. He needs you here."

"Am'mā, I've got a contract here. I'm happy here. I'll visit later in the year, alright?"

"No, Kandiah. It is not alright."

There was no love in my mother's words, no affection, and definitely no desire to see how I was doing. Fortunately, an announcement over the loudspeaker indicated assistance was needed with a new arrival.

"I have to go. There's an emergency," I lied, knowing my team wasn't in that area today.

Mum didn't even say goodbye before she hung up. I knew I was a disappointment to my parents, but I felt so much freer over here. I could live as myself, and part of that had to do with Henry.

I was still guilty that my parents were obviously stressed. I'd try to call tonight and perhaps speak with my father.

"This is nice." Henry had his head in my lap, and I ran my fingers through his hair.

After cricket training, I'd whipped up a quick fish curry for dinner. Henry had insisted on doing the dishes and told me to sit on the couch with a cup of tea he'd made for me.

"It is," I replied softly. "You know, I've been playing this morning's activities on loop in my brain all day. You're an excellent teacher."

"I don't think so." Henry laughed, a huge smile on his face. "I mean, you didn't need to learn much."

My phone pinged next to me with a message from one of my sisters telling me she was concerned about our father.

"Everything okay?" Henry asked, still smiling.

"Just my screwed-up family." I sighed. "My family is into emotional manipulation."

Henry grunted, clearly not approving of their tactics.

"Yeah, well, they hate the idea of me being over here."

"Is it control?" Henry asked. He grasped the hand that wasn't stroking his head and just held it to his chest.

"Yeah. That's part of it. They can't understand that I want to live a life they haven't planned. They thought I'd take over Dad's accountancy business, and they'd find me a nice woman from their congregation, and we'd marry and have a couple of kids and live in their neighbourhood and have dinner with them a few times per week and worship with them on Sunday, and go to home groups and, and, and."

"And now you're a doctor on the other side of the country living with a man who thinks you're incredibly sexy—who only sees you as a housemate, I might add—but can't wait to feel your cock again, who can't remember the last time he set foot in a church." Henry sat up, breaking our contact. "Was that your parents?"

"My sister texted me. Mum texts in all caps, but she rang me at work today." I stared at the floor, embarrassed to think that Henry had the perfect family and mine was a screwup.

"Hey." Henry's voice was soft as he placed a finger under my chin and drew my head up so he could look into my eyes. "It's not on you. Your role in life is not to make your parents happy; it's to make you happy. Were you happy in Perth?"

"No," I whispered.

"I can't wait for you to meet Christian this weekend. His parents divorced when he was eight, and he was made to spend every second weekend with his dad, even though his dad kept telling him what a piece of shit he was and that his mother was a whore. Now, I should add, Lena is the most amazing woman, and I don't think she's had a relationship since her marriage ended. But anyway, Christian started refusing to see his dad when he was fifteen, and his dad dragged them to court where the magistrate said Christian was old enough to make his own decisions. He hasn't seen his dad since."

Henry stroked my jaw as he spoke, and I relished the contact.

"Now, I'm not saying break all contact, but remember, you aren't responsible for their happiness." Henry leant in and placed a gentle kiss on my lips.

"Let's go to bed." I smiled at Hen as I reached for his hand.

"But I'm not tired," Henry replied coquettishly, his eyes blinking rapidly with his head tilted sideways.

"Good." I laughed as I dragged him to his feet.

We brushed our teeth side by side in the bathroom before heading to my room. I undressed slowly, glancing at Henry, who was doing the same.

"You know…" Henry bit the side of his lip, a look of desire in his eyes. "I usually sleep naked."

"I can try that." I smiled, eager to feel Hen's skin against mine again.

Starting off naked was wonderful. Our bodies wrapped around each other immediately, with Henry draping a leg over me as our arms intertwined. I still couldn't believe how amazing his kisses were. The juxtaposition of firmness with a soft overtone was hard to describe but wonderful to feel.

Our cocks rubbed together between us. I could feel beads of precum leaking from mine, but either I was producing much more than usual, or Henry also was leaking. The thought of this made me groan. I moved from kissing Henry's lips to kiss along his jaw and down his neck as he threw his head backwards.

I wanted to kiss down his chest and over his abdomen until I took his cock in my mouth, but we held each other too tight. Our cocks were duelling between us, and I was amazed how turned on I was by this rutting. We didn't speak with words, but our bodies communicated a desire and longing.

Henry pinched one of my nipples harder than I would have expected, which saw me almost come undone. Instead, I pressed my groin closer. The hand that pinched the nipple moved between us and wrapped around both of our shafts. Pressure from fingers on one side and another cock on the other was not something I'd ever even thought of.

"I'm…" I tried to speak, but kissing was much more fun.

We were both desperate to be closer to the other, his hand working our cocks, and mine digging its fingers into his smooth back. Suddenly, Henry threw his head back as he roared out an orgasm. The sound and feeling of warmth between us from his cum saw me erupt, too.

"You know I wanted to blow you, right?" I whispered as we both levelled out our breathing.

"We'll get to that." Henry smiled as our eyes locked together. "I'm just going to grab a cloth. I don't think we dirtied the sheets again, but if we did, I'll lie in the wet spot."

"Thank you." I placed another kiss on Henry's lips as he returned from the bathroom with a cloth and wiped me clean.

"No, thank you," he replied jovially. "I haven't had this much fun in ages."

"I like your cock." I smiled, even though I could feel my cheeks reddening. It wasn't like me to speak like this.

"That's good, because I like yours, too. I think it's because it's attached to you, and you are fast becoming a very special person in my life." Henry sounded sincere as he brushed some hair off my forehead.

He was fast becoming a special person in my life too. I was lucky this wasn't a relationship, because that might lead to heartbreak. We'd maintain our friendship, not that I could ever see myself moving on from sex like this. In a day, Henry had already ruined me for other men, and we'd only really rubbed each other's cocks. Imagine what I was going to be like once I started sucking him and we started penetrating each other. Perhaps I was indeed screwed, but it was easier to live in denial.

Chapter 15

Henry

I t was fortunate we'd agreed we weren't in a relationship, because I could see myself being swept up in the romance of spending time with Ken.

His kisses stole my breath. The way he ran his hands through my hair and over my face before he scratched down my back gave me goose pimples both at the time and when I thought about the experience later. He made my body come alive in a way no one else ever had. Somehow, Ken picked up on cues and could tell if I liked something or if he needed to change tack. I would never have guessed he was as inexperienced as he says he was. It's not that I doubted him, but he needed such little guidance.

It's like I was addicted to his touch. Even little things like brushing past him in the kitchen or lying with my head in his lap as we watched telly together at night brought so much pleasure and made me want to be closer to him.

Perhaps it had been fortunate that our rosters had coincided this week. It wouldn't usually be that way. Both of us also had the weekend off together. I couldn't wait to introduce Ken to Christian. Not as a partner, of course, but as someone who had quickly become important in my life.

Each night, we'd snuggled in front of the television before both of us decided there was nothing on we wanted to watch. We then headed to bed early and rubbed against each other until we came. It always struck me as heteronormative to insist on penetration being the pinnacle of sex. Don't get me wrong, having my prostate stroked in a certain way can get me off quicker than a Kardashian can press publish on a social media post, but usually, it's the friction against my cock that really brought me undone. I wasn't greedy where that friction came from, be it a hand, a mouth, or even another cock as our bodies pressed together.

So, I'd stroked Ken, and he'd stroked me. He'd hinted so many times he wanted to blow me, but I didn't want that to happen for the first time at the end of a long day or as we were rushing to get ready for work. Ken wanted me to teach him how to, well, have sex, and I was planning on taking my time.

I was currently writing notes about a patient who was convinced he was a microwave when Giles poked his head around the door.

"Got a minute?" He was all serious as he leaned against the door-frame in his navy scrubs. I daren't tell him that Ken rocked them much better than he did.

"Sure." I saved my note and pushed my chair out as Giles sunk into the empty seat next to me.

Giles told me about the patient he'd just been to see and how he didn't think the antipsychotic medications were any good for her heart. It was such a shame, as she'd been stable for the first time in ages, and we were hoping to discharge her.

"I'll let Simone know." Simone is my registrar. Giles ran his hand through his hair. It was something all us boys did, even though I'd never noticed Mum or Dad do it. "Cheers. You coming to Mum and Dad's tomorrow night?" I asked, my foot resting on my knee.

"I'm on call this weekend, but Bee will be there with the girls even if I'm not. You know how much she loves Lena." Lena was Christian's mum. Bridget's mother died when she was a teen, and she had been adopted by my mum, as well as Christian and Emily's mums.

"You're bringing Ken, aren't you?" One side of my brother's mouth lifted.

"He knows he's invited," I replied, hoping I sounded as nonchalant as I did in my head. Ken had told me he'd see, and I didn't want to beg. It was something someone in a relationship would do, and we weren't in a relationship. This had become my mantra, and I almost believed it every time I recited it silently to myself.

"Want to come over tonight? I was going to pick up takeaway. The girls would love to see you."

"Can't tonight." I picked off a pretend piece of lint from my thigh. "Christian's dropping off my mattress."

"Bet you can't wait to sleep in a bed again. That couch must be pretty comfortable though if you're this calm and collected after a week on it. Anyway, see you tomorrow, I hope." Giles stood and was out the door after a punch to my bicep. I should have known that was coming by now; it was his MO, but I was always so slow to get him back. One day, he wouldn't see me coming.

I thought about his comments about how relaxed I was. There was no way I was going to tell my older brother that I'd been sharing a bed with my housemate. Sure, I might have introduced partners to my family early on in past relationships, but this wasn't a relationship, and I didn't want my family getting the wrong idea.

"... So, he runs through the back door out onto the deck." Christian is laughing so much that there are tears in the corners of his eyes. "And he says, 'Mate, I need you to kiss me. She doesn't believe me when I say no'."

"And did you?" Ken asked in a soft voice, engrossed in my friend's story of a party in our last year of school.

"Gross, no." Christian scrunched his face and poked out his tongue as if he was about to vomit. "But sure enough, she came out after him, and I just said 'Mel, you know he's gay, but I'm not, and I think he's a fool for not seeing how fucking hot you are'."

"And..." Ken's eyes were wide as I sat back in my chair, my arms crossed and my head shaking.

"We found a spare room, and I made her forget Henry Hartman ever existed." Christian smirked, recounting the tale.

"Ah, but you forget." Henry removed one hand from his gripped bicep and pointed at his friend. "You arranged a date for the following Friday, and she stood you up, and you saw her making out with Sharon Summers in the park."

"True. And I understand they're both still together after ten years." Christian laughed. "Let me know if you need to kick me out. You probably want to get up and make that bed up. That couch doesn't look that comfortable."

"I'm liking these stories." Ken smiled as he looked at me. If I didn't know better, I'd think he was making eyes at me. "Besides, another night with him in my bed won't be a total hardship."

I'm glad I wasn't drinking, as I would have sprayed it everywhere.

"I thought you two were together." Christian clasped his hands together as he shook his head, a huge grin on his face. "Bloody hell, Hartman, you waste no time, do you?"

"It's not like that, really." I looked at Ken, wondering why he'd even come out with our sleeping arrangements as he had. "I mean, we're both clear. It's not a relationship, it's a mutually beneficial arrangement."

"I'm warning you now, Ken." Christian turned to face him and placed a hand on his shoulder. "He'll become all clingy and have your wedding planned by the end of the weekend. You'll be running back to Perth before you know it."

"I think I'm safe." Ken almost smiled, but I sensed apprehension as he quickly shot a glance my way. "Hen's explained his clinginess and how he's screwed up his relationships in the past, so we are lucky we aren't in a relationship, aren't we?"

I knew the question was rhetorical. This was the most out of his shell I'd seen Ken since I'd met him. He was usually so reserved and pensive, and yet here he was, laughing with my best mate. He needn't have worried that Christian wouldn't like him, as Christian liked anyone and everyone. There's a way he talked to those around him that made them feel at ease.

This must be why Ken opened up to him so easily. It had been a great evening. Ken arrived home just as Christian pulled up, and we all dragged the mattress upstairs. Val had sent a box of chocolates as an apology, but Christian had left them in the ute all week, and they were well and truly melted.

Ken cooked one of his curries for dinner and seemed proud when Christian commented that although he'd been looking forward to my parents' cooking tomorrow night, he could easily have more curry. Mum and Dad are major foodies and always create amazing dinners.

During dinner, it also struck me that I hadn't thought about work after hours all week. I got on well with the team around me and was warming to our clients, or patients, on the ward. Some of them were mad as a cut snake, but I hoped we were doing some good with the treatments that were offered on the wards.

Yes, it was early days, but I was enjoying my job for the first time in, well, forever really.

"I've got it." I tried to swat Ken away as he tried to help load the dishwasher.

"It will be quicker if we work together," Ken replied, bending around me more for a cuddle than to assist me.

"You're not helping." I laughed as Ken ran his fingers up and down my chest under my shirt.

I kicked the dishwasher door closed before spinning to face him, a smirk on his mouth and lust in his eyes.

"What—"

"Shh..." Ken cut me off as he reached down and started undoing my belt before unsnapping the buttons of my fly. "I like the way your bum looks in these jeans." Ken kissed down my neck as he reached a hand inside my boxers and drew out my quickly stiffening cock.

He dropped to his knees and, with our eyes locked, he took the head of my cock in his mouth, swirling his tongue over it and moaning as if he'd found water in the middle of the desert. Without the moan, this would have felt amazing, but with it, it was otherworldly.

Sure, there were signs Ken wasn't experienced at giving head, but my body didn't care. Ever so slowly, Ken took more of me inside his mouth, maintaining eye contact as his sucking intensified. His hands cupped my bum cheeks, kneading as if he wanted to draw me deeper. In my brain, I was telling him to grasp the root of my cock as he sucked, but I couldn't form the words.

He coughed as I hit the back of his throat and withdrew a little, but he didn't stop the sucking. His tongue stroked the underside of my cock, producing the most amazing sensations. Our eye contact broke as I threw my head back and moaned. I wouldn't last long. Once again, Ken attempted to take me deeper, but he was beaten by his gag reflex. It didn't deter him, and what he did was still amazing. My entire body tingled, and my balls felt tight as they begged for release.

With one hand gripping the counter behind me, I stroked the other through his hair. I wanted to grip the back of his head, but he needed to do this at his tempo. Ken's eyes were so dark with arousal that it was hard to tell where the iris met the pupil, and when our eyes met again, I felt like I was gazing deep into his soul. My breath hitched, and I bit my tongue as his tempo increased, and soon, I was erupting inside his mouth. I tried to pull away, but he wouldn't let me.

Some cum escaped his mouth and dripped onto the ground, but I didn't care. Hoisting a hand into his armpit, I tried to pull him up. The confident cock-sucking Ken of a few minutes ago had gone, and he looked almost scared of what my reaction would be. I simply pulled him to me and smashed into him with my lips, tasting myself in his mouth.

"I, I'm sorry," Ken whispered as we broke our kiss.

"Why? That was fucking epic." I was still drunk on the endorphins, but I managed to put my cock back in my jeans.

"I wanted to wait for you to show me what you like, but I got restless, and I, well, I wanted to..."

"Hey." I stroked his cheekbone with my thumb as I cupped his chin. "I'm sorry I didn't warn you I was going to come."

"I wanted you to." Ken looked a little happier as he smiled and gazed into my eyes. "I'll, um, go upstairs and..." He adjusted himself in his jeans.

"I could repay the favour," I replied as I rubbed his cock through his jeans, causing him to moan.

"I didn't do it because I wanted it myself." Ken frowned as his eyes looked down.

"Let's go upstairs together." Tilting his head, I planted a soft kiss on his lips. "I want to make you feel as amazing as you made me. I'd say more amazing, but I don't think that's possible."

Ken grabbed my hand as we climbed the stairs together. This non-relationship thing was going rather well.

ALL WEEK, Val had been texting me silly memes and things. It was her way of apologising. As much as I missed having her around, I enjoyed having my brothers close to me again. Val still had a few years left of uni, and I hoped that when she finished, she'd find her way back to Cassowary Point.

> STINKY:
>
> So, Christian delivered the mattress then? Is all forgiven?

> Maybe. And maybe he didn't really need to. Ken and I have decided to be housemates with benefits.

> STINKY:
>
> Yeah right!

> No, true. You know how I can get when I'm in a relationship. This way, we can have fun, and I don't need to worry about smothering him.

> STINKY:
>
> I give you two weeks to fuck this up!

> Thanks for the vote of confidence. We're off to the market. Have fun at work.

It was another fun morning at the market. I didn't run into any family members, but an old schoolteacher and some friends of my parents. To people on the outside, we must have looked like the idea of domestic bliss, talking together and Ken passing me bags to carry. I needed to look into getting a trolly of some description to carry all his purchases.

Ken insisted on grabbing some flowers for my parents. I didn't object, as it meant he was coming to dinner after all. He'd tried to argue it was for family, and I told him I wouldn't enjoy myself if I knew he was home alone. I also used my nieces as bribery and said they'd asked to see him. This was true from what Bridget told me when I bumped into her at the hospital during the week.

The only stipulation Ken had on accepting the invitation was that he could prepare something to add to the feast. Dad said they were going to fire up the barbecue, so Ken agreed to bring a salad.

It shouldn't have surprised me that he wouldn't bring just any salad. He found all manner of vegetables, which he told me he was going to roast together and mix with herbs and tinned chickpeas with a dressing of preserved lemons and garlic mixed with oil. My stomach rumbled as he talked about it.

We'd grabbed a coffee and shared an almond croissant before making our way home.

As the vegetables we'd chopped roasted together, we talked more about our families. I didn't like the sound of Ken's parents and could see why he had escaped. His sister, Abha, had messaged whilst we were out saying that their dad was stressed but wouldn't go to the doctor. Ken had refused to reply.

In some ways, I didn't blame him, but I also knew that I could never do that. I was close to my mum, dad, brothers, and sister. I was close to Bridget and Emily and would like to think that when Val found her one, I'd be close to him or her, too. Ken seemed to be closer to his other sister, and he told me he'd call her soon to get her side of the story.

Ken showed me how he made the dressing for the salad, keeping an ever-constant eye on the oven.

Sure, I'd cooked with my parents over the years, but nothing was as fun as this. I enjoyed spending time with this man. In the week I'd known him, he'd shared some intense things, and I'd done the same. In my head, I was almost disappointed we'd agreed to no relationship, as Ken was the real deal. I chastised myself for thinking this way and tried to remind myself that it was all part of my repeating patterns.

"Abha's always been as intense as my parents." Ken stirred the dressing through the chickpeas and held a spoon to my lips so I could taste it. My groan indicated how good it was. "Dipti's different. We never see her much, as she and her family live further away."

"Who knows what the future holds?" I said as Ken covered the bowl with a wax wrap. "Families come in all shapes and sizes after all, and, as Mum and Dad often say, found family can be the most precious of all."

The importance of having Ken at the dinner with my folks wasn't just that I enjoyed spending time with him, but I also wanted to show him that his history of family was different and that there were many examples of family around the table today.

Christian's mum, Lena, escaped an abusive marriage and brought up Christian by herself. She's always been supported by my family and was often seated around our dinner table. The same with Emily's mum, Rosa, whose husband left her for his secretary when Emily was in high school.

The last thing I wanted was Christian's prophecy from the night before coming true and Ken fleeing back to Perth. I wanted to give him reasons to stick around, even if we weren't more than housemates.

There was nothing about Ken that I found I didn't like. He was like no one I'd met before, and yet, I wanted to learn more and more about him. I wanted to cook with him and have friends over for dinner and take him to my folks' place for Saturday dinner or Sunday brunch. I wanted to show him restaurants in town that I thought he'd like.

We'd discovered that we both enjoyed hiking and had decided on our next day off together we'd go out together.

I caught myself daydreaming and tried to rein my thoughts. It had only been a week, and we were just housemates. As much as I loved spending time in the kitchen with Ken, we'd only ever be just friends, and I needed to be okay with that.

As we waited for the vegetables to cool, we cleaned the house. I'd thought we'd divide it into upstairs and downstairs, but Ken suggested we do it together, which was lots of fun. To think that a week before, I'd planned to escape from spending a day with this man, and now, this week, I couldn't get enough of him. Life was easy, and it was good. I was smiling and enjoying things, and Ken was the reason.

Chapter 16

Ken

Having never been in a relationship, I probably didn't recognise what Henry and I had fallen into. In the month since he'd moved in, we'd shared a bed each night. Even when I had late shifts, Henry would pull me close to him when I climbed into bed. When we woke, our bodies were pressed together in one form or another.

It wasn't just in bed, either. We spent most of our free time together, be it at cricket, or at the market on the weekends, or simply watching something on telly, one of our heads in the other's lap. It was convenient, sure, but to me, it was more than that. There was a sense of belonging I'd never felt before. I may have suggested Henry teach me things, but I'd never expected him to show me how amazing just spending time with someone else was.

Coming home one Saturday morning, after I'd worked all night, to find Henry snuggled up to my pillow, gentle puffs of air leaving his mouth in regular intervals, made my heart swell. Our plan had been to go to the market together, but I was knackered. Instead, I stripped off my scrubs and climbed into bed. I wanted to shower, but I wanted Hen's arms around me more.

"Mmm... You smell better than your pillow." Henry sounded like he'd swallowed a handful of gravel, but his arms were welcoming. "Good night?"

"It was shit." I sighed, relaxing into Henry's arms and gripping his forearms to draw him closer. "Six kids in a stolen car wrapped themselves around a tree. Four were dead at the scene, one we worked on for a while, but she'd lost too much blood. Looks like the driver was the only one wearing a seatbelt, and now he's got spinal damage and probably won't walk again."

"That sucks. Were you on the team looking after them?" Henry brushed his lips against my shoulder, never loosening his grip.

"For the driver, yeah. He reeked of rum. What a fucking waste."

My parents had instilled such a fear into me that not only would they punish me if I did anything wrong, but God would smite me from above, reigning judgement without mercy. My upbringing was based on fear. Fear of my father's belt, fear of God's wrath, and fear that I would be a disappointment.

I was still a disappointment. Abha had been texting me half the night, complaining I'd left her and Dipti to look after our parents. Her texts were full of the same language and judgement my mother had been using on me, complaining they had children to care for and someone needed to look after my parents. My parents didn't need a guardian. I suspect my sisters were just complaining that our parents were spending more time with them now that I'd moved away. I'd rather not think about them anyway, and get lost in Henry's arms.

"Do you still want to go to the market?" Hen was still holding me tight.

"Not really." I sighed. "I need to shower. Want to join me?"

Henry threw the doona off the bed and almost ran to the bathroom, suddenly awake. The shower was steamy by the time I stumbled into the room.

"You're exhausted, you poor baby." Henry held out a hand to help me into the shower. "Let me wash you and tuck you up in bed."

My body was used to Henry's touch, but his body near mine still had the same effect, and my cock was soon at full mast.

"I want you to fuck me." I turned as Henry finished washing my back, having paid special attention to my bum. "I want to feel you inside me."

Henry swallowed, seemingly surprised at my forwardness. "I haven't wanted to rush you," he said, sweeping my wet hair off my face.

Taking the cloth from his hand, I rinsed it before loading it with the body wash Henry loved and started washing his chest. Sure, I was tired, but I was also incredibly aroused. So was Henry. I could almost swear his cock twitched when I made my suggestion.

After washing each other, which took much longer than it should have because we kept stopping to steal kisses, we stood outside the shower and dried ourselves.

"Are you sure?" Henry was so sweet the way he rubbed a hand up my stubbly cheek.

"Never been surer," I replied, grabbing his towel to hang up next to mine. "You're going to have to guide me, but I'll tell you if I don't like something."

Nothing Henry had done to me so far had been anything close to unpleasant. He'd left a hickey on my chest that you could almost see through my V-neck scrubs, but I wore it as a badge of pride. I trusted Henry enough to know he would take care of me.

"I've got lube," I said as we walked into the bedroom holding hands. "But, fuck, I forgot condoms."

I was angry with myself for not even thinking about condoms.

"I've got some. Wait here." Henry held out a hand as he ran from the room into what we called his room, even if he had never slept there. "Here." Henry almost panted as he ran back into the room, a strip of condoms landing on the bed. "I'm overdue for STI screening, but I haven't had sex since my last screen, so it would just be making sure nothing was missed last time, you know, window periods and all."

Henry's cheeks reddened above his beard, and he rubbed the back of his neck with his hand.

"I've never been tested, but, well, you know…" I trailed off, embarrassed that Henry was so much more experienced than me.

"You must think I'm a whore getting regular testing. I was on PrEP for a while too, but I stopped it a few months ago when I wasn't having sex."

"Not at all." Reaching out, I stroked Henry's beard. "I thought it embarrassing that you're so much more experienced than me, and I hope I don't let you down. I mean, I want this, which is why I asked."

It was my turn to close the distance between us and lock lips with my housemate. In the back of my mind, I knew it was silly referring to him as that, as I knew we were much more, but I also recognised it helped Henry deal with his past relationship traumas.

My kiss was urgent. The shower had woken me up somewhat, and there was no way I could sleep until I'd come. In sharing saliva, we shared so much more: desires, dreams, hopes. I hoped Henry could see this. Breaking from the kiss, Henry pushed me back onto the bed, and I landed with a bounce.

"Nuh-uh," Henry scolded as I attempted to climb to my hands and knees. "I want you on your back so I can look into your eyes as I fuck you. I want to see your neck tense as I wring pleasure from you, and I want you to see what you do to me."

My heart was beating a thousand beats per minute. I could only imagine how blown my pupils were, and my cock dripped precum at Henry's words. Pulling me to the edge of the bed by my legs, Henry dropped to his knees before licking from the tip of my cock, down over my balls, past my taint until he found my puckered hole. His tongue swirled in circles, depositing saliva before probing into a place only his fingers had been before.

When Henry had fingered me whilst blowing me a couple of weeks ago, I almost levitated when I came. It was like nothing I'd ever experienced. But a tongue was different. I could feel his whiskers brushing against me as he lapped away. Lapping turned to a probing. I never realised how sensitive my hole was, and even though Henry wasn't touching my cock, precum was pooling on my stomach.

"Don't." Henry was firm when he saw my hand come down to touch my cock. "Hands above your head."

I liked the Henry who took control. He knew what he wanted. It was clear he'd done this a few times before. It reminded me of when we'd tried edging last weekend, which had been torture at the time, but amazing when he finally let me come. His method of control was different to my parents, though, in that it came out of care and concern, not fear. I was almost tempted to say it came from love, but it was far too early to be placing labels like that on things.

He could have rimmed me for hours and I wouldn't have known, but I didn't think it was that long before he laid on top of me, kissing me. Knowing where his tongue had been was strangely erotic. Eventually, though, he rolled off me and went to my drawer to grab the lube.

"Where do you want me?" I asked in a soft voice, looking around the large bed. I was unsure of so much.

"Wherever you'll let me." Henry smiled as he stood next to the bed, gazing down at me. "How about you lie at the top of the bed and use the pillows to make sure you're comfortable? Now, at any time, tell me to stop, and I will."

I knew I'd never tell him to stop. I wanted this so much. I wanted to be joined to him. I wanted him to enter my body and use it for his pleasure.

The crack of the lube bottle being opened broke the silence that had engulfed the room. My cheeks clenched as the cold lube touched my hole, courtesy of Henry's fingers.

"Sorry," he whispered with a huge grin on his face, showing he was anything but.

The groan that flew from my throat when his first finger penetrated me was met by a burning intensity in his eyes. He wanted this as much as I did.

A second finger joined the first. There was pain, but it was a pleasurable pain. I knew nothing bad was going to come from it, only good. Whilst opening me up with his fingers, Henry leant up to kiss me. It wasn't the frenzied kissing of before, but tender and sweet, sucking my bottom lip between his teeth.

"Are you ready?" he asked, as he reached for a sock that lay next to the bed to wipe his fingers on. I didn't want to ask what it was doing there.

"You tell me," I muttered back, biting the same lip that he had had between his teeth seconds before.

I was well aware that Henry's cock was both wider and longer than mine, and I'd always thought myself to be slightly above average. I knew it was going to be an effort to take it, but I wanted it so badly.

Henry rolled on the condom and slathered it with lube. He then squirted some more around my hole.

"Bear down as if you're—"

"Taking a shit. Yeah, I know." I wasn't sure where my snark had come from, but it made Henry laugh.

Henry pushed the latex-covered head against my puckered hole. The second my muscular ring gave way and allowed the head of Henry's cock to enter was like nothing I had ever experienced. I hadn't realised I'd been tense until I released around him. Henry's eyes were on me, looking for signs, including the nod I gave for him to continue.

He was slow and steady, inching deeper and deeper inside of me until I felt his balls press against me. I'd never invested in a dildo or plug, and I wondered if this made the experience better or worse. I felt every millimetre of his cock as it entered me, the pleasure indescribable. My back arched, and I gripped the sheets. I could feel my heart hammering, not with anxiety or fear, but with a relief that I was finally getting what I'd always wanted.

"Fuck, you're tight." Henry closed his eyes as I worked my pelvic floor. "You better stop that if you don't want me to blow straight away." Beads of sweat were on his forehead.

For a moment, he opened his eyes, and we simply gazed at each other, knowing we were as close as we were going to get. I went to move my hand to my aching cock, but Henry shook his head. He gripped my thighs as he started a slow tempo of thrusts. I needed more, and he knew this, but he maintained his rhythm, teasing me until I was begging for more.

It didn't take long before his tempo increased, though. He wanted this as much as I did. Henry wiped his hands through the pool of precum on my belly. There was so much, one might have assumed I'd come, but this assumption would be wrong. I was as aroused as I'd ever been. I needed to do something with my hands to stop me touching my cock, not wanting to disobey Henry's order. I ran them through his hair, trailing them down his neck, causing his head to tilt back. As he thrust into me, I grasped his chest and used my thumbs to stroke his nipples, causing him to groan in pleasure. Henry hit my magic spot, and my cock twitched. Leaning back, he hit it again and again, watching me moan as my head rolled from side to side.

He pistoned deeper, and I relaxed. It felt like we'd been doing this for a lifetime. There was no pain now, only pleasure. It was a pleasure I wanted more of. It felt so amazingly perfect, what I'd been missing all my life. Henry looked at me with hooded eyes, as if I was the only other person on the planet. His cock was hitting more than my prostate, though it was hitting my heart too. This was what it was to be so close to someone you wanted to share everything.

"I'm gonna..." Henry started, and I reached for my cock, but before I could, I felt the telltale tingle at the base of my spine and my balls dragging up before my climax erupted all over my chest and stomach, a rope of cum even hitting my chin. I'd never felt anything like this. It was as if every other orgasm I'd felt had been bland and underripe, but this was fruit prized by royalty and served in only the top restaurants. It took this experience to open my eyes and show me how it should always have been.

Henry wasn't far behind, grunting as he tried to get deeper inside me. I yearned to feel his warmth hitting me and vowed I'd get tested as soon as possible.

As my breathing slowed, I reached out for my lover, drawing him down until he lay on top of me.

"That was..." I had tears of jubilation in my eyes as I wrapped my arms around Henry and simply held him. "It was perfect."

"What can I say?" Henry laughed, his head buried in my shoulder, and I wished I could see his face. "I'm an excellent teacher."

My heart sank. We hadn't talked about it, but I thought we'd moved on from his idea of flatmates with benefits. I'd obviously seen more in his eyes and actions than he had. It just went to show how much I didn't know about relationships myself. Perhaps I just needed to be happy with what we had and try to keep my heart out of it.

"Can you read this one, please, Uncle Ken?" Millie's round blue eyes pleaded with me as she climbed onto my lap with yet another picture book. Mia had decided she wanted to play with dinosaurs today, and her sister was more than willing to take her place on my lap.

I'd slept a few hours after our amazing sex yesterday morning and then last night pretended to be asleep when Henry climbed into bed. We'd been to the market this morning and played cricket in the afternoon, and now we were at Bridget and Giles' place having dinner. Hillary and Charlie were due to arrive any minute. I wasn't sure who'd been avoiding whom, but Henry made it clear our sex meant much more to me than it had to him.

This shouldn't have surprised me. He'd told me he didn't want a relationship, and he obviously wasn't getting clingy with me, so I had to believe he wasn't as into me as I was to him. I had no one to talk to about all the emotions consuming me. I could have called Billie, but she knew Henry, and I didn't want to put her in an awkward position. Instead, I'd wait and see what happened. I didn't want to tell Henry how I felt for fear he would straight out reject me. So, I'd keep on keeping on and hope he recognised we had something special together. Well, I thought we did. Until he categorically told me otherwise, I'd believe that there was hope, and I'd just wait for him to wake up to himself.

I was reading to Millie about a very hungry caterpillar, a story I wasn't familiar with even though it had been around since before I was born, because my parents ensured the only story books we read were biblically based.

"Look, look, it's a butterfly." Millie almost screeched in my ear as I turned the page to show the multicoloured butterfly. "Look, Mia, the caterpillar became a butterfly because it ate a lollipop and a cupcake. Mummy—"

"No." Bridget was firm as she reached out for a carrot stick and dipped it in the hummus I'd brought. "You don't need to become a butterfly. But you can have some cucumber or carrots if you like."

From the side of the couch, Millie produced yet another book, but I got out of reading it when her grandparents arrived.

"How are you, Ken?" Charlie Hartman asked as he sank into the chair next to the couch on the spacious deck.

I wasn't sure where Giles and Henry got their height from, as Charlie and Boyd were both shorter than my six foot, and Hillary was shorter still.

"I've just finished a string of nights, so I'm still tired, sir." Charlie was someone to be looked up to and revered. He was one of the leading cardiologists in the country and had chosen to work in Cassowary Point.

"None of this 'sir' business. It's Charlie, alright? Did you finish this morning?" Charlie leant over and grabbed some vegetables and dip.

"No, yesterday," I said, still nervous in this man's presence.

We talked about the accident on Friday night. It was all over town, even though Cassowary Point was too large to call a town. Henry was quiet. Every so often, he'd look over at me and smile, but something had changed.

I figured I'd ruined things by pushing him yesterday morning, and, even though both of us had enjoyed it, it wasn't where he wanted to go. Our rosters were all over the place in the coming week, so it wasn't as if I'd need to be around him a lot.

This made me incredibly sad to contemplate. In a month, I'd come to love our sleeping arrangement and what went with it. I loved waking up to a quick blow or hand job, and I'd thought our kisses were out of this world.

"Easiest five bucks I'll make from you, Gilbo." Hillary nodded her head at Giles as they walked up the steps with platters of barbecued meat in their hands. "Hammy, my lad, are you or are you not in a relationship with the wonderful Kandiah here?"

I wanted the ground to open up and swallow me. Charlie shook his head and rolled his eyes at me as if to apologise for his wife's behaviour.

"Gee, thanks, Mum." Henry shook his head and let out a slow breath. It was clear he was working out what to say.

What did I want him to say? I wasn't entirely sure of that either.

"We're housemates, Dr Hartman," I said, hoping I sounded more confident than I felt. "Why would we want to ruin an amazing friendship that's developing?"

"Kandiah, it's Hills or Hillary, please." She smiled at me.

"Well, you can call me Ken, then." I wasn't snarky, nowhere near as snarky as I'd been in bed with Henry, but for the first time, I felt like I was standing up for myself with people from an older generation. My parents would have been mortified by my behaviour.

"Do you prefer Ken?" Bridget asked as she brought a salad out from the kitchen and fastened Mia into a highchair.

"Yeah, I do," I replied, standing and moving to the table. "If I had my way, I'd change my name to Ken Kandiah and be done with my father's surname."

"I know all about that." Bridget smiled at me as Giles pulled her chair out and placed a kiss on her head as she sat. "I don't really know your story, but you won't regret untying yourself from people who do not enrich your life."

Maybe Bridget was right. Maybe it was something I needed to consider. But first, we needed to eat. Henry looked at me from across the table as I cut a chop into pieces for Millie, who had determined I was her favourite adult. "Thank you," he mouthed with a smile.

I was beyond knowing what was going on, and I just hoped that what Henry and I had would be enough and that my heart could withstand the battering heading its way.

Chapter 17

Henry

I willed my sister to pick up her phone early on Monday morning. I'd snuck out of bed. Ken was working late, so he was still sleeping, but I needed to talk to someone. Christian was back at the mines, so Val it was. I was freaking out and needed someone to talk me down.

There was an expletive, followed by the sound of a phone falling to the floor. "What?" Val croaked.

"I need your help." I knew my voice was an octave higher than usual.

"It's like"—Val paused, and I could imagine her peeking through one eye to check the time on her phone—"six thirty. Are you banged up?"

"No." I stretched out the vowel.

I was walking towards a coffee shop near the hospital but didn't want to talk there in case someone heard me.

"I've done it again." I sighed. "I've caught feelings."

Val sighed. "Who is he?"

"Ken. My housemate. We were meant to be housemates with benefits, but then, he's just so lovely and sweet and kind, not to mention sexy as all fuck, and he asked me to teach him about sex and stuff, because he's had this sheltered life, but he hasn't needed to be taught anything, and he's just... I love him. I mean, well, I'm smothering him, and he's the best man I've ever met, and I want forever, and—"

"Slow down, Romeo." I could hear Val clicking the switch on the kettle. "Has he said you're smothering him?"

"No, but he will. And I'll have to find somewhere else to live, and I'll see him around the hospital, and everyone will be all over him because he's just amazing." I stopped on a street corner, not pressing the button to cross, grateful there weren't too many people around.

"Start from the beginning." Val yawned.

So, I did. She knew about the kiss at the gala ball and the bed situation. I raved about Ken's abilities in the kitchen and how visiting the market with him was so much fun. Even though he was naturally quiet, he'd drawn in the folks at the cricket club and cast them under his spell, too. Just this weekend, when he took two wickets in an over, the team couldn't shut up about what an addition he was to the team, and he was. I've never seen him work, but I could imagine that quiet confidence shone through with patients, too.

"... And he just..." I paused, still standing waiting to cross the road with more cars coming now. "He's like a best friend, too, but different to Christian. I mean, I can't lose that. I just can't smother him."

"What is in the water up there?" Val laughed. "I mean, between you and Boyd..."

"Thanks, stinky. But I rang for advice."

"From your twenty-year-old sister? Jesus. My advice is to back off a bit. Has he shown he wants more than this housemates with benefits arrangement?"

I thought about it. "Perhaps I'm reading into things that aren't there. I mean"—I let out a short huff—"I'd like to think he wants this as much as me, but it's just wishful thinking. It's just me seeing things, and I should be seeing the patterns of my past relationships. I mean... Fuck. He's incredible. He's the most incredible man I've ever met, but I know I've said that about others before, but this is different, and I know I've said that before, too, but..."

"Look, I'll be up in a couple of weeks. We'll do some stuff together, okay? Plus, I want to meet this Ken. Perhaps you need to tone it back a bit, though? I mean, I know what you can get like when you get love on the brain. Just take it slowly or something. Fuck. What would I know? Just, I don't know, just, slow down, perhaps?"

"Shit, you've got exams." I felt awful for waking Val up when she needed to be rested.

"I'd already pressed snooze, Hammy. It's all good. Have a good one at work, okay?"

"Thanks, stinky. Good luck. Bye."

Val wasn't the best person to talk to, but she was the only person I could think of who could talk me down from the ledge I felt like I was standing on. She hadn't really offered me any advice, but she also hadn't told me I was being an idiot.

I grabbed a coffee and pot of muesli and yoghurt and headed for the park opposite the hospital. It was a cooler morning but still lovely to sit outside. Birds created music in the trees, and I got to watch the sun come up. I needed to back off with Ken, but I wasn't sure how. Outside of work, we were almost joined at the hip. We played cricket together, and my family insisted he come when I caught up with them.

Ken was an amazing bed buddy, and it was more than the sex. I enjoyed talking with him and loved the way we gravitated towards each other under the sheets, usually waking up entwined in one another. It had been lonely when he was on nights, but I needed to ensure I didn't become dependent on him. That would lead to smothering and turn him against me. Val offered little in the way of suggestions, but she was right in that I needed to step back a bit. I needed to create space and ensure that I didn't suffocate any chances of a future together.

Closing my eyes, I couldn't help but dream of a future with Ken. A life where we worked together and lived together. Maybe children. Ken would be an amazing father. Emily talked of her ovaries spinning when she spent time with Millie and Mia, and I felt that pull to reproduce, too—to raise another human being. I didn't care about biology. Being able to raise a child with Ken by my side suddenly seemed like an amazing goal.

Shit. I was doing it again. I'd just explained to Val why I needed to back off, and here I was imagining our future. No, I needed to play it cool and give Ken time and space to come around to the possibility of a relationship. It would be hard, but it was necessary so that my past didn't keep repeating.

"Henry." Jack, my consultant, had poked his head through the door to the junior doctor room straight after handover. "Got a minute?"

I followed him to his office and took the seat in front of his desk. He didn't look upset, but he'd always been chill about everything. He pulled his chair around and sat beside me.

"I just wanted to pass on how much the team has appreciated having you here the last month or so, and I was wondering what your plans are."

The new rotations would start in a couple of weeks. I hadn't even thought about it. There was something about working in mental health that appealed to me. For the first time, I felt I was making a difference as a doctor, and I was only a very junior one, the lowest rung on the ladder.

"I'm liking it here, and I feel like I fit in." I couldn't help but be relaxed in Jack's presence.

"You did a house doctor year last year in Brisbane, no?" Jack asked, his elbow leaning on his desk.

"Yeah. And I never found a specialty where I felt like I fit until I came here, so that probably says something."

"You're an excellent doctor, and you're great with our clients and staff. If you want to stay, I'm happy to help you with an application to the college to train and become a psychiatrist." The sincerity in Jack's words came through in his eye contact and the gentle smile on his face.

"So, there's a place here next term, then?" I asked, trying to hide the excitement that I might have finally found my place in the world of medicine.

"Indeed, there is." Jack almost laughed. "And we'd love you to stay."

It didn't take me long to think about it. "Sure." I smiled.

"Good. Now, not wanting to throw you in the deep end, but Jamilla is off sick and due to work four nights starting Thursday. You'd get tomorrow and Wednesday off, and then Monday and Tuesday next week." Jack looked at some paperwork. "You'll be on with Becky, one of the senior registrars. I'll just get you to head to emergency today though and shadow whoever is there so you know what's required."

Talk about being thrown in the deep end, but I knew enough about Jack to know he wouldn't set anyone up to fail. I'd not spent any time in the emergency department, even though I knew that there were mental health staff there to deal with clients who presented.

After finding the office where the mental health staff hung out, I was shown to the break room and stashed my lunch in the fridge. This change had come at a good time. Ken had Friday off this week, but I'd be sleeping. From memory, our days off wouldn't sync for a couple of weeks now. This was just what was needed to overcome my nature to smother him and drive him away. It could only be seen as a win-win.

I trailed a registrar called Cooper, who I'd never met before. Cooper explained that he usually worked in the community but had been seconded to the ED for a few weeks, and he was looking forward to having a break from community work.

Any chance I could have had for forgetting about Ken was long gone, though. I was in his territory and, even though I knew he didn't start until after lunch, I kept looking for him around the ward.

"Henry, are you coming to the dark side?" Armon slapped me on the shoulder as we met in the corridor.

"No." I shook my head, knowing the emergency department was not for me. "I'm doing some nights and might end up down here, so I figured I'd better see what happens."

"I'm still in awe of Ken's wickets yesterday. See you at training, yeah?"

"Ken's working lates, but I'll be there." I waved Armon off as he scurried down the corridor towards his next patient.

Cooper and I went and saw a patient who'd been sitting in the department most of the weekend waiting for a bed on the ward. They were floridly psychotic, thinking the television was talking to them and telling them to start a revolution.

As I finished up my notes back in the small broom cupboard that was called the psych office in the department, Cooper turned to me. "So, that physio, he mentioned Ken. Does he mean Dr Ken, who works here?" Cooper tapped his pen on the desk.

"Yeah. He's one of the interns in the department," I replied as I hit save and turned to him. "Why?"

"So, are you and he..." Cooper let the question trail off as he raised his eyebrows.

"We're housemates." I didn't want to talk about this. I wanted to claim Ken and say he was mine, but he wasn't. We were simply housemates with some amazing benefits.

"So, he's not seeing anyone?" I knew Cooper was nervous, but did he have to start every question with a 'so?'

"You'll have to ask him. I'm grabbing a coffee. Do you want something?"

I just wanted to change the subject. Deep down, I recognised how special Ken was, and no doubt, many others were bound to think the same. I needed to distance myself from him and make sure I enforced the boundaries we'd set. We were just housemates with benefits, after all. I doubted Ken saw me like I saw him. Anything I'd thought I'd seen in his face when we'd fucked on Saturday morning was merely endorphins. No guy ever saw in me what I saw in them, and I couldn't expect Ken to be any different. Not that I was unlovable, but I was too intense.

No matter how much I tried not to, I couldn't stop thinking about Ken. As I stood at the sink in the break room and jiggled a tea bag in my cup—there'd been no coffee left in the pot, and I couldn't be bothered starting another one—I not only thought about Ken and his disdain of tea bags, but the way his hands looked as he scooped tea into the gently warmed pot at home. I thought of the same hands and how they trailed down my chest on Saturday morning as we joined for the first time. I thought of the ways I wanted to stroke him and trail kisses behind my caresses all over his chest. And, of course, I thought of the way I wanted to run my fingers through his silky hair, brush it away from his eyes, and caress his face. I was screwed.

Lost in my thoughts of my housemate, I hadn't noticed my sister-in-law appear next to me.

"I forget they only have these crap tea bags in here." Bridget leant across me and grabbed the milk. "Rarely see you down here. Usually, I get to bump into Kandiah."

"He doesn't start until this afternoon." I stirred some milk into my cup before placing the carton back in the fridge.

One thing I liked most about Bridget was she wasn't one for gossip. She never questioned about relationships or talked about who'd been seen holding hands or leaving or coming to work. She was also secretive. I recalled asking if they were going to have another baby, and she simply said "No," whereas the look I received from Giles could have killed at one hundred paces.

"Thanks for last night." I leant against the bench as I talked, grateful the room was all but empty. "I moved back to be closer to you all, and sharing food and talking like we did reminds me I made the right decision."

"Yes, well, I was almost late this morning. I couldn't get Millie out the door, as she was building a pile of books she wants Ken and only Ken to read to her." Bridget laughed.

When I first started studying with her at uni, I would never have imagined her as a mother. She was so focused on her studies, and all she wanted to do was succeed at medicine. The way she had combined her success as a doctor with family life made my heart smile. Knowing the obstacles Bridget had overcome gave me hope that perhaps, one day, there might be a future with a decent relationship for me.

"HEY!" Ken's eyes shone as we almost bumped into each other as I left the broom cupboard I now called our tiny office. My skin sizzled as he steadied himself by gripping my forearm, and I wanted to place my hand over his to keep it there.

"Nah, I work here," I blurted out, as I pulled away from Ken's touch, only to realise he hadn't asked me what I was doing here after all. "Sorry, I'm tired. There's been a roster change. I'm going to do nights over the weekend."

"You didn't sleep well?" Ken's brow furrowed as he looked up at me.

"I woke up early." I shook my head. What should I say to Ken? "I'll probably be asleep by the time you get home. I've got tomorrow off now."

"Cool." Ken smiled. "I start late again, so I can cook us brunch or something."

"There you are." Cooper came barrelling out of the broom cupboard, only to almost bump into Ken and me.

"Sorry. I was just off to see the new client in Bed 11." My eyes were stuck on Ken. I wanted to lean over and kiss him and tell him I wanted so much more than being just his housemate with benefits, but I needed to back off. "Ken, do you know Cooper? He's one of the psych registrars."

Even though they just shook hands, I was jealous of Cooper touching Ken. Fuck. This was going to be near impossible.

"I'll see the, um, new..." I pointed towards the area our new client was in.

"I'll catch you up." Cooper was also looking at Ken as I scurried down the hall.

The lady in Bed 11 didn't need an admission. She lived on the streets and knew what to say to get a warm bed, a sandwich, and a cup of coffee. She regularly had her antipsychotic depot injection and was managing as well as we would have expected. There was no sign she was going to harm herself or others, so I told her I'd let her sleep for a few hours.

Cooper called me soft when I went back to the broom cupboard. He hadn't bothered coming to check on my assessment, but he knew the patient.

"Got a hot date with Ken?" I asked as I typed the password into my computer. My fingers were so stiff—as was the rest of me as I waited for Cooper's response—that I had to retype it to get it right.

"Nah." Cooper sighed. "He told me he's not seeing anyone, but there's someone he's keen on, and he's waiting for the right time to ask him out."

My heart sank. Ken was keen on someone. I had no idea who. His words further deepened my resolve to keep my distance, though, and ensure I reinforced the boundaries we'd set for our arrangement. Sure, I hoped we could still have some fun, but as long as I was sleeping in Ken's bed, things were bound to get messy.

The walk home from work was tedious. At work, I'd convinced myself I needed to make up my bed and sleep there, but during my short walk, I'd told myself I could have one more night in Ken's bed. This conviction strengthened when I threw my keys on the kitchen bench and saw a note from Ken saying he'd made a curry and there was plenty in the fridge for me. He'd even signed the note with 'XO'.

I tried to persuade myself that my feelings for Ken were the same as the feelings I'd had for all my other short-lived boyfriends over the years. This was pure lust, just as it had been with them, and I hadn't worked out how to separate lust from love.

> How was your exam?

I texted my sister, pretending to be a thoughtful brother.

STINKY:

Great! I think I aced it. How's Ken?

> Complicated.

STINKY:

You know what to do. Back off. Don't smother him. Let him come to you if he has feelings, or else you'll chase him away.

> I think I'm too late. He told a colleague he's interested in someone and waiting to make a move. I've probably smothered him already.

STINKY:

Oh, Hammy. I'm sorry.

> Meh. You still got one exam, no?

STINKY:

Thursday. Same as Boyd and Emily. We're having a virtual party together on Thursday night online. You should join us.

I'll be working nights, but thanks.

I flicked off the television I hadn't really been watching and trudged upstairs to Ken's room. It smelt like him, and I'd be sad to sleep across the hall. Tossing and turning, I tried to sleep, but it never came. My body relaxed when I heard Ken's key in the door downstairs, and I pretended to be asleep as he came and stripped before getting in the shower.

The sensible thing would have been to sleep across the hall, but I couldn't bring myself to, not tonight. I'd been holding Ken's pillow, but I placed it back where his head would soon lie and pretended to sleep as I waited for him.

When Ken climbed into bed, my arm reached for him, drawing him to me. He must have known I wasn't asleep, but he didn't show it, instead whispering, "Good night, Hammy," as he snuggled into me.

Chapter 18

Ken

I should never have asked Henry to fuck me.

It changed things. Sure, I'd never been in a relationship before, but despite what we said about housemates with benefits, I thought it was more than that. I was falling for Henry Hartman, but Henry had shown me in the last few weeks that the feelings weren't reciprocated.

Our rosters had been all over the place, but that didn't explain why Henry made up the bed in his room and used it whilst he was on nights. I had loved coming home from nights and finding Hen in my bed, but him moving to his own room made it clear that he wanted his space.

And there had been so many uncomfortable moments. That day I found him working in the ED, my heart leapt for joy when he almost bumped into me. I wanted to give him a quick kiss and hold his forearm, but it wasn't the time or place. Then Cooper, the doctor Henry was working with, asked me out. I've got no idea if he asked Henry about me, but he seemed to think I'd jump at the chance of drinks with him after work one day. I told him I was keen on someone else and plucking up the courage to ask him out for a drink.

It wasn't a lie. I'd like nothing more than to take Henry out on a date. I wanted to sit in a restaurant and gaze into his eyes as we held hands across the table and rubbed legs under it. But it was very clear that Henry didn't see me like that. Perhaps I should have accepted Cooper's offer.

When I got home from work that night, Henry pretended to be asleep. Climbing into bed, I almost let out a huge sigh when his arms reached for me and held me tight. I felt secure. I felt wanted. I felt, well, loved.

The following morning, I'd planned on cooking up a huge brunch. Food and cooking were something I'd always loved, but it had been amazing being in the kitchen away from my mother. There were no jabs about putting in too much of this spice or not enough of that. As a doctor, I knew that if you tried to get to the heart through the stomach, you were doing something wrong, but I thought for Henry, I'd try. But he was gone before I woke up, leaving a note saying he was helping his younger brother and his girlfriend study.

I cooked up a feast anyway and tried to enjoy it myself. When I got home from work, I was pleased to see he'd eaten the leftovers I'd placed in the fridge for him. This time, he was asleep when I climbed into bed, and he didn't reach over to hold me.

When I have a day off, I never usually set an alarm. Imagine my dismay when I woke a few hours after Henry should have finished his night shift to find my bed empty and no sign he'd been in it. It was the first time since Henry moved in that he'd worked nights. I crept downstairs, thinking he might have been the type to sit up for a few hours before attempting to sleep. His keys were on the kitchen counter where he usually left them, and when I went upstairs again, the green scrubs I'd seen him in as he blew into the emergency department as I finished the night before were in the washing basket in the bathroom.

It took me ages to realise he was sleeping in his room. I wanted to open the door and check he was alright, but I received the message loud and clear. Tears pooled in my eyes. There was both a sadness and a feeling of hurt, realising Henry no longer wanted to share my bed.

Henry had decided I wasn't worth it. The sex we'd had was probably so below what he was used to, what with my inexperience. I thought it had been amazing, but I had nothing to compare it to. Well, except for those poor attempts at sex with a woman that I'd decided didn't count. I'd been stupid to think any differently. My parents had been right all along about how hopeless I was.

In the afternoon, I wandered to the local fish market and bought some marlin and prawns to make a fresh curry. It was almost ready when Henry appeared in the kitchen.

"Something smells nice." He leant in behind me as he looked over my shoulder. He sounded tired.

"Sleep alright?" I knew my voice sounded higher pitched than usual, but I needed to pretend everything was hunky-dory.

"So-so." Henry moved to the sink and poured himself a glass of water.

I wanted to ask him about sleeping in his bed and not mine, but I was too nervous. I'd obviously misread things and didn't want to make things worse by showing him how much I valued what we had. Henry claimed he was the one who stuffed up his relationships, but I had stuffed this one up. I didn't know how, though. Perhaps I'd smothered him, suffocated him like he claimed he did. Whatever it was, it felt like crap.

Dinner was quiet. Henry was quiet. He looked exhausted as he blew out the door towards the hospital for his next shift. There was no kiss, just a *thanks* for dinner.

I was working all weekend, and our paths hardly crossed. Henry stayed in his bed and in his room for most of the time, and I tried to stay downstairs in case he wanted to spend time with me. I felt so much for my housemate that I was willing to take any scrap he might throw at me in terms of his attention.

What struck me most was that although I missed the intimacy we'd shared over that short period, it was the time spent talking about everything and nothing that I missed more. Missing his kisses and cock paled in comparison with the conversations we'd had. Now we were ships that passed in the night. Housemates with few benefits as far as I could tell. I had no idea where I'd gone wrong, but this was obviously the new status quo. I was going to have to learn to accept it, whether I liked it or not, even if my heart jumped every time I saw Henry or thought about him.

He'd made his position clear, and I needed to respect it, no matter how much it hurt.

The last thing I wanted was to push him away further and see him move out. In my head, I'd planned we could study together and both become psychiatrists and live a happily ever after. I couldn't believe I'd got it so wrong.

OUR NEW ROTATIONS had been posted for a while, and I was due to start cardiology in a week. I would be glad to see the back of the emergency department, that was for sure. Sure, I'd liked the variety, and the fast pace meant shifts went quickly, but there were so many weekends and nights. I'd wanted and planned to ask for a psych rotation, but I wasn't sure how Henry would take it. Instead, I got to work with his family.

When I'd got to work this morning, there was an email from Charlie Hartman's administrative assistant asking me to meet with Charlie this afternoon. As one head of the cardiology department, this didn't surprise me, and I let my supervisors in the ED know that I'd be leaving early.

"Ken, come through." Charlie had the same smile as Henry, even if his came with added lines on his face that added to the feeling he really was pleased to see me. "I feel like I haven't seen you for weeks, what with your roster in ED and Henry picking up all these extra shifts. You are joining us on Sunday, though, I hope. Val, our youngest, was planning on coming up a couple of weeks back but forgot to put in with work that she needed time off, so she'll be here Friday. It will be amazing to have everyone under our roof for a meal, and, of course, Hillary and I would love to see you there."

I wanted to tell him I'd have to check my roster, but both of us knew I had the weekend off before starting in his department. "You sound so excited to have Val home." I changed the subject.

"I am, I am, but I didn't bring you here to talk family. Now, we have four main cardiology teams here at the hospital. As you can imagine, it's been a challenge having so many Hartmans around. I'm aware you are sort of a Hartman by association now, and—"

"Sorry, sir," I interrupted, feeling the blush that had crept across my cheeks, "but as much as I appreciate gathering socially with you, I can't see how being Henry's housemate makes me an honorary Hartman. If it would make things easier, I'm happy to not socialise with your family whilst I'm on the cardiology team."

I looked at my hands sitting in my lap, my fingers forcefully intertwined.

"Ken." Charlie removed his glasses and held them in his hands. "I know you said at Giles and Bridget's that you and Henry were just housemates, but it seems you have developed a strong friendship too." The way Charlie said friendship showed that he thought there was more to us than that.

"That may have been then, but Henry's made it pretty clear over the last few weeks that we're housemates and nothing more. Now..." I swallowed hard, amazed that I could be this forthright with someone. "I don't think you called me here to talk about your son."

"No, no, I didn't. I wanted to talk about your rotation here and reassure you that you won't be on the same team as Hillary, Giles, or myself."

"Thank you, sir."

Charlie took in a deep breath, and I was ready for him to remind me to call him Charlie, but he leant back in his chair and tapped his glasses on his desk.

"Where do you want to end up?" he asked.

"Psych. But I'll probably move away to train. I mean, Henry appears to be loving his time there and has found his calling, and I don't think I could..." I pulled myself up before I blurted how much it would hurt to see Henry at work each day.

There was silence, and I wondered if I should add on to my last brain fart, but I'd already said too much.

"Well, Ken, I'm meeting with all the interns this week who will join us next week. Please remember my door is always open, and you are more than welcome to come and see me about anything, work related or not."

There was a subtext there. Well, I thought there was, but I didn't want to ask. I didn't want to tell Charlie Hartman how cold his son had gone on me after we'd had amazing sex together. Perhaps I should look up Cooper and see if he wanted to grab that drink.

I WONDERED if I had grown up in a family that showed effective communication if I might have been able to ask Henry what I had done wrong. We finally had a weekend off together, and he still wasn't sleeping in my bed. Henry wasn't up when I came down to the kitchen and brewed a pot of tea. I placed some bacon in the oven to crisp up and mixed some pancake batter. I needed comfort, and light and fluffy to contrast the lead weight that hung over me.

Henry hadn't appeared, but I heard music coming from his room. It sounded upbeat, but when I went upstairs to use the bathroom, I heard Bernard Fanning lamenting a breakup. I could relate, however, I wasn't at the stage of wishing Henry well.

I felt ignored and insignificant. This silence from Henry was worse than if he'd told me he didn't want me anymore. I wasn't even worth that.

I grabbed my shopping bags and walked to the market. The sun peeked out from behind white, fluffy clouds, and many would have claimed it was the perfect day, but it did nothing for my mood. I found it hard to find joy in the smell of the herbs at the market or the bountiful produce that would usually get my creative juices flowing and a weekly menu developed in my head.

Carrying my own bags didn't help. I liked Henry insisting on carrying everything, even when I tried to grab some bags from him or refuse to hand over my latest purchase.

Feeling my phone vibrate in my pocket, I grabbed a coffee and a seat around the large communal table at the edge of the market space. I'd seen a few colleagues and was being recognised more and more by different stall holders. It gave me a sense of community, of belonging. I needed to put thoughts of Henry aside and focus on the good things.

My phone was not one of these things.

AM'MĀ:

KANDIAH CALL.

AM'MĀ:

CALL NOW.

Somewhere along the line, I'd missed a call from my mother, but I wasn't going to listen to her voicemail at the market. I was about to pocket my phone once again when the screen lit up with her incoming call.

"Am'mā, I thought it was early there and was going to call later." The time difference was a couple of hours, and I always use it as an excuse to avoid contact.

"We need you, Kandiah." There was no question from my mother about my tired voice or the sounds of people in the background. No question how I was. No question of how Cassowary Point was treating me. "It's your father. He's not well. He's having turns and getting confused."

"What sort of turns?" I rubbed my thumb and forefinger over my closed eyes and hoped I sounded concerned enough.

The truth was, I wasn't concerned. My mother had always complained that something was wrong with my father. His cholesterol was slightly high. Am'mā was convinced he was at death's door. His blood pressure had crept up, so to her, he was about to have a heart attack. Once, she'd confused an ingrown toenail for cancer and told me I needed to do something for him. I booked him into a GP.

"He ignores me." I couldn't imagine why. "And he pretends he doesn't hear things when I talk to him. Then he mumbles."

This was not new behaviour for my father. As much as he controlled my mother and made it clear he was the head of the house and his word was gospel, my mother was a nag. They were codependent in their skewed view of love. No wonder I was having issues communicating with Henry.

"Have you taken him to the doctor?" I asked, taking a sip from my coffee that was rapidly getting cold.

"What will he do?" My mother's shrill voice told me she didn't want an answer from me. "He needs you. You need to come and tell him to do the right thing."

Do the right thing? Did I hear my mother correctly? If my parents knew I'd had sex with a man, they'd disown me. I was concerned, though, that my father's overall grumpiness towards me was now being directed at my mother.

"And you need to pray for him," my mother continued. "God tells me you haven't been praying enough. Are you reading scripture?"

"Am'mā, is he treating you alright? He's not yelling at you or hitting you?" A silent yawn escaped, which was more from lack of sleep than having to talk to my mother, or so I told myself.

"Kandiah," my mother chastised, "your father is a good man, a godly man. He needs you here. I need you here." Her voice didn't soften as she spoke. We were bound to go around in circles with this conversation.

"Look, Am'mā, I can't break my contract here. I'll see if I can take some leave and come and visit though, okay?"

It wasn't okay, and I ended up listening to my mother's rant about my sisters not doing enough for their husbands.

After several minutes, I needed to get my mother off the phone. Her call exhausted me. "I have to go, Am'mā. My taxi's here."

She all but hung up on me, a muffled farewell followed by the slam of a phone in my ear. I suspected one reason she hated the cordless phone and her mobile was that she couldn't slam it down when she was done with you.

I hadn't ordered a cab or an Uber. I'd just thrown my empty coffee cup in the bin when I turned and saw Henry's mother.

"What a pleasant surprise seeing you here, Ken." She greeted me with a kiss on my cheek. "No Henry?"

"He was still sleeping, I think," I lied, my eyes blinking rapidly.

"Lazy bugger." Hillary laughed. "I was just grabbing some things for Val. She got in last night, and, like her brother, she is also still sleeping. Gosh, you are weighed down with bags." She reached out to me. "Here, let me take a couple."

"No, I'm fine, seriously. I was just going to grab a cab home."

"Nonsense." She linked her arm in mine as we walked past a stall selling homemade soaps. "I'll give you a lift. I'm finished here, anyway."

Hillary was a different insistent to my mother. She wanted to make things easier for me and help me. I was glad when we talked about work in the car and not Henry. She told me how excited she was to have me around the cardiology department and how Bridget had sung my praises from my time in O&G.

Whereas my mother tore me down, Hillary tried to build me up.

"Now, we will see you tomorrow night, won't we?" Hillary asked as we pulled up at the gates to our townhouse.

"I'm not sure. Some guys from cricket have organised a dinner and want me there, and I..." I trailed off when Hillary placed her hand on my thigh.

"Just know you are very welcome in our home, alright?" Hillary looked at me with an enormous smile as she gave a gentle squeeze to my leg. "Now, I won't come in, and if I don't see you tomorrow, I'll see you at work this week."

I thanked Hillary for the lift as I grabbed my bags from the back of her SUV. I'd thought Henry was like his mother, but something had changed. He'd gone from showing care and concern to ignoring me. I had no idea what waited for me behind the front door to the townhouse, and I was almost nervous to turn the key, but we were still housemates, and I needed to get past this sadness that we'd had something great that I'd somehow ruined.

Chapter 19

Henry

Had I fucked up? Probably. I knew I had to stop smothering Ken before I drove him away, but staying away was so hard. We were barely talking. I was making up excuses to not be around for fear that I would draw him close to me and press his body to mine. I wanted to feel his beautiful soft lips and his tongue as it glided through my mouth, wanting to taste me more than any of the amazing food he'd created. As much as I adored his cooking, it always tasted better on his lips.

I could see few benefits of us being roommates now. If I talked with Ken about the situation, I would blurt out about how much I was falling for him, and I'd probably even declare everlasting love. I didn't know if I loved Ken like that, but it felt different to all the other men I'd thought I'd loved. Home life was torture. We'd had this amazing thing, and then I'd blown it.

With Ken, I not only wanted to make his life brighter, but I loved the way he took care of me, too. He was still cooking, which I suspected was the primary way he showed people he cared, and he'd do little things like fold my laundry if he found it in the dryer. I'd even heard him listening to songs that I'd been playing.

I had an extensive list of mainly love songs I listened to over and over. I mean, the playlist was several hours long. It included music that spoke to me of the sort of love I wanted to find in the world. Over the years, I'd added songs about heartbreak, too, but nothing matched the way my heart felt at the moment.

Ken had made pancakes for breakfast. I'd heard him in the shower, and my cock swelled when I thought of him naked, water dripping down his hairy chest that I loved so much. I came downstairs when I heard the front door close and assumed he'd left. He'd left pancakes and bacon for me. Even after the pancakes were warmed in the microwave, they were still fluffy and made me wish I'd been down to share them fresh.

Neither of us were slobs, which was lucky, as I was a naturally clean and tidy person. I'd finished mopping the tiles downstairs when Ken returned.

"Shit, I'm sorry," I said as Ken almost tripped over the bags of produce he'd obviously bought from the market. "I should have gotten up early and driven you."

"It's all good. I bumped into your mum, and she gave me a lift home." Grabbing some bags Ken had left at the door, I took them into the kitchen. "I've got this." Ken pulled the bags from me and didn't even look at me as he piled mandarins into the fruit bowl, his voice lacking the warmth I'd come to crave.

"I'm, um, I'm off to catch up with Boyd. We're going to see a movie or something this afternoon." I should have invited Ken, but I couldn't trust myself. I wanted to sit next to him in a dark theatre and share a bucket of popcorn.

I grabbed my keys from the place I always threw them on the bench and made my way to my car. A cappella voices filled the car as soon as I turned on the engine, reminding me that fools rush in. I'd been so foolish with what I'd done. I'd bulldozed my way into Ken's life and fallen for him. He'd said he wanted someone to tutor him so he'd have some experience when he met an actual boyfriend. There was no way he saw me as boyfriend material. I'd explained to him how dysfunctional I was when it came to relationships, and I didn't want a relationship, did I? I just wanted to be with Ken, to go back to sharing a bed and whispering sweet nothings to each other as our arms wrapped around each other and our noses touched as we shared a pillow.

Deep down, I knew I wanted my cake and to eat it, too. I wanted the intimacy of a relationship, but living with Ken deepened things rapidly. Staying the course I'd set needed to be my focus. Plus, Ken already had his eye on someone. It was probably one of the guys at cricket. Now I needed to avoid cricket, too. Why did I always fall so hard, so fast?

"I THOUGHT we were meeting at the cinema after lunch." Boyd greeted me at the door wearing sweatpants and nothing else. "Em and me could have been in the middle of something."

"Looks like you've been there, done that." I laughed as he showed me into their tiny apartment, and I perched on one of the kitchen counter chairs.

"We're both bloody insatiable. Plus, look at her; she's everything, she's perfect." Boyd definitely had hearts in his eyes when he spoke of his girlfriend.

"Hey, Hammy." Emily appeared from their bedroom, her hair wet and her feet bare. "I thought we were meeting after lunch."

"I needed to get out." I let out a sigh as I shook my head. "See, I've gone and fallen for Ken, despite telling him about my relationship past, and I've had to back off or else I'd smother him, but I've gone all icy on him, and I don't think he knows what's happening, and I don't know what's happening, and, oh, have you seen how fucking sexy he is? I mean, that bum, it's—"

"I get the picture. Sort of." Boyd laughed. "What does Ken think?"

Emily had switched on the kettle and brought out some jasmine tea. It was all she drank. Boyd didn't drink tea or coffee, but he kept Coca-Cola in business with his consumption of Diet Coke.

"I don't know," I hissed as I looked at my hands on the counter. "He wanted a tutor, and he's found someone he's keen on, anyway."

"Sorry, back up." Emily poured water over the leaves in the pot. "A tutor in what? I thought he was an intern, too."

"Yeah, he is. He, well, his parents are ultra Jesus freaks and would have disowned him if he brought a man home, so he's, like, never been with a man, even though he's gay, and... Shit, this isn't my story to tell." Bile rose in my stomach as I shared things I wasn't sure Ken wanted me to. "Can you forget that, please?" I looked at Boyd, knowing Emily wouldn't share anything if she was asked not to.

"Sure, but you fooled around together?" Boyd leant against the fridge, having grabbed a can of his beverage of choice.

"He's the best kisser I've ever met, and the way our bodies fit..." I trailed off, reminiscing about the things we'd done.

"I get the picture." Emily poured me a cup of tea and slid it in front of me before moving to the fridge to stand with her boyfriend.

"But he's found someone else, you say?" Boyd asked, clearly enthusiastic to learn more about my sordid tale of woe.

"Yeah. Probably someone from cricket or work." I could feel tears welling in my eyes as I thought about Ken with someone else.

"His loss." Emily tilted her head to the side as she leant against Boyd's shoulder. "There's something about you Hartman boys. You're all such lovely men."

"It's our big cocks, babe. Whatcha up to tomorrow?" Boyd asked me as he finished his drink and threw the can in a box next to the fridge meant for recycling.

"Cricket in the afternoon. Not that I really feel like it. Plus, we have family dinner with us all." Mum had messaged me to remind me Ken was invited. I wanted him there so much, but, again, I knew I'd make a fool of myself at the same time by being all heart eyes over him. I was just as bad as my brothers and their love for their partners, except mine didn't return my feelings.

"There's a group of us from uni going on a hike if you want to join us." Boyd played with Emily's hair, making me recall the feeling of running my hands through Ken's luscious locks.

"That sounds good. If I miss cricket, I miss it." I tried to sound enthusiastic, but it was challenging.

Boyd explained where we were going. I'd hiked it before, and it was a nice place, especially at this time of year. I'd told myself I wanted to do more hiking, so this was an excellent opportunity for that.

"Don't tell me you've convinced Val to come?" I smiled, trying to laugh but failing.

"Of course not." Emily drew away from Boyd and poured more tea. "She and I are going shopping."

"She'll hate that just as much." This time, I managed a chuckle.

"Yeah, but she needs some things. It was her idea, actually." Emily became so animated when she talked about her best friend. She and Val had a strange friendship, despite their two-year age gap, and Val treated her like the sister she never had, despite her being loved up with our brother. It was weird, but it worked and always had.

THE HIKE WAS AMAZING. It was everything I loved about being in nature, the sounds of the birds and other animals in the rainforest, the smells of the native plants that I didn't experience in Brisbane, and the lush greenery that surrounded us. A couple of Boyd's medical student colleagues wanted to pick my brain over specialties, and I think I almost convinced one of them to give psych a go.

When we reached the top of the peak we'd climbed, I found a rock and sat in silence for a while. I thought back to my last months in Brisbane and how I'd hated my job, and I compared that to now loving my job but hating not having Ken. I wasn't sure how I was going to get over this. Perhaps immersion therapy would be good, and I would just make sure I saw Ken with his new love interest over and over until my brain registered that he wasn't into me like that.

Psych was showing me how to read people better. I'd always thought I'd read people well, but Jack pointed out things that I missed from time to time. I'd definitely missed signs with Ken. It had seemed like he was into me. I thought that being the first man to be intimate with him, we had something special. It felt special to me, but feelings aren't reality.

It surprised me that when I arrived at my parents', Emily and Val were talking with Mum about what a great guy Ken was.

"I mean, he hates it as much as me. He was telling me how Billie took him shopping before the gala and that's set him up, but I'm glad you convinced him to get that gorgeous shirt." Val turned to Emily and finally took a breath.

"I mean, that aqua popped against his dark skin. I hope he wears it tonight," Emily said as she popped a cube of cheese into her mouth.

"Hey, Mum." I leant around her and pretended to stir the gravy she was tending to over the stove. "I thought we were having lasagne."

"No, your sister wanted roast lamb." Mum swatted my hand away, and I gave her a kiss on the cheek.

"Good choice, stinky." I grabbed some of the cheese the ladies had been nibbling on. "Gilbo here yet?"

"He's out the back with your dad and the girls. Bridget was called into work, but she should be here soon." Mum shooed me away as she poured more wine into the empty glasses in front of the three of them. Boyd appeared with two bottles of beer and made a performance of twisting the caps off with his forearm before making out with his girlfriend.

"It's a shame Ken's not coming," Mum said wistfully, as she placed the empty wine bottle in the recycling bin before reaching for another.

"Nah." Val took a big swig of the wine that had been poured for her. "He's had enough of grumpy Hammy, I think. He's made the right choice."

"Yeah." Emily pulled away from Boyd, but he kept kissing her neck. "I hope they enjoy the movie as much as we did yesterday."

Fuck. I coughed as beer went down the wrong hole at this conversation. Ken was going on a date wearing a new shirt that the women thought suited him and seeing that film, which, although billed as an action film, had a powerful theme of romance throughout. Someone else was going to taste Ken's lips tonight. I wondered how far they'd go and if he'd bring him home. My heart hurt, and any hope I might still have a chance with Ken evaporated.

It would probably be better if he brought him home. I mean, I could then accept that Ken would never be mine and start moving on. Living with him, though, would make that hard.

I was subdued throughout dinner. Boyd, Emily, and Val had all received their results and aced their exams. Emily and Boyd were talking about travelling to Thailand over Christmas, which surprised me. None of us had done a great deal of travel. It was something I'd thought about but never acted on. As kids, Mum and Dad would rent a beach house over the summer for us all, and we would gather there, usually with our grandparents.

There was so much of Australia I hadn't even seen. I'd never been to Perth, where Ken was from. I'd probably never go now that we were, well, I wasn't even sure what we were.

Bridget arrived and told the tale of being called in when the registrar on call came down with something and there were twins on the way. This led to Giles retelling the story of the first time Bridget caught a baby, a story we'd heard repeatedly. Val told us about a guy she'd been seeing who was also a law student, but he'd sent her a text that morning saying his girlfriend was out of town and Angus might like to come over.

"I mean, we were never serious, and I didn't even think we were exclusive, but he was shocked when I texted back and told him he had the wrong number, and he then rang me." Val took a deep breath. "Poor guy. We had a heart to heart, and it turns out his parents want him to have a girlfriend, but he's bi and met this Angus, and they have this great connection that he and I never had."

Val continued with her story. It showed the sort of family we were in that no one batted an eyelid, even though Millie and Mia were sitting around the table with us. It also made me think more about Ken. I wondered how many other people still had families that couldn't accept their sexuality. I'd like to think there were less and less, but perhaps it was wishful thinking.

It shouldn't have surprised me that Ken would want to move on and experiment more. I mean, when I first went to Brisbane for uni, I hooked up with lots of guys to experience as much as possible. I shouldn't have thought that Ken would want to spend his time with just me. There are probably lots of other guys out there who would give Ken what he wanted and what he needed. Deep down, I just wished it was me, but I needed to accept that it was not.

"Where's Uncle Ken?" Millie had come and sat on my knee after she finished her dinner.

"Do you want me to read you a story? I'm sure Gammy and Gramps have some books around." I stroked my niece's hair, and she looked like she was half asleep.

"I think we need to go." Giles picked Millie up as Bridget gathered a wide-awake Mia in her arms.

I needed to go, too, and find out what, or who, would greet me at home.

THE TOWNHOUSE WAS quiet when I got home. I could hear our neighbours watching a movie next door with screeching tyres and gunfire. There was no noise from upstairs. I never knew if Ken's bed squeaked the same way Billie's had, because I was usually in it with him.

After a shower, I decided to just head to bed and read. Val had tried to get me into some thriller she said was amazing, but I kept putting it down for weeks on end and forgetting what had happened. It wasn't late when I heard a car door slam downstairs.

"You right to get inside?" Who was that talking to Ken? I tried to think of the guys at cricket. It sounded like Ben, but I thought he had a girlfriend.

"Yeah. Thanks." Ken laughed in a way I'd never heard before. "Oops!" There was a crash, and I figured Ken must have had a few drinks.

"You sure? Is your room upstairs? I can help you." Yeah. This was Ben.

"Nah, man. I'm totally fine. See..." Ken slurred as I heard the door open downstairs. "Thanks for tonight. It was, well, it was amazing—the best night I've had in ages. We should do it again sometime."

"Yeah, but not on a Sunday. Perhaps Friday night?" Was Ben asking Ken on another date? Shit. "I'll see you Tuesday, and we can work it out then. Say hi to Henry for me."

"If he talks to me," Ken mumbled. "I have to work tomorrow. I need to sleep. G'night, sweet Ben."

"See ya, Kenny. And sweet dreams, alright?"

Ken wasn't a big drinker, and I'd never seen him drunk. He had his first day in cardiology in the morning, and I wondered how he was going to fare with a hangover. Was he expecting my family to go soft on him? I didn't think he realised how seriously we all took medicine. It wasn't a joke. Part of me wanted to protect him and say that he was sick and tell him to stay home, but the other part was angry that he'd gone on a date with Ben. I mean, Ken and Hen were bad enough when considering our names, but really, Ben, too?

Sleep wouldn't come. I could have sworn I heard Ken at my door saying good night, but it was probably a dream. I rued the carpet upstairs and wished we had creaky floorboards like at Mum and Dad's, so I could hear if he was stealing away from my room.

THERE WAS no sign of Ken in the morning. He still had an hour before he needed to be at work, but usually, he'd be downstairs cooking breakfast. I wanted to poke my head into his room to check he was okay, but that was a bad idea. I missed sleeping in Ken's bed and knew that if I went up there, I'd tell him I thought I was a better choice than Ben. So, I sent him a text.

> Hey. Hope cardiology goes okay.

I wanted to add something about my family, but I had no idea what I wanted to say. Instead, I headed out early and grabbed a bagel and coffee before I started my day. No doubt I would spend it worrying about Ken.

Chapter 20

Ken

What had I been thinking? Ben and some guys from cricket had been asking me to go out for a few drinks with them after the match for weeks, and this week, I relented. We'd planned to see a movie, too, but the bar had been too comfortable. I'd ended up telling them about Henry and how he'd ghosted me despite still living with me.

I'd drunk far more than I ever had before, the guys plying me as I opened up more and more. Ben told me about his girlfriend and how he had issues communicating with her to begin with because his parents had been so dysfunctional. I needed to sit down with Henry and talk. Perhaps I could explain to him I liked him a lot, and even though I suggested early on that I didn't want a relationship, living without him had been so hard, and I'd do almost anything to go back to where we'd been.

Even though I'd washed my sheets, I still hadn't washed the pillowcase Henry had slept on. It no longer smelt of him, but I snuggled up to it anyway each night, thinking that his head had touched it. I wished he was with me now, kissing me and rubbing against me until we both came. There'd been no way I could have had dinner with his family and not spent the night yearning over him. I would have made my feelings very clear, and even young Millie would have picked up on them.

There was more light than usual peeping through the blinds in my room when I heard my phone beep. It was probably another text from my family. I grabbed it and jolted upright in bed when I realised I'd slept through my alarm. The sudden movement made my head throb. It was a text from Henry simply wishing me well on my first day in cardiology. Shit. I was going to be doing my first day with a hangover.

After a quick shower, I saw Henry had ironed my scrubs for me. He kept doing these little things that made my life easier. He'd mopped downstairs whilst I was at the market on Saturday, after also cleaning the bathroom. Now he'd found time to iron for me. It was as if he was sending mixed signals. Still, they gave me a little hope he might be receptive when I spoke to him after work.

I remembered getting home last night and barely being able to get my key in the door. I stood at Henry's door for ages, leaning my head against it, wishing he would sense me there and open it. It was a pointless exercise, and I suspect sober Ken would have worked that out. Instead, I wished him good night, and I think I had actually voiced this before leaving a kiss on the timber. Who was I trying to kid, though? Sober me had been saying good night at his door for weeks now. It was hopeless. I was hopeless. I needed to accept Henry no longer saw me that way, if even he ever had.

There was just enough time to rustle up a basic omelette on toast. Henry had left my teapot out with the tea canister next to it and a packet of painkillers. He must have heard me come home.

I'd heard Henry's father proclaim on more than one occasion that tea made everything better. I suspected that my parents held a similar philosophy. However, for them, I think it was less about the chance to sit down and talk with someone and more about the reminders of a home that none of us had lived in.

At uni, I'd read a bit about second and third generation migrants, especially those from non-European backgrounds, and there were a lot of similarities, whether you'd arrived in Australia from Asia, Africa, or Latin America. There were large Indian populations scattered around but fewer Sri Lankans. I was often confused for being Indian myself, and I'd had more than one patient tell me they were surprised they could understand me when I spoke to them. This feeling of not fitting in wasn't new. I was used to disappointment and feeling like an outsider, but the feelings after Henry cast me aside cut far deeper.

There was no way I was going to psychoanalyse my parents and their reactions to tea, especially with a pounding head. With Henry not here to drink the other half of the pot I'd brewed, I placed it in a travel cup and made my way to work. I was glad for sunglasses, even though it was technically winter. It was still warm enough that I didn't need a jacket in the mornings, and I suspected I would have tilted my head to catch the sun had I not imbibed too much last night.

Giles was already waiting in the handover room when I arrived, but we were the first ones there. So much for believing I was running late.

"Missed you last night, well, Millie missed you more than most because you read stories better than anyone apparently." Giles laughed as I took a seat next to him. "Did you have a good evening?"

"Yeah. The guys from cricket took me out for drinks, and I may have had one or two too many." I leant back and closed my eyes, too nervous to see Giles' reaction.

"Sounds like fun." I glanced over to see Giles smiling. "Henry thought you were on a date."

"What?" I sat upright, my eyes bulging, my voice louder than it should have been. My head did not appreciate any of it.

I wanted to question Giles more, but another couple of registrars and three of the other new interns joined us, along with the doctor who'd been on all night. How could Henry think that? I'd had an enjoyable morning with Val and Emily. When Val texted me saying she was going shopping with Emily and I should join them, I'd been surprised. I didn't even know she had my number. Val and I bonded over our mutual disdain for shopping, but Val needed some new clothes for her upcoming placement at a law firm, and Emily had a brilliant eye for fashion. She even convinced me to buy a striking aqua shirt.

Both of them had tried to get me to come to their family dinner, but I told them the guys from cricket had been bugging me for weeks to join them for a drink after our game. It was a handy excuse and meant I didn't have to tell them that Henry had been ignoring me and wouldn't want me there.

Val was just as kindhearted as her brothers. She reminded me a lot of her mother in that she loved to laugh, talked with her hands, and aimed to make everyone feel at ease around her. She was vague when she asked me about Henry, and my replies were probably more vague. I wanted to come out and ask her about why her brother had ghosted me, but I simply told her what a great guy I thought he was, and I really enjoyed living with him. Which was true.

After a brief meeting with my new team, I joined them on rounds, glad that I didn't have to write up the notes from our encounters, as I was still getting my head around things. It would have helped if my head wasn't still pounding, too.

My phone had been blowing up in my pocket. There was no way I was going to glance at it on my first morning in a new rotation. Whoever it was could wait. It was probably my family telling me how useless I was again in not being there and not becoming an accountant. No doubt I'd be reminded how I needed to pray more and read my Bible.

"Dr Dissanayake?" The ward clerk came up to me with a Post-it note. "Your sister, Dipti, called. Can you please call her straight away?"

"Go, we've got this," Mikel, the consultant, whispered as he placed his hand on my shoulder. "Family comes first."

I made my way into the empty doctor's room and sat at one of the computer chairs. Having my family call the hospital was a new one. I sighed as I picked up my phone to see over a dozen missed calls from both of my sisters.

Dipti's phone didn't even ring before she answered. "Kandiah, it's Daddy." My sister was sobbing. "He's in the hospital. Come, please."

SITTING AT 33,000 FEET, I had time to breathe. I'd thought Dipti was overreacting. I rang the hospital they were at and spoke to the registrar in the ED who was looking after my father. She told me he'd had a haemorrhagic stroke and was still unconscious. I'll never forget the kind but forthright tone she used to tell me it was unlikely he would survive, and she recommended I find my way to his bedside, even if it was to say goodbye.

I'd spoken to my mother as well, which had been a mistake. She blamed me and told me the stress that I'd placed on my father had caused this. I told her I was coming home. She just cried. I should probably have felt guilty that I hadn't been there for them, but I blamed my hangover for preventing this. I didn't hesitate heading home, but I suspect it was more a sense of guilt I knew I'd feel if I didn't go.

Mikel found me in the doctor's room, and when I told him what had happened, he helped me arrange a flight and told me to take as long as I needed. I'd run home, changed out of my scrubs, thrown some clothes in a case, and caught an Uber to the airport. I'd forgotten my phone charger, but I was on a flight that didn't have Wi-Fi, so I simply turned the damn thing off. It wasn't like the person I wanted to speak to was speaking to me, anyway.

For over four hours, I'd have time to sit here and think. I should have grabbed a book, but I was just glad I'd been able to get a seat on one of the few direct flights from Cassowary Point to Perth. The stress of my father's condition had made me forget about my headache. I tried to feel sad for him and was prepared to land and discover he had died, but I felt angry rather than anything else. He didn't deserve a family who dropped everything to be at his side.

My mother had told me their congregation was praying for my father, and they were expecting a miracle. I knew the miracle would be him being alive when I landed. From what the doctor had told me, the damage from the ruptured vessel in his brain was extensive, and I knew from spending time on the stroke ward as a medical student that it was indeed a catastrophic bleed. There was no coming back from this. I don't know if being a doctor helped me process this news, but I liked to think that even if I still held the faith of my parents, I wouldn't be so naïve in my thinking.

Despite being sandwiched between two middle-aged women, I was glad they didn't want to talk throughout the flight. I tried sleeping, but my brain was too wired. I had no idea if I'd left Cassowary Point for the last time. My mother would need me. I doubt she'd be able to cope without my father. He told her to jump, and she simply asked how high. He managed the finances and gave her money each week for groceries. He told her what to wear and who she could speak to. He was a controlling prick. I was almost shocked at my thoughts. Being away from Perth had given me a distance to crystalise exactly how I'd been treated by the people who were meant to want the best for me. My father had never wanted what was best for his family, but rather what was best for him.

It would be expected that I'd step into this role as the son of the family, despite being the youngest. I'd have no trouble getting a job at a hospital in Perth, but that would mean breaking my contract at Cassowary Point. I knew they'd be understanding, considering the circumstances.

But it would mean leaving Henry. This thought was the first that brought tears to my eyes. Perhaps I should just learn to deal with it. Henry had made it clear he didn't want me as part of his life, and I had to respect that. When I closed my eyes, I could still picture his gorgeous light-brown eyes and feel his coarse beard caressing my skin.

I thought of messaging him and telling him about my father, but I figured his family would tell him. It wasn't that I was seeking sympathy from him. I didn't want him to contact me because he felt he should or it was the right thing to do. He should contact me because of what we had, or what I thought we'd had. It was my inexperience that saw me understand things inaccurately. I'd asked him to fuck me, and he had, and he'd not enjoyed it, obviously. I mean, at the time, he said he had, but there must have been something off about it.

What disappointed me the most was I'd never know what I did wrong or what I could change for the future. Not that I saw a future with anyone, well, anyone other than Henry.

Dipti's husband, Gayan, met me at the airport, but he made it clear I was an inconvenience. He simply dropped me at the hospital and made his way back to work. It amazed me how different the Hartman family was to mine. If something had happened to one of Bridget's relatives, I was sure Giles would have dropped everything to be with his wife, and the whole family would have rallied around her.

Walking through the large glass doors of the hospital reminded me of a placement I'd had here as a student. It smelt the same as Cassowary

Point Hospital, but it was three times the size. The volunteer at the information desk directed me to the first-floor palliative care ward.

It shouldn't have surprised me that Abha's husband was also absent. My sisters were comforting my mother as two nurses worked to move my father in the bed, propping up his hip and back with pillows to prevent pressure sores. With Abha and Dipti seated on either side of my mother and none of them attempting to greet me when I entered the room, I made my way to my mother, placed a hand on her shoulder, and kissed her head.

The three of them said nothing.

"You must be Kandiah." One nurse looked at me with kind eyes.

"Yes," I replied, drained from the emotion and the travel. "Is there any change?"

"We're keeping your father comfortable."

"Thanks. Morphine? Midazolam?" I looked at the machine trickling medication slowly into my father's stomach.

The nurse nodded. I knew the drill.

"He doesn't need medication. God will heal him." My mother sounded angry. "Our minister will be here shortly to lay hands on him and bring him back to life."

The nurse glanced at me, and I closed my eyes and shook my head. There was never any point arguing religion with my parents. "Now that you're here, Kandiah, I'll call the doctor." The nurse smiled before leaving the room with her colleague.

"Am'mā," I spoke softly. "Appā had a stroke. He will not get better from this."

"Nonsense." My mother scoffed. "God. Will. Heal. And I've seen the shows. They can operate and take the stroke away these days. Why aren't they operating?"

"Am'mā." It was hard to remain calm, but I tried. "There are two types of strokes. Appā had the type where the blood vessel bursts and not the type where there's a clot. I thought we had his blood pressure under control, but usually, high blood pressure leads to this type of stroke."

"He didn't need those tablets. He stopped taking them months ago."

I had to bite my tongue and count to ten to stop myself from playing a blame game. The doctor came and reiterated what we already, well, what I already knew. My sisters were quiet, and I didn't know what they were thinking. I knew from experience that families came in all shapes and sizes, but today I looked at mine as an outsider. Distance had given me a greater understanding of how dysfunctional we were. I'm sure, to many, we would have looked normal, but we weren't healthy. There was definitely no fun in our dysfunction.

It was as if I'd been looking up through a window my entire life, and I'd seen sunshine and clouds, but now there was a thermometer in the aperture telling me it was actually icy cold on the other side. If I came close to the window, I'd see that the ground was hard, and the trees had no leaves.

"I'll stay with Appā tonight," I told my mother and sisters, trying not to sigh. "But first, I'll head home and cook up some food for your families, Abha and Dipti."

"You shouldn't do that." My mother shook her head, but she still sounded angry. "My girls can provide for their families."

"I know that." I swallowed. "But I enjoy cooking, and it will give me something to do."

"Take my car." Dipti stood, and I saw her eyes were bloodshot. "I'll walk you out."

We'd left the ward before I let my anger get the better of me, stopping and banging my fists against the concrete wall.

"Come here." Dipti drew me into a hug.

"He stopped his blood pressure tablets, Dip. I mean, why?"

"Because of their fucked-up views of religion." I'd never heard my sister swear before, and I'd never heard her talk about my parents' faith like that. "I'd love to have a talk with you alone sometime. There's..." She paused as I drew away from her embrace. "There are changes... I think I'm the one responsible for Daddy's attack."

Dipti had always called our parents Mama and Daddy. She had tears in her eyes, which she wiped with her sleeve. "Can you come back tonight?" I asked.

"Gayan won't be happy, but yes." Dipti looked downtrodden and sounded exhausted.

Of my sisters, I'd always been closer to Dip. She was eighteen months older than me and much more carefree than Abha. It surprised me when she agreed to marry Gayan soon after she turned twenty-one. I'd always suspected she'd done it to escape my parents, but I assumed she escaped into a similar situation. He was from my parents' congregation, after all, and he held the same beliefs as my father.

I'd referred to my parents' house as home at the hospital. However, when I arrived, it felt anything but. The paramedics had left wrappers from different supplies they'd used to help stabilise my father before transporting him, and I cleared them up so my mother wouldn't have to see them. Whilst the curries were simmering, I even ran a vacuum around, knowing my mother did this each morning and would be upset it hadn't been done.

This house was so different from the townhouse Henry and I shared. Sure, it was clean and tidy, but it was cluttered with religious paraphernalia. My father's Bible sat next to his large armchair. I contemplated putting it with my things to take to the hospital. However, I decided it would simply reinforce their delusions.

I looked at my phone and thought of texting Henry. Ben had advised I reach out and open the lines of communication, but that was before all this had happened. I had no idea what was going to happen, other than my father was dying, and there was a possibility I would need to stay. There would be no point talking to Henry and showing my feelings if I wasn't returning to Cassowary Point.

Once again, everything was a mess, and there didn't appear to be any way out of it. My attempts to leave Perth and forge a life of my own had been dashed, and I was bound to stay here and care for my mother like the dutiful son she wanted me to be. There would be no time for love or intimacy, especially not with another man. My life was not my own. I sank to the floor as loud sobs erupted from me. This was not the weeping and wailing I'd heard about in the Bible, but a visceral reaction to how hopeless everything was. The whole experience with Henry had been for nothing.

Chapter 21

Henry

The rotation of interns saw a sudden change in my roster. Why they kept doing this, I didn't know, and it pissed me off to no end. I could have said no, but staying on until 10 p.m. then doing three evening shifts in a row had not been the plan.

I'd thought I'd finally be able to talk to Ken after work whilst I cooked dinner for him. His head was probably still thumping after his drinking session the night before. I had no idea what I wanted to say, but I needed to get past the whole ignoring each other and accept Ken was moving on.

The thought of him being with Ben still hurt. I'd had the experience of being the token gay guy for bi-curious men wanting to test if they did like cock or not, and I wanted to protect Ken from men like these. I didn't know Ben's entire situation, but I thought he had a girlfriend. Perhaps Ken knew all about this and understood what he was getting himself into.

It was probably what I'd end up back doing, trawling the apps and being picked up by random guys just looking to get their dicks wet in arse instead of pussy. I'd always been vers, but I found most bi-curious guys simply wanted me to bottom. That Ken had asked me to top was huge for me, and I thought he knew how special this was for me, at least. At least I wasn't drinking. I chuckled to myself, thinking about how brief my relationship with Jack Daniels had been back in Brisbane. Perhaps I should have been pleased about this and that I hadn't turned to the bottle after Ken moved on. He'd set boundaries, and I was the one to ignore his desire to be just friends.

The day dragged. I thought of texting Ken and telling him I'd order a pizza to be delivered, but he hadn't replied to my text from the morning wishing him well. Whoever said that absence made the heart grow fonder knew what they were on about. I was craving Ken's touch, his smell, and his taste. I cursed listening to Val and my brain, thinking I could just stay away from someone I'd grown to care so deeply about in such a brief space of time. It made me almost chuckle when I figured I was smothering myself with thoughts of Ken. I'd turned inwards and couldn't stop thinking about him if I tried.

Even if he was into Ben, maybe I still had a chance. I could ask Ken on a date and show him how I'd wine and dine him. For me, sex had been mind-blowing, but it obviously hadn't blown Ken's mind. I couldn't blame him for wanting to experience more. Perhaps in time, he'd realise that what we'd had together had been magical, and he'd return to me. I knew I'd wait.

When I'd split from other guys, there'd been little heartbreak. One moment, I'd seen them as being the one for me, the next, they'd shown me the door, and I was simply moving on. I didn't want to move on from Ken, though. I wanted to show him how special he was... he is, to me.

Tuesday morning, I'd slept in a bit and didn't hear Ken leave for work. When I finally made it downstairs, it didn't look like anything had been touched from the night before, and there were no extra dirty dishes in the dishwasher. The teapot and tea I'd left out for Ken to brew his morning cuppa also hadn't been touched.

My heart sank when I imagined him spending the night with someone else. Being the sadist I was, I took my time ironing my shirts, before grabbing Ken's scrubs from the dryer and ironing them, too.

I thought of calling Val and grabbing a quick bite before my shift but decided against it. She didn't need my grumpy face. Instead, I made my way to the hospital library and flicked through some journals. Nothing caught my eye, and I was still in the same Ken-related funk I'd been in for weeks.

Wednesday morning, there was still no sign Ken had been home. I knew I was tired, but I still burst into tears seeing the teapot where I'd left it Monday night. He'd found someone else.

My phone pinged with a text.

STINKY:

Hey, Hammy. Did you say you were free for dinner tonight?

Nah. Roster change. I'm free now if you want to grab brunch, but I'm not the best company.

STINKY:

How's Ken?

How should I know?

STINKY:

I thought you might have contacted him, that's all. Pick me up?

See you in 10.

"So, you haven't heard from him, then?" Val jumped into my jeep and fastened her seatbelt. I simply shook my head. "Giles seemed to think it was serious."

That would be right. My brother probably talked Ken into seeing someone else. I was fighting back tears so hard that I couldn't pull out of my parents' drive.

"Well, from what Mum and Dad were saying, the guy sounds like a prick, but good on Ken for turning the other cheek."

And now my parents were in on it, too. The tears fell, and I sobbed into my hands.

"Oh, Hammy. Let's come inside and have a cuppa, okay?" Val was hugging me across the centre console. "We don't even know if he's dead yet or not."

Wait, what? "Who?" I croaked through my tears.

"His dad." Val looked at me as if I had multiple heads. "Who did you think I was talking about?"

"I'm confused. Ken's dad?" Nothing was making sense. My nose scrunched and my brow furrowed as I looked at Val for answers.

"That's why Ken flew to Perth on Monday. Because his dad had a stroke. Didn't you notice he wasn't home?"

"But..." My voice was high and screechy. "Why didn't anyone tell me?" Oh my god. Poor Ken. I knew he didn't get along with his father, and I could only imagine what he was going through. "I have to get there to be with him. No. He doesn't want me. He wants some other guy. He went on a date. I've fucked it all up."

Val dragged me inside our parents' house and sat me at the kitchen counter whilst she made us a coffee.

"I figured because you weren't with Ken in Perth, you didn't care about him as much as he does about you." All colour drained from my face as Val spoke.

She told me about their shopping day on Sunday and how Ken wouldn't stop talking about me but admitted to them that he was upset that I'd ghosted him despite living together, and he figured I didn't like him anymore.

"But I was smothering him." I threw my hands in the air and almost screamed at my sister. "I told you I needed to step back."

"Did you step back a bit or step back altogether? He thinks you hate him and can't work out what he did wrong. I'd figured you'd just moved on like you usually do."

Poor Ken. "But Sunday. He went on a date." My head was spinning as I tried to make sense of everything.

"He went out with the guys from cricket to get advice from them about how to handle you, ya boofhead." Val laughed as she placed a coffee in front of me. "I thought you mustn't have been serious about him when you didn't join him on Monday when he flew to Perth."

"I didn't know... I'm fucking besotted with him." Tears dripped into the coffee Val had made. "I was scared of losing him. What must he think of me? He thinks I hate him. Oh fuck. I have to get there. I have to go now." My words tumbled out of my mouth far faster than I would normally speak. My hands shook as I pressed them to my temples.

Val settled me down and helped me book a flight. Jack was understanding when I told him I needed to take the rest of the week for personal leave, and I might not be back for a bit. I didn't call Ken to tell him I was coming. Instead, I rang three hospitals before I came across the one that his father was in. It's amazing what receptionists will tell you when you tell them you're Dr Hartman and have been trying to find Mr Dissanayake for a clinical trial he is part of.

I COULDN'T GET a direct flight and had a two-hour layover in Sydney. Normally, I'd people watch, but I was too worried about how I'd stuffed everything up. Val had said that Ken was as heartbroken as I was, and yet, he'd said nothing. I mean, neither had I, I suppose. I wrecked everything. My parents modelled amazing communication, and I'd not even stopped to ask Ken how he felt. Why wasn't I honest with him all along?

I'd found out that Ken's dad was on the palliative care ward, so I knew he was not expected to pull through. My thoughts weren't with the dying man, though. They were with Ken. He thought I hated him, which was so far from the truth, it wasn't funny.

In the past, I'd tried to pin down when I started falling for people in the fast way I did. I grew up in a family full of love. Whilst my parents were affectionate towards one another and to their children and now grandchildren, Mum and Dad had always been their own people. It was Manuel who first told me I was smothering him. He used the exact phrase when I told him how amazing I thought he was and how I could imagine spending my life with him. Sure, I was twenty-one, but I loved the feeling of being with someone as special as I'd believed Manuel was. Looking back, I could see that I saw him through rose-coloured glasses. He had his faults, just as I did.

I'd never had issues with hooking up for a night either. Sure, one or two guys had turned into more than one night, but it was always clear it was just sex. Nothing with Ken had felt like just sex.

Ken tried to pretend it was casual, and we were experimenting, but when I'd had hookups in the past, I'd never stayed the night, and here we were, Ken and I sleeping together and holding each other.

I wanted to think Val was right and Ken did like me and saw me the way I saw him, but I wasn't hopeful that things could go back to the way they were. I'd hurt this amazing man with my stupid actions. Trusting the opinion of the sister seven years my junior was probably a mistake, but she knew me so well, and if it wasn't for Val, Ken and I wouldn't have shared a bed in the first place.

The flight to Perth was full, and I was stuck in the centre seat. My headphones were on, and I was listening to the gravelly voice of Nick Cave. The passenger in the aisle seat was chatting to the person across the narrow gap between seats. I had no desire to know what they were on about. The lady in the window slept, and I just wanted the plane to speed up so I'd be there faster.

Landing just before ten at night, I headed straight to the hospital. Val had arranged accommodation nearby for me. For all her forgetfulness, it appeared she could be organised when she wanted to be.

It was a risk turning up at the hospital long after visiting hours, but it was one I was willing to take. I wished I looked professional and was wearing a suit instead of jeans and a hoodie. At least the hoodie kept me warm. It was definitely cooler in Perth than Cassowary Point, that was for sure.

Flashing my hospital ID from Cassowary Point, I asked the security guard at the front desk to direct me to the palliative care ward. I didn't know if Mr Dissanayake was still alive, let alone if Ken was still there. I wasn't sure what I'd do if he wasn't.

"Can I help you?" I'd pressed the intercom outside the locked ward and a tired voice had answered.

"Good evening. I'm Dr Hartman. I've come from Sydney,"—well, that wasn't a total lie—"and I'd like to see Mr Dissanayake or his family if possible. It's late, I know, but it's for a medical trial."

"Buzzing you in." Whoever it was sounded totally disinterested.

I pulled the heavy door and made my way to the nurses' station, thinking that hospital layouts all seemed rather similar.

"Dissanayake?" A nurse barely looked up from her phone to see my nod. "Room 16."

Walking down the corridor, my pulse started racing. I hadn't thought this through. Turning up at a hospital at nighttime to see someone I wasn't sure wanted to see me was not my smartest move. Perhaps I should just come back later. I had no idea what I'd say or even if Ken was there.

I felt my heart tighten when I came to the room and saw Ken sitting there, his father lying in the bed. I was about to knock on the open door, but Ken sat back in his chair and started talking.

"I fucked up, Appā. And yeah, I swear. There's so much about me you never bothered learning about. You never saw me as Kandiah, your son. I was always a disappointment, someone who didn't meet your expectations. Well, you know what? Your expectations don't matter anymore. If they ever did at all. You may hate that I'm a doctor, but my colleagues think I'm good enough. You may hate my sexuality, but guess what?" Ken had stood, his arms flying around about him as he spoke. "I'm gay. I enjoy having sex with men. It's not a fucking sin. It's who I am and just as part of me as anything else."

Ken kept his voice low, but there was venom in his words. "And I won't start on the way you've treated your wife and daughters. You know how unhappy Dipti is, but no, 'divorce is a sin' you say. Well, so is hitting your wife. Don't worry. I'm helping my sister like any decent human being should. But you? You never listened. You never listened to me, or my sisters, or my mother, or anyone apart from your church. Well, well done. It's gone and killed you. I hope you're happy."

Ken slumped back in his chair, his father still unconscious in the bed. His shoulders shook, and he leant forward to rest his arms on his legs. Silently, I walked in and placed my hand on his shoulder.

"Feel better?" I whispered.

Ken jerked in the chair, almost falling off. "You're here?"

"I didn't know until Val told me this morning. How is he?"

"Almost dead, but not quite." Ken huffed out a sound that others might have believed to be a laugh, but it was more a sign of acceptance of the situation.

Ken had dark rings under his eyes, and his hair, which was usually so well kept, had been pushed every which way from his fingers running through it. I wanted to just hold him, but I wasn't sure how he'd take it.

I wanted to provide comfort, but I couldn't be sure it would be accepted.

"Are you staying overnight?" I asked, moving to stand closer to him.

"Yeah." Ken stood, reached out, and threw his arms around me. "We don't want him alone when he goes. Well, Dipti and I don't. Abha and Mother are convinced the Lord will heal him."

It felt amazing holding Ken in my arms again, and I drew him closer. I held the back of his head to my shoulder as he started crying, running my fingers over the strands of hair at his neckline to comfort him.

"We just need to move him and change his pad." Two nurses knocked and entered the room. "Do you want to grab a cuppa?"

I led Ken out of the room, holding his hand. "What?" I saw him chuckle as he swiped at a tear.

"It's nothing."

"Sure?"

"It's dark," Ken warned.

"You've met me." I squeezed his hand as he opened the door to the visitor kitchenette.

"Dad always told me I'd be with a man over his dead body, and I feel like saying, not quite, but almost."

We both bent over, we were laughing so much. I'd heard the speech Ken had given his father, and there seemed to be plenty of things going on. Now wasn't the time for me to do anything but apologise.

"I'm sorry I ghosted you. I know now isn't the time, but it was wrong of me, and I should have just talked to you, and perhaps we can have that talk in the future, because I know you've got a lot happening at the moment."

"So, I did nothing wrong?" Ken sounded wounded. He had dropped my hand and used it to fiddle with some loose skin around his thumb, not looking at me.

"No, no, no. Not at all." I bit my knuckle to stop myself from declaring undying love. Now wasn't the time.

"What?" Ken placed his hand on my arm. Fuck. After everything I'd done, and all I'd put this gorgeous man through, he was still looking out for me. I needed to make things right and ensure this man never escaped my grasp again. I'd been such a fool. I didn't deserve anyone like the amazing Ken, but I was going to try.

"It's not the time. Just know it wasn't you, it was all me and my hangups. I'm here to support you through this with your dad."

Being a ward where families waited for loved ones to die, the small kitchen area was well equipped. It even had a teapot and a selection of lovely teas. Ken was in his element, brewing the pot exactly how he liked it. An older woman came in walking with a stick, her grey hair limp, a large cardigan hanging off her frail body. Her eyes were rimmed with black, just like Ken's, her face covered in lines that showed years of facial expressions.

"You're still here, too, Mavis?" Ken asked.

"He's a stubborn bugger. Is that Darjeeling?" she asked.

"Please, have my cup. I should get going." I looked at my watch, even though I was well aware of how late it was.

"Are you sure?" The older lady pushed Ken out of the way before adding a dash of milk into the teacups and pouring the tea in bursts, the same way I recalled my grandmother doing when I was younger. "Now, who is this fine gentleman, Kenneth?"

"Mavis, this is Henry, he's my..."

"Housemate and friend," I finished for him. Fuck. I should have said boyfriend. But what if Ken didn't want my apologies? Shit. He looked like he did. There was pain in his eyes at my declaration of him being a friend. I was blowing this.

"I might be old"—Mavis stirred the tea before placing the spoon in the sink—"but I'm not blind. My Rachel's been with the same woman for twenty-five years. My grandson was here today with his boyfriend. My Reg wanted to march in the Pride Parade, but he wasn't up to it. We watched it on the television, though."

I liked this woman. Ken carried her cup of tea as she toddled back to her dying husband's room.

"We've been married sixty-three years, and even on his deathbed, Reg takes my breath away. I hope you two have a life as full as ours has been." Mavis reached up and touched an arthritic finger down my cheek before she entered the room her husband was dying in, and we went to Ken's father's room.

The nurses were just finishing hanging more medication for Ken's dad when we reentered the room. There were no signs death was imminent. His breathing was still regular, and he looked peaceful. One nurse went to fold out the seat that turned into a bed, but Ken stopped him, telling him he'd be fine to do it himself.

"I should let you get some rest," I whispered as I took Ken's hand in mine and studied it, wondering what it would look like after sixty-three years with me. I was sure that, to me, it would be just as soft as it is now. "Please call me if anything changes or if you need anything. I'm not... I'm not here to cause trouble with your family. I'm here for you. Perhaps if your mum's sitting with your dad tomorrow, we could grab lunch or something?"

"I'd like that." I looked up to see Ken smiling. "Thank you for coming." Ken leant over and placed a tender kiss on my cheek. The brush of his lips made me feel a hope I hadn't really dared feel until now. Perhaps it wasn't the clusterfuck I'd thought it was.

As I walked out of the hospital, my hand still pressed where he'd kissed me. It was a horrible situation to be in the middle of, but perhaps he still liked me despite all I'd put him through.

Chapter 22

Ken

Henry was here. In Perth. He'd come to see me.

I could hardly believe it. I almost thought I'd dreamt his hand on my shoulder, and seeing I could count on one hand the hours of sleep I'd had this week, that wasn't as strange as one might have thought. Had Henry heard my rant at my father? I was angry, sure, but it didn't excuse my behaviour. Just another thing to put down to my exhaustion.

It wasn't just that the fold-out bed was uncomfortable, but I believed I needed to be there keeping a vigil over my dying father. There's been no change since I arrived, and I must have dozed off, as I woke to a commotion in the hallway. It was still dark outside. I looked at my phone. It was just after 4 a.m. No doubt the nurses would be around soon to move Dad.

I'd never realised before just what an amazing job they did. Sure, they'd saved my back frequently, but the way they truly cared—not only for their patients, but their families—made me treasure their work even more. I'd need to ensure to respect them even more when I was back at work.

Work. I sighed, thinking about how amazing they'd been. Mikel had texted me Monday evening to say they were thinking of me and to let them know if I needed anything. He also said there was no reason for me to rush home. I know he meant Cassowary Point, but over the last couple of days, I'd been stressing about where home was.

Initially, I thought I'd need to stay and help care for Mum, but when Dipti opened up to me in the coffee shop about how Gayan was abusing her and that my parents said they would disown her if she left him, I knew I'd made the right decision to leave Perth. Dipti was a shell of her former self, and I wanted to help her. Abha could stay and help our mother.

The days blurred together, but at some stage, I'd thought I could move with Dipti and her children, Luke and Sarah, somewhere safe. Right now, they were staying with my mother. Gayan did nothing for his children except work to bring home the money. I doubted he'd want anything to do with them. Before Henry arrived, I hadn't even thought about returning to Cassowary Point. Now, though, things had changed.

My mind was all over the place. I was far too tired to make any serious decisions. I sat on the edge of the bed and held my head in my hands as I slouched forward.

"How's it going, Ken?" Mavis placed her hand on my back. I hadn't heard her come in. "The nurses are turning Reg. I see your old man's hanging on, too."

"Yeah." I sighed, sitting upright and turning to face this old woman who had taken me under her wing the last few days. "Cuppa?"

"I was going to ask the same thing. I think it's time for an Earl Grey." Mavis had hooked her arm through mine as we wandered down the corridor to the kitchenette. "He seems nice."

"Who? My father?" I stopped and scrunched up my face in disgust.

"No, your fella." Mavis patted my arm.

"It's complicated." I sighed again as I grabbed the teapot and heated it with the boiling water that was on tap while Mavis grabbed the tea canister.

"Life's complicated, my son." Mavis had tears in her eyes as she looked up at me with a smile.

"My family won't accept I'm gay. They threatened conversion therapy when I was younger, so I hid it."

There was a small table in the corner of the kitchen, and Mavis placed our cups there and took a chair, pulling out the other for me.

"My parents disowned me when I married Reg. I was pregnant with Rachel, our eldest, you see. They would have had me adopt out the baby, but Reg and I were in love. Heck, we still are." Mavis chuckled.

"But you married him, anyway?" I took a sip of the tea.

"I was twenty-one, and he was twenty-two and had a job with the railways. My parents couldn't understand me being with a blue-collared gentleman, not that they ever referred to him as a gentleman. I had a choice to make: my parents, who had always been standoffish and aloof, or a man who loved and cherished me. It wasn't a hard decision to make in the end. Family is what you make it, and often the family you find brings more blessings than the one you were born into. Well, it did for me."

I thought about the family I'd found in Cassowary Point. It wasn't just the Hartmans but also the folks at the cricket club. There was no way for me to tell why Henry was here unless I spoke to him, and that was what I'd do.

"Ken." Yoshi, one of the nurses on duty, came and knelt beside me. "I've called the doctor, but your father's died."

I wondered how I'd react when it happened. Would I feel relief or sadness? I felt neither. If anything, I felt a sense of emptiness. "I should have been in there," I whispered.

"It's coming up seven years that I've worked on this ward, and you'd be amazed the number of times someone waits until they are alone to slip away." Yoshi was so gentle with his voice. "Would you like me to call your mother or sisters?"

"No." I shook my head. I needed to do that myself.

Mavis took my hand across the table and squeezed it. "His pain and suffering is over."

His may have been, but mine was still there.

MEDICINE HAD TAUGHT me that life was not black and white, and there were many, many shades of grey. Pastor Samuels had never received this memo. He'd been the pastor at my parents' congregation since I was a young boy. I'd seen him wave his Bible in the air as he preached fire and brimstone on Sundays, reminding everyone to accept Jesus as their personal saviour if they wanted eternal salvation.

"There will be scripture. And songs, so many songs." Pastor Samuels had his eyes closed as he looked towards the heavens while we sat around the kitchen table at my parents' home the day after Dad died. "And Kandiah." He looked at me as if he was judging me, which I knew he was. "You will give the eulogy."

"Actually—" I started before I was cut off by my eldest sister.

"No, I will give the eulogy. My dear Appā would not appreciate sinners speaking in the house of God." Abha shot a look at Dipti and me that showed how disgusted she was with the two of us.

Henry hadn't met my family, and I'd hardly spoken to him since he'd arrived. I'd told them that a friend from Cassowary Point had flown in, and Abha had immediately rolled her eyes. She'd always been frosty, but this was something else.

I looked at my sisters and mother as they and Pastor Samuels had their eyes closed while they prayed. Their prayers went on forever. Am'mā had been quiet since Appā's death. She hadn't come into the hospital when I called, telling me she'd see him in paradise. Dipti was trying to hold things together. She'd sent Luke and Sarah to school today, and Abha was pressuring her to return to Gayan tonight.

It had only been six months since I left Perth, and yet, I felt like I'd returned to a parallel universe. I knew my parents were fundamentalist in their beliefs, and I thought this had rubbed off on both of my sisters, but that my mother and eldest sister could condemn my other sister for wanting to leave an abusive marriage was unfathomable to me. I didn't care that Abha didn't want me to deliver the eulogy. I wasn't sure what I'd say, and I knew I'd have a hard time praising my father and saying what a wonderful man he'd been when he'd been anything but to me.

The prayers continued, with my mother mumbling away as she grasped Abha's and Pastor Samuels' hands. My phone started vibrating in my pocket, and I was glad it was on silent. If only the pastor would finish up and let me get on with my afternoon. I was dying to see Henry. We'd texted this morning to see how each other was, but it had been brief, and there was only so much you could say in a text.

Dipti had put Luke in my old bed to sleep while they'd been staying here, and I didn't want to change things around, so last night, I offered to take the couch. I was so tired, I would have slept anywhere. It hadn't been the most comfortable night, but it was more comfortable than the couch in our townhouse. *Our townhouse.* It was strange to think of it like that. Billie and I lived there for longer than Henry and I had, yet I could hardly remember what life was like in it before Henry.

"Through Jesus, our heavenly Jesus whom we love, and Jesus whom we adore and worship, and Jesus is Lord and"—the pastor didn't even stop to take a breath, his head shaking as he continued as he had for the last half hour—"we worship and adore our Jesus forever and ever. Amen."

It was finally over. Abha and Dipti both excused themselves to collect their children from school, and I was left with my mother and the pastor. I had hoped he might have lost his voice after praying so hard for so long, but he hadn't.

"Tea, Pastor Samuels?" my mother asked. I couldn't tell if it was out of politeness or a desire for this man to hang around longer and save her from having to spend time with me.

"No, my little lamb." Pastor Samuels grasped her hands in his. "The Lord has inspired me, and I need to write a sermon. Kandiah"—he kept hold of my mother's hands, but his tone became deeper—"remember, sins of the flesh are the most heinous and will land you in hell, meaning you will not be reunited with your Appā or your heavenly Father. Resist all temptation and look to the Lord."

It wasn't just anger that consumed me at these words, but also a sadness at the misguided beliefs this man held. To these people, love was seeing a woman being forced to stay with her husband who hit her because God said that marriage is forever. It wasn't two men caring for each other and going out of their way to make the lives of the other easier, of making each other smile and laugh. Of comforting them, and flying across a continent when they discovered the other one was having to watch his father die.

If their views showed love, I wanted no part in it.

"Thank you, Pastor Samuels." I stood as he did and shook his hand. "I'll reflect on your words."

I tried to remain neutral in my tone, but I suspected I had failed. Perhaps he saw it as me being over emotional with his caution about my life and his words having some effect. If only he realised the effect was not the one he wanted.

My mother went to make tea.

"I'm going for a walk," I said as I rubbed my forehead. My mother went to open her mouth. "The pastor's given me food for thought."

My mother clutched her hand to her chest and beamed with pride.

I could see my mother watching me through the front window as I closed the old chain wire gate and started down the footpath. When I was out of sight, I dragged my phone from my pocket. I had three messages from Henry.

HENRY:

Hey. How's things? The guy at the hotel suggested a Swan River cruise, so I'm sitting on a boat heading to Fremantle. Apparently, I can catch a train back. Let me know what I can do to help.

HENRY:

Hey again. Just had the best fish and chips I've ever eaten for lunch. The batter was so crispy, and the fish was so fresh and moist. You would have loved it.

HENRY:

Well, that was an experience. I turned the wrong way at the station and got lost. Ended up calling an Uber and am now back at my hotel. Hope things went okay with the pastor. I know you love to cook, but let me know if I can send food or anything. I'm trying so hard not to smother you, but it's a real challenge. Okay. I'll stop texting now. You're busy. I don't expect replies or anything. I really am thinking of you.

Hey. Can I join you for dinner?

HENRY:

> That sounds perfect.

I'll be about an hour, maybe a bit longer.

HENRY:

> I'll see you when I see you. xx

The kisses at the end of his message made my heart swell. Even if Henry and I were just friends and that was all we'd ever be, that would have to be enough. Henry showed more love in simple messages than my parents or Abha showed with their anger and shame. I so wanted to work things out with Henry, and I hoped tonight might be the start of that.

I COULD HAVE CAUGHT the bus to the city. That would have been the more economical thing to do. It's what I told my mother I was doing. She asked what time I'd be home, and I was tempted to say tomorrow morning, but I simply told her I'd let her know if I'd be late.

Deep down, I hoped Henry would ask me to stay. His messages had taken away the anger from the pastor's visit, but getting back to my parents' house and having my mother ask me 1,000 questions about why I was going out and who I'd be with...

"Is he a good Christian boy?" she'd asked me, as if that was the most important aspect to anyone I should come across.

"He's one of the best men I know, Am'mā."

He had been. Until he ghosted me.

So, here I was, sitting in an Uber that collected me at the end of my parents' street. The anger that had been bubbling under the surface started rising like steam on top of a lake. How dare Pastor Samuels and my mother put their beliefs before what was best for my family? I knew religion was important to them, but surely family was, too. The things Dipti had told me... She'd shown me photos of the bruises on her arms from where her husband grabbed her and held her far too tightly.

To me, it was incongruent to talk about a God who loved and cared for us all and then to not care about your family. To believe that your daughter must stay with her husband because of vows made before God. Well, Gayan had made vows, too, to love and protect his wife, and here he was, happy to belittle her and lay hands on her, and not in a religious sense. There was no point in me trying to explain to Pastor Samuels, my mother, or Abha that I didn't have a choice who I was attracted to. Breasts didn't do it for me. I was attracted to men, and insisting I be with a woman because it fit their idea of what was acceptable would not change my core being.

Then there was Henry. I was angry at him for his actions. Sure, we'd agreed to be housemates with benefits, but surely he felt the magic between us. I'd never been in love before, but I felt myself falling for this man, only to have him ignore me.

I was surprised when Cooper asked me out on a date. The irrational side of me wanted to say yes, to rub it in Henry's face that someone found me desirable. Instead, I told him there was someone else. There was. Henry Hartman. This infuriating man had gotten under my skin, and I'd dreamed of a life with him. Had I smothered him? I know he talked about how he was all in on relationships, but surely he could see that I was, too.

His actions had hurt me. He hadn't talked to me about things, simply changing our relationship by sleeping in his room. I knew our rosters hadn't helped, but I suspected he picked up extra shifts to avoid me. Yet here he was now when I needed him. I felt more supported by this man I'd known for months, rather than my family. He showed more care and concern and even love than my own flesh and blood.

Henry had left a key for me at reception. I stepped into the lift and held the key against the sensor before pressing the eleventh floor. With my arms crossed against my chest, my foot tapped as the lift rose, and I was glad I was alone. I could feel the pain from my teeth grinding together, but my nerves were on edge. When the lift stopped, I got out and made long strides towards Room 1105.

It took three attempts for me to get the door open, and I was just about to kick it when Henry appeared, having opened it for me.

Storming past him, I drew my jumper over my head and started undoing the buttons on my shirt, pulling the tails from where they were neatly tucked into my jeans.

"Hey." Henry's voice was soft as he stood on the other side of the room.

"Just fuck me, alright?" I could feel the spittle spraying as I talked. "I may not have been any good last time, but I need to learn. And tonight, I need to feel."

"Ken." I hadn't noticed Henry walk towards me. I was too busy kicking off my shoes and trying to undo my belt and jeans. "Ken." Henry placed his hands on my arms as I bent over to step out of my jeans. Fuck. I wasn't even hard. It wouldn't matter, because he was going to fuck me. "Ken." Henry was louder this time, forcing me to look at him. "I can see that you're angry."

Well, hello, Einstein.

"Angry? Why wouldn't I be? My father died. I had to spend an afternoon with Pastor Samuels, who told me I was going to hell if I slept with a man. My mother thinks my sister made vows to her husband, so she has to stay with him and turn a blind eye to his treatment of her. And then..." I paused. "And then you reappear as if nothing has happened. You fucking ghosted me. I was good enough to stick your dick in, and then you ignored me. So, yeah, I'm angry. But I'm here now, and I've got two holes and a heartbeat, so come on..."

I dragged my briefs down my legs and went to kneel on the bed.

"Hey." A fully clothed Henry pulled me down onto the bed and held me. I wanted to cry, to sob and let it out, but there were no tears. "I'm sorry."

"What was that?" I snapped.

"I said I'm sorry." Henry stroked my hair as he held me to him.

"Well, you should be. You broke my heart when you refused to sleep in my bed and stopped talking to me." I was still short with Henry, indignant at his actions of the previous weeks.

"You know I stuff up relationships because I smother or suffocate people. I was so scared of doing that to you." Henry sounded almost unsure as he spoke, and I felt like turning to face him, but I didn't. I was lying here naked, after all.

"Ghosting someone is a pretty surefire way of ending a relationship, too."

"Yeah, I kinda see that now." Henry at least sounded sheepish. "It wasn't helped when you told Cooper you were interested in someone. I can still feel that knife twisting."

"I was talking about you, you boofhead!" At least Henry had made me laugh.

"Really?" Henry held me tighter.

"I think my words to Cooper were, 'I'm flattered, but there's someone else, and I think he and I have a real future together if he just gets his head out of his arse'."

"Really?" This time, I turned to face a shocked-looking Henry.

"No! I told him there was someone I was really keen on, and this guy gave me goose bumps when he brushed past me and made my heart explode when he smiled."

"So"—Henry took a deep breath—"you were feeling the same things I was?"

"It would seem that way, yes." I tilted his chin with my finger and placed a tender kiss on his lips.

"I know you're underdressed at present"—Henry laughed as he ran his hand through my hair before pressing it against my cheek—"but can we go out to dinner together, like a date?"

I paused before I answered. Part of me wanted to remain indignant and refuse Henry's rationality. But I couldn't put myself, or him, through further pain. "I'd like that."

The tenderness between a fully dressed Henry and a naked me wasn't sexual. It felt deeper than that. We'd barely skimmed the surface of talking about what had happened before we'd both rushed to Perth, but it was a start.

For the first time in a long time, I had hoped that maybe things might just work out between the two of us.

Chapter 23

Henry

When Val told me about Ken's dad, my first thought was I needed to be in Perth to support him. Memories of him being in my bed and what we had done were forgotten. It was deeper than that.

In my time alone, when Ken had been with his family, I'd reflected on my past relationships. The common theme from my exes was I'd smothered them, suffocated them, and pushed them away in my enthusiasm. Yes, we'd had dates, but it all led to sex. I'd introduced them to my parents and siblings, but they'd never got to know them. It was as if I'd found a trophy or prize I wanted to display.

This seemed strange coming from a family that epitomised love. They lived love every day. Sure, Mum and Dad had had some doozy fights over the years, but they'd even fought with love, most fights being about how one of them saw the other not living up to their potential or encouraging them to do something the other didn't want because it would place more burdens on them.

Once, Mum wanted Dad to go away with some colleagues who were heading away for a long weekend of wine tasting down south. Dad insisted Giles had a footy game on and wanted to be there for it. As an adult, I can look back and see how stupid the argument was. Dad ended up going with the guys, and Giles survived not having his father there to cheer him on for one match.

Over and over, they'd shown they wanted the best for each other and their family. I remember school friends being shocked when I mentioned Dad had stayed home from work with me when I was sick once. To us, this wasn't unusual. Dad was involved in our lives. I still wasn't sure how he and Mum balanced their amazing careers with raising us, but I suspected a lot of it was because of the support of Dad's parents.

It was like that with Ken. I wanted the best for him. I wanted to make his life easier and be someone he could lean on. The intimacy we'd shared had enriched our friendship, our relationship. He'd stripped as soon as he walked into the room. Sure, I wanted to ogle his body and would have thought nothing about getting lost in it, but it wasn't the time. I didn't just lust after Ken. It was so much deeper than that.

I reached for Ken's hand as we left the hotel. There'd been no reservations made for dinner. I looked in both directions we could have gone, and we both shrugged our shoulders before I guided Ken to the left.

The streetlights illuminated our path, and our hands added warmth to each other that somewhat overcame the chilly evening.

Pausing outside an old church, we heard an organ playing. The door was open, and the lights inside projected the colours of the stained glass onto the outside garden. Ken looked at me, and I squeezed his hand.

"It's open." Ken bit the side of his lip. "Could we perhaps have a look?"

"Of course." I smiled back. I'd do anything for this man.

The inside of the church was much more modern than the exterior. An enormous poster greeted us at the door with a rainbow background. Its words were simple: 'All are welcome here, for God is Love'. Pews had made way for comfortable chairs, and banners with images of doves were hung from the ceiling. I'd always loved stained glass windows, and these were exceptional. There was a mix of old and new with a contemporary window of simple coloured glass mixed with more traditional windows depicting famous biblical stories.

The organ played music I wasn't familiar with, but Ken hummed along.

There was a woman sitting at the front of the church dabbing her eyes with a tissue. As we walked closer, Ken let out a small gasp.

"Mavis?" It was indeed the same woman from the hospital.

"Oh, Ken." She stood and took Ken's face in her hands. "How lovely to see you."

"Reg?" Ken had dropped my hand and gathered the woman in a hug.

"Yesterday morning. It's a relief, really. His pain is gone, and he's with our Lord."

"We heard the music," Ken spoke rapidly, as if he needed an excuse to be here.

"It's my Rachel's, Sarah."

"I have a niece called Sarah, too." Ken played with his fingers, his head bowed.

"A lovely biblical name. Ah, Rachel, did you meet Ken at the hospital?"

A woman who looked as though she was in her late fifties appeared wearing a patchwork skirt and a pink shirt with a clerical collar.

"I don't think so, but Mum's talked about you. Welcome to St Andrew's."

"You're... you're the minister?" Ken's voice was high as his eyes bulged.

"Yes." Rachel smiled. "It's the purple streaks in the hair, isn't it?"

We all laughed.

"I'm shocked, I suppose." Ken's brow furrowed. "I mean, all afternoon, I've had my mother's pastor telling me I'm going to hell for being gay, and I've listened to my mother and sister blame my other sister for wanting to break her marriage vows because her husband is abusive."

"And here I am, a minister?" Rachel laughed.

She moved the chairs into a circle so we could sit and talk to each other. I suspect it was mainly for her mother's benefit.

"I'm sorry that's your experience, Ken." Rachel leant towards him as she spoke, her hands in her lap. "That's not the Jesus I know. My Jesus talks of love and compassion and helping people regardless of their creed or colour. Just look at the story of the Good Samaritan. What do you believe?"

Ken took a deep breath and looked at the window in front of him. It showed Jesus holding a lantern. "I'm not sure."

"And that's okay. Here." Rachel held out a business card. "Take this and call me anytime."

"I'm sorry, your father's just died too, and I'm keeping you from your family." Ken went to stand.

"You can't stop Rachel from working." Mavis laughed.

"I had a meeting about securing more funding to help the homeless in this area that I wanted to attend. Sarah pops in after work most days to play the organ, and Mum..."

"This is where Reg and I were married all those years ago. I can still feel that kiss as he lifted my veil after the minister declared us husband and wife."

The music had stopped, and another woman walked down the aisle wearing pink overalls and combat boots.

"This is Sarah, Rachel's partner. She's actually a speech therapist at the hospital, but she took today off and brought me in here." Mavis held out her hand, which Sarah took before coming and standing behind her mother, bending over so her arms draped over her shoulders.

I could see Ken's confusion over this interpretation of the religion he'd grown up with. We'd not observed any religious practices, and I had no faith, but I sensed this was important to Ken.

Ken's stomach rumbled, reminding us that our mission had been to find somewhere to eat. We made our farewells, Rachel reminding us that the church was open during daylight hours usually, and we were always welcome.

As we walked down the steps from the church, Ken reached for my hand.

"Thank you for that." He glanced at me, making my heart swell.

"For holding your hand?" One side of my mouth turned upwards.

"Ha-ha. My mother wanted to know if you were a Christian man. I didn't think that telling her I'd heard you pray when I meant I'd heard you calling God's name as you were balls deep inside me made you one, so I left it. But please know I was tempted."

This man shocked me. We hadn't talked about what happened between us, and yet, here we were, walking down the street, looking like a couple. Perhaps it was time to voice what had happened and see if we did indeed have a future together like I hoped we did.

WE'D STOPPED for dinner at a small Italian restaurant that looked busy. The food had been great, but the conversation was a little stilted. I didn't want to open up to Ken in public, but I also wasn't sure if asking him back to my room would be appreciated.

On the walk back to the hotel, we didn't hold hands. I was too busy focussing on a dried cuticle on my thumb, wondering how to broach the conversation we needed to have.

"Do you have a curfew?" I looked at Ken, once again taken in by his beauty.

"I'm a grown man, but I can see why you'd think that." One side of his lips rose.

"It's just…" I paused and took a deep breath. "I want to talk with you and explain why I did what I did, not that I can excuse it, and see if, maybe… I sort of, well, I do, like, I want…" I was going in circles here. "I want things back the way they were, but different, too."

"I think I need to come up then." It was Ken who reached for my hand this time, taking it in his, leading us through the hotel's massive glass doors towards the lifts.

This was it. I'd had days, weeks even, to play what I wanted to say, but I still had no idea what words to use. I was scared that if I told Ken what I really thought, then he'd run a mile. Yet he hadn't this evening. He'd been receptive to our hands joining, and he'd even wanted sex when he first arrived.

Standing outside the room, I placed the card in the lock and turned the handle. This was going to happen. I paused, holding the door open. Ken entered, and I was glad when he sat in the lonely armchair in the corner. As for me, I was second-guessing myself. I wanted to sit on the bed and hold hands as we talked, but I didn't know if we were there yet. Instead, I rocked on my feet and ran my fingers through my hair.

"Are you going to sit?" Ken asked quietly as he swallowed. Perhaps he was as nervous as I was.

"I should, yes."

I perched on the edge of the bed—far enough away from Ken that I couldn't touch him but in his line of sight. Inhale, two, three, exhale, two, three. I practiced the breathing I'd seen Jack use on clients who were close to panic on the ward.

"Where to start?" I let out another breath and looked at the ceiling. My foot was tapping on the ground, and I gripped my hands, hoping Ken couldn't see that they were shaking. "So, I told you I fall easily and hard, and I end up smothering my partners."

I looked over at Ken, who nodded. I took another breath. If I didn't tell Ken how I felt, I'd never know his reaction. He was either going to send me away or tell me he felt similar feelings. I mean, he'd held my hand this evening. That had to mean something, surely.

"You told me you wanted to learn about sex, and I went and fell hard for you." Sweat clung to my brow as panic rose in my throat. I knew my voice was higher than usual, as the words tumbled quickly from my mouth. "Except it wasn't like before."

"So, the sex was bad." Ken hung his head and played with his fingers.

"No." The exclamation left my mouth in a rush, and my breathing quickened as I jumped down the bed and took his hands in mine. "It was amazing. And that's part of what confused me. Like, it was constantly amazing. Here we were, sharing a bed, and we seemed to be on the same page sexually."

My thoughts went back to those days, and for the first time in weeks, I felt blood rush to my cock.

"But it was more than the sex." I let out another deep breath as Ken looked up at me, his brows furrowed and his head tilted to the side. "It was seeing you read to Millie and the way you interacted with my family. It was cooking with you and sitting and sharing a meal together before snuggling on the couch and watching whatever trash we could find. It was watching you bowl at cricket games and feeling such pride when you took a wicket. It was so much more than just sex." I took a deep breath, letting my words settle.

"I was a total idiot, though. Instead of talking to you, I retreated. I could blame Val, but her advice to back off was sound, except I probably could have spoken with you about my reasoning. Then, when you refused that date with Cooper and told him you were keen on someone else, I never imagined it could have been me. I thought you wanted to experience intimacy with lots of different people, and I couldn't blame you for that."

Ken's shoulders started shaking, and I saw a smile creep across his face as he laughed. "And here was me thinking you put Cooper up to it and the sex had been so bad, you couldn't wait to be rid of me."

"Yeah. Our rosters didn't help, but it was shit communication on my part, and I'll own up to that." I shook my head. "And you went out with the guys from cricket, and I thought you were out with Ben. Fuck, I've been stupid."

When I said these things aloud, I realised just how misguided I'd been. I'd had great examples of effective communication from my parents, and I ignored them. Perhaps I'd been doing this in all my past relationships.

"I've got a lot going on at the moment." Ken looked deep into my eyes, as if he was glancing at my soul. "I wasn't sure where I was going to go after we bury my father, but I can tell you Cassowary Point is firmly a favourite."

I let out a sigh, glad I hadn't chased Ken away altogether.

"I need to look out for Dipti, though, and Luke and Sarah, of course." Ken took a large swallow and looked at me with worried eyes, as if I wasn't going to like what he had to say.

"I get it. I really do. Your family needs to come first. How old are Luke and Sarah?" I knew so little about Ken's family, whereas he knew so much about mine.

"Luke's eight, and Sarah's six. I don't know if Gayan's going to let them leave the state." Ken's expression slid into a frown. "I might need to stay here to make sure they are all okay."

"Have you spoken to a lawyer?" Ken shook his head. "Val probably has some contacts. Do you want me to ask her?"

"Would you?" Ken's deep frown eased a bit as he exhaled this question.

"Of course." I squeezed Ken's hands. "I'm assuming Dipti doesn't work outside the home?"

"She was a bookkeeper for our father when she left school, but she stopped that when she married Gayan. She's the one in the family who should have studied accounting."

In my mind, I was ready to ask my parents if Dipti, Luke, and Sarah could stay with them whilst we set them up in Cassowary Point. Ken obviously cared deeply for them.

"What about your other sister?"

"Abha?" Ken's eyebrows rose as he shook his head. "She's been brainwashed by our parents."

We sat in silence for a few minutes. My breathing had evened out. I stroked Ken's fingers as I kept hold of his hands. This was a good sign that he was on the same page as me or was at least adjacent to it.

"I don't want to scare you"—Ken's head shot up as I spoke—"but if you end up over here because of Dipti, then I'd be happy to move, too. I'm sure we could both get jobs over here."

"You'd do that?" Ken's eyes glistened at my words.

"If you want me, I mean, I know I come on strong, but I'd like to see where the two of us could go, and I feel we could go almost anywhere together."

"I've missed you so much." Ken wiped away the tears that were spilling down his cheeks despite the smile on his face.

"Yeah?" I asked to a nod from Ken. "That feeling is totally mutual."

We both stood and wrapped each other in a hug. Ken shook as he cried, and I simply stroked the back of his head as he laid it on my shoulder.

"You've had a rough few days." I could have comforted Ken forever if that was what it took.

"I'm just relieved you don't hate me." Ken laughed, pulling away from me, snot dribbling from his nose. "Although you might do now; I've got snot on you."

"Never." I smiled. Ken wiped his nose with his sleeve, and I gripped his face with my hands. Our lips met in a gentle and somewhat chaste kiss. Sure, we had passion in our lives, but there was also a tenderness, which I yearned for. Something I hadn't experienced with anyone else.

"You know I'd ask you to stay, and you can if you want, but I don't want to cause even more friction with your family."

"Thank you." Ken smiled as he looked at me with sparkling eyes.

It was so hard to put him in an Uber to head back to his parents' home, but it was necessary. I stood on the kerb and waited until the lights of the car vanished around the corner. It had been an emotional evening, but at the same time, it had been necessary.

KEN and I spent time together over the weekend. Despite not having a kitchen in my hotel room, we went to a farmers' market on Saturday and grabbed some bread, cheese, and salami to make sandwiches for lunch. On Sunday, I met Dipti. She'd got away for a bit and spoke to a lawyer friend of Val's for over an hour.

Both evenings, Ken apologised for not taking me to meet his mother. I knew it was a challenging time, what with the funeral tomorrow. Ken had even tried to insist I didn't need to be there. I told him I'd go, but I'd sit at the back.

The Christ Resurrected Vineyard Fellowship met in an old cinema. Even though the lighting had been totally replaced, emulating that of a concert venue, the seats and curtains remained. Ken had warned me the service could go on for a long time. He sat at the front comforting Dipti and her children. I assumed Gayan sat next to Luke. Abha, her sons, and her husband sat with the lady I guessed was Ken's mother.

I hadn't been to many funerals in my life. One of Giles' uni friends had died, and that had been a sombre occasion, but this was different. There was a rock band at the front, even though they played more laid-back music than what I assumed they usually played. The pastor wore an ill-fitting grey suit and waved his Bible around as if it was a shield.

After about an hour of songs, prayers, and scripture, Abha took to the microphone to give her eulogy. She spoke of a man who sounded nothing like the man Ken had described to me. The congregation was told how loving and caring her father was and how amazing he was to her sons. She spoke of her parents' marriage being the example of Christian marriage all people should aspire to. I was the only person who gasped when she actually said that her father's only disappointment was his son and his other daughter who could not live up to his Christian values, and how sad he was going to be when he would not be reunited with them in heaven, as they would be burning in the pits of hell.

The pastor thanked Abha for her words and invited other members present to come forward and share their memories of the deceased. People stood and spoke of the way Mr Dissanayake took care of the financial records for the congregation and there were never any errors. I hardly saw this as something worth noting, but it was important to this man. Another man said he had aspired to live as Christian a life as Mr Dissanayake and used him as an example in his marriage. I almost pitied his wife and children.

Others stood and spoke about how the deceased had been received into God's heavenly kingdom, and they were excited to see him when they made the pilgrimage. The pastor looked around at those present, checking to see if anyone else wanted to come forward and share some words.

It could have been anger at Abha's eulogy, but I stood and made my way down the steps from the back of the auditorium towards the microphone.

"Good afternoon." I jumped back from the microphone as a squeak was heard around the venue. "Sorry about that. I'm not used to speaking to crowds like this. My name's Henry Hartman..."

Chapter 24

Ken

"**M**y name's Henry Hartman, and I didn't know Mr Dissanayake at all, but I can imagine he had some wonderful traits." My eyes were so wide I wouldn't have been surprised if the eyeballs popped out and started rolling along the floor. Dipti reached over and grabbed my hand, giving it a squeeze, and I forced myself to close my jaw, which had dropped towards the ground when Henry stood up to speak.

"You see, I'm a friend of Kandiah, or Ken, as I know him. He's actually my housemate, and we work together." Henry took a breath. He'd be heckled out of this place if he mentioned we were lovers. "But, yeah, mostly, he's an amazing friend. Now, as I said, I didn't know his dad. Ken's told me bits about him, but even if he hadn't, I would think he must have had some great bits to him because he raised a man like Ken. Actually, Abha, Dipti, and Ken, you're all reflections of your parents, and Abha..." Henry nodded to my sister who sat there with a clenched jaw and flaring nostrils. "I know this isn't the place to talk about how kind and considerate Ken is and what an amazing contribution he makes to the patients he comes into contact with, as well as others in the community. I mean, someone recently reminded me that God is love, and Ken embodies the notion of loving your neighbour, and I think he must have gotten that from his father."

Henry was stirring the pot. He looked around at the people gathered and stepped away from the microphone, sending me a glance and a smile that conveyed he was in my corner.

"Thank you." Pastor Samuels stood at the microphone again and said something else about the Holy Spirit guiding so many people to say such nice things about my father. I don't think it was any spirit that guided Henry.

There were more hallelujahs, songs, and yet more prayers before we were dismissed and filed past my father's coffin. Apparently, it was too hard to get it up and down the steps, and the undertakers had used an old goods lift to transport it in. There was to be a private cremation anyway, so it wasn't like we needed to follow the coffin anywhere.

The ladies of the congregation had put on a feast in the foyer area. I didn't want food. I wanted to be out of there. The whole place felt foreign. As a child, I'd feared putting a foot wrong in church because of what my parents would say. Now I felt like an outsider. I didn't feel bad that I didn't belong. In fact, it was a relief. It was like we'd sung in the service: I once was blind, but now I could see, even if what I saw was not what the intention of the song had been.

I wasn't sure if I still had faith in God. I definitely didn't believe in the God my parents worshipped.

People I didn't know approached me with comments about being sorry for my loss. It didn't feel like a loss. Perhaps it should have, but I was sick of being put down for who I was. Yes, I was gay. Yes, I was a doctor. Yes, I lived on the other side of the country. Henry believed I was a good person, and it was time for me to believe this, too.

"Hey, I've been trying to get to you for ages." Henry placed a hand above my elbow, squeezing gently. His voice was soft and deep toned. "You alright?"

"Yeah, I am." My voice was relaxed. "Let's get out of here."

Gayan had left as soon as the service was over, no doubt heading back to his office. Dipti had left with the children, telling them she'd get them an ice cream. There was no reason for me to stay.

As we made our way through the crowd, Henry asked if I needed to say goodbye to my mother or sister. I simply shook my head as I took his hand in mine.

"THANK YOU FOR SPEAKING UP." I still held Henry's hand in the back of the Uber.

"I had to say something." Henry's eyes narrowed, and his eyebrows pulled together. "I'm sorry your mother and sister aren't what you need."

"It is what it is." I sighed.

"Well, for what it's worth," Henry continued, "I'm not actually sure that we are a product of our parents and their environment, and, to be honest, I'm not sure if your father did have any redeeming qualities. He seemed to be full of hatred from what you've told me."

I thought about what Henry said, both now and in the service. My father didn't beat my mother like Gayan did to Dipti. He worked hard to bring home money for the household. In his own way, he loved his family, but his love was conditional. We needed to follow his rules to be worthy of it. I was no longer willing to follow these rules. Escaping to Cassowary Point had been the start. Meeting Henry had been another catalyst. And now Dad dying.

"Val's been amazing with Dipti." I closed my eyes and laid my head back against the seat. At least something seemed to be going right. "Gayan has told her he wants nothing to do with her or the children if she walks away. I mean, he wouldn't know how to care for them, anyway."

"So, they could come to Cassowary Point?" Henry spoke quickly, as if I'd just promised him a puppy for Christmas.

"Val's already arranged with your parents for them to stay with them for a bit, and apparently, Christian's mum has a possible job for Dipti, too." I turned my head to Henry, my body feeling lighter than it had in weeks. He wasn't finished, though. "Millie's already telling everyone about her new friend, Sarah. Bridget's been investigating all the local schools in the only way she can—with precision and an eye for excellence—so she can help Dipti find somewhere for the kids."

"Your family's amazing." That Henry had done all this for Dipti, knowing it would help me, was amazing.

The car pulled up at the hotel Henry was still staying at. He was flying home tomorrow night, as he needed to get back to work. I clambered out behind him and couldn't help but notice his pert backside in his suit pants. As much as I appreciated it, I was sick of having him do nice things that helped me. Now was the time for me to do things to him that made us feel better than nice.

"I'm not staying at my mother's tonight." I brought Henry's hand to my lips. His Adam's apple bobbed as he swallowed.

"It's a little cold to be staying on the streets, isn't it?" Half of Henry's mouth rose, a twinkle in his eye.

"I don't care where you sleep, but I'm sleeping in your bed."

There'd always been a spark between the two of us, right from the gala ball. When he first moved in with me, it may have been sexual, but my feelings for Henry were much more than lust. Before meeting him, I had little idea of what love was. It hadn't been modelled to me growing up and had been stifled by the actions of my parents trying to force me to be someone I wasn't.

"Did you want a drink or something?" Henry asked, his usual confident demeanour absent in the crack of his voice.

"I think I want something, yes." We were still standing outside the hotel. Leaning over, I stroked Henry's cheek. "I want you, Henry Hartman."

"I'm—" Henry blew out a breath. "I'm likely to suffocate you and become overbearing."

"No, you're not." I laughed, causing Henry to look up from the shoes that he had been inspecting. "In the past, you've found guys who appreciate all you can do with your tongue, your hands, and your amazing cock," I whispered into his ear, not wanting the people rushing past us to hear. "But I appreciate that, and also, I appreciate you and the amazing man you are. You talk about how good I am, but I'm not even half the man you are."

"Perhaps we're both good people?" Henry placed a hand against my chest and lightly gripped my jacket lapel.

We both reached forward together and pressed our lips together. I'd totally forgotten where I was until I heard a horn beep. Jumping away from Henry, I pressed my fingers to my lips.

"You're a beautiful couple." An older man in a suit walked past us, a large smile on his face.

"Come on." I reached for Henry's hand and led him inside.

"You're not running?" Henry asked as we waited for the lift.

"Not away from you, no."

I thought back to the gala and how I'd run from that amazing kiss. A lot of my reasoning at the time had been about fear of how others, especially my family, might see me. I'd never be good enough for my mother or Abha. I was, however, good enough for Henry.

Inside the lift, I pushed Henry against the back wall before grabbing both his lapels in my fists and crashing my mouth into his. The taste and feel of his lips transported me to another plane. The way his beard brushed against my face as his tongue tangoed with mine had me hard in a microsecond. I'd felt something for this man the first time I saw him, and those feelings had only deepened. Sure, I may have questioned them when we weren't really talking, but I recognised Henry was something special.

The doors opened again, and I pulled away, only to see we were still on the ground floor. A woman pushing a pram entered and swiped her card before pressing the floor she wanted. Henry did the same, both of us giggling. The young mother smiled throughout our ascent.

"Have a great day, you two," she said as we left on our floor.

It took Henry two attempts to open the door to his room. It probably wasn't helped that I leant around and grabbed his cock through his pants, rubbing up and down as I remembered how it felt in my mouth. The usually extremely tidy Henry surprised me by kicking off his shoes and not even watching as they flew across the room before he undid my tie and threw it on the ground.

"Slow down." I traced down the side of his face from the edge of his eyebrows to the dimple on his chin.

"We've only got tonight, Ken." Henry was now busy undoing the buttons on my shirt.

"Henry." He paused, hearing his name on my lips. "As far as I see it, tonight will be the first of many."

I was too scared to say I thought we had forever, but that was how it was in my head. I couldn't imagine not having Henry in my life.

"You're serious?" It was probably more a statement that came out in Henry's husky voice.

"I was planning on showing you how serious I am." I tried to sound coy, but I failed, my desire for Henry coming out all too quickly.

Henry had stopped undressing me, so I leant over and undid his tie before removing it and winding it around my hand, placing it on the bench near the door. I removed his jacket and hung it in the wardrobe we were standing next to and started undoing the buttons on his shirt. All the while, I tried to maintain eye contact, hoping to convey exactly how serious I was about this man.

I was head over heels in love with him, but I wanted to show him rather than blurt it out. Henry undid his cuff links before shaking off his shirt and tossing it to the ground. Holding up a finger as if to tell me to stay there, he rushed into the bathroom. In the mirror, I could see him opening and closing many of the zippered compartments in his toiletry bag.

"Come on," he almost grunted as he opened what must have been the last pocket. "Bingo!" He held up a strip of condoms before turning them over to check the date. I saw a small bottle of lube in his other hand.

My cheeks reddened at the memory of Henry inside me, and my cock leaked at the thought he was going to do it again. It had been far too long.

"I was thinking..." Henry swallowed as he walked me to the bed, him dressed only in his trousers, me with my shirt half undone and my shoes still on my feet. "I want you to fuck me."

My amazement at Henry's request was hidden by a slow breath. I knew how much this meant to him. He'd told me of the men who'd used him for sex before discarding him. I undid the remaining buttons on my shirt and the cuffs. I paused and looked at Henry as he stood in front of me. The sound of me undoing my belt buckle broke the silence in the room and saw Henry whip off his belt before undoing his trousers and dropping them with his briefs.

The urgency wasn't a fear of this being our only time. It was a desire to show Henry exactly what he meant to me.

Pushing Henry to sit on the bed, I knelt between his legs and brought his face to mine. My lips met his before they travelled across his jaw to his earlobe. I gave a gentle suck and nip before trailing my lips down his neck. The groans that I felt vibrate through his chest as I trailed to his nipples showed me I was doing something right.

"Fuck," Henry breathed as I took a nipple in my mouth, twirling my tongue around the areola before sucking and pressing the bud of the nipple between my teeth.

After worshipping both sides of his chest, I kissed down his abdomen, finding the trail of hair that guided me to his erection. Sucking one of his balls into my mouth, Henry spread his legs further as my head dipped lower. Releasing it, his eyes were hooded as I looked up at him, and I swiped my tongue across his engorged cock. If his cock felt as hard as mine, then I knew he was bordering on pain.

I'd tried taking Henry deep in my mouth before with little success, but today felt different. Sucking gently, I took it little by little past my lips, egged on by his moans and groans. I might have flinched a little when he hit the back of my throat, but I continued, proud I could take more than ever before. Henry's fingers combed through my hair. I could feel him getting closer to release, and even if he tried to push me away at one stage, there was no way I was stopping. Tilting my head, I looked up to see Henry playing with his nipples, his bottom lip between his teeth. Seeing him like this saw more blood rush to my cock. Even when Henry had fucked me, I don't think I'd been as turned on. I hoped sex would only ever get better.

Edging back along his shaft, I increased my suction as I twirled my tongue over the head of his cock. Henry gasped as jets of semen hit my mouth. A small trail dribbled from my mouth as I tried to swallow as much as I could.

Henry was panting as I sat back on my haunches. He reached

towards me, and, wrapping his arms under mine, he drew me up until we were both lying on the bed.

"That was amazing." He licked the cum I hadn't reached with my own tongue before drawing me in for another kiss.

Henry's cock was still hard as I reached over and grabbed the lube. I remembered what he'd done to me, and, well, I knew the basics of a prostate examination from medical school, but this was so much more.

I lubed up my fingers and Henry's hole before pushing a single digit in. His cock jumped as I passed the ring of muscle, and I grinned as I saw him once again bite his lip. Moving in and out with my finger, I gave him time to acclimatise to it before he nodded at me, giving me permission to add a second one.

"That's so..." Henry let out a slow breath along with a quiet moan. "Can we just skip to your cock? I need to feel you inside me."

"So much for me being the grasshopper. You're the one needing patience." Henry chuckled as I reached for the condom.

I was lying behind him. Henry raised his leg as I smothered my latex-covered cock with even more lube. It was on the tip of my tongue to tell him how much I loved him, but I tried to let my body do the talking. My cock knew where it wanted to be. I actually didn't think it would have minded being inside Henry's mouth, or in his hand, or even sandwiched between our bodies. It looked forward to once again having Henry's foreskin stretched over it as he stroked both of us as if we were one cock.

But for now, it was pushing inside this special man. When I'd fucked Kayla, I'd come, but it had felt nothing like being inside Henry. Sure, it was a different hole, but there was more to it. Henry felt hot and tight. My cock felt like it had found its way home. I bit down on Henry's shoulder as I felt my balls against his. I wanted to withdraw and actually fuck him, but I was already so close to coming, I knew I had to pause.

"You feel amazing." My voice was breathless.

I withdrew a little before pushing back, slowly developing a rhythm that saw both of us fill the room with sounds that made no sense except to convey the euphoria we were experiencing. My hand, still slick with lube, reached around and grabbed Henry's still engorged cock. It jumped at my touch. My hand matched the rhythm of my thrusts, and I knew I was about to detonate.

"I'm... I'm..." I couldn't talk and simply exploded inside the condom, at the same time feeling the cum from Henry's release on my hand.

We lay there for several minutes, catching our breath as I held Henry close to me.

"You know," Henry mumbled, "even before this, I knew I felt something for you, but I can definitely swear I've caught more feelings for you now."

"Me too, babe, me too."

Chapter 25

Henry

Even if Ken told me I couldn't possibly smother him, I was still slightly wary of being too, well, too much, I suppose. Even if I had fallen fast before, this felt totally different. It was so much more than the amazing sex. It was wanting to appreciate him and just be together.

That last night in Perth, we'd hardly slept. Ken joked it was lucky we'd be apart for a few days, as our cocks were rubbed red raw. It had been so hard getting on that plane alone, but Ken promised me he wouldn't be too far behind. I'd been the last to board, and I knew they were getting close to calling my name over the intercom.

"I hate leaving you in tears," Ken had whispered as we both wiped away the streams that flowed from our eyes.

"I hate leaving you, full-stop." I tried to laugh, but it simply saw snot trickle from my nose.

"Just remember, we'll both be listening to the same playlist for the next few hours, I promise."

I'd introduced Ken to my taste in music. He hadn't heard many of the songs before, even though they were oldies, and he loved the meaning behind some of them. I'd laughed when he'd even added a few songs to the list himself, songs he'd found when he'd searched for Australian love songs. Some, I questioned if he'd listened to the lyrics, but he made me laugh as he belted out "Alice? Alice? Who the fuck is Alice?"

I knew he wouldn't be listening the entire time I was on the plane. He went to Reg's funeral. Even though he hadn't known him, Mavis had been a good friend to him in the hospital. I didn't care if Ken had a faith in a higher being or not, but I didn't want him to dismiss any form of faith because of his parents' attitudes. I hoped that being amongst Mavis and Rachel's congregation, he might have some idea of how others practiced their faith in a more inclusive manner.

Even though Gayan pretended he didn't want to see his children again, Dipti let them have a last dinner together as a family, no matter how dysfunctional that family was. Gayan thought nothing of back-handing his wife across the face in front of the children after their meal. Ken said it was the first time he touched her face, but it would also be the last. Neighbours had called the police, who helped Dipti, Luke, and Sarah escape to a women's shelter for the night. They also helped Dipti arrange a protection order so Gayan couldn't come close to her.

I'd told Ken that even though I didn't have thousands of dollars saved, I'd give all I had to get Dipti and the kids over here to Cassowary Point. It was something we'd argued about. Well, argue was a loose term, but Ken had refused and insisted I make it up to him by sucking his cock as soon as he landed back here. I wasn't sure who was the loser in this situation. In the end, the women's shelter helped arrange flights at a huge discount. Ken managed to get on the same plane, and I was now at Cassowary Point airport waiting for them all.

It was Saturday afternoon, and I was relieved they'd changed my roster so I wasn't on call. Ken had messaged me from Perth airport telling me they were there waiting to board, and he'd see me in the pickup area. His concern had been about the cost of parking. I was in Giles' SUV, Bridget arguing that Sarah would need a booster seat. There was no way they'd fit in my three-door jeep. I wasn't even sure if Ken understood that I would have parked illegally and paid a thousand dollar fine if it meant I saw him sooner than the pickup bay.

He was so much more than a pickup.

He was my everything.

I'd contemplated flowers or a teddy bear for Luke and Sarah, but I stood at the gate empty-handed. I hadn't tried to sit, instead, I paced, glad to see the sign change to say the flight had landed. There had been talk for years of non-travellers not being allowed through security points at Australian airports because of security threats, but I was glad it was still permitted.

The first few people from the flight started appearing. A family with a screaming baby rushed past, the father trying to soothe it by bouncing and putting a pacifier in its mouth. Nothing was helping. More people were coming. I looked through the doors and saw no sign of Ken. Other families sauntered past, and now there were just dribs and drabs of people stretching their legs after a long flight.

"Sarah!" I heard Dipti's terse shout as Sarah ran around the corner, spreading her arms out wide as if they were wings and she was an airplane. "Wait for us, please."

Sarah wasn't going to wait. She'd seen me and was barrelling through, making plane noises. An airline employee looked at her as she ran towards me. I'd spent little time with her, Luke, and Dipti, but she seemed pleased to see me. This had to be a good sign.

"And we went whoosh." Sarah made a swoop with her arm as if a plane was taking off. "And then we were inside the bird, and now we're here. Oh, and I had fizzy drink on the plane."

"An abundance of fizzy drink thanks to Uncle Ken." Dipti greeted me with a kiss on my cheek as I stood, while Luke hid behind her back.

"Hey." Ken's low voice went straight to my cock. I was sure he realised that biting his lip, like he did, was a major turn-on. "Come here."

It felt amazing to be in his arms again. We both had one arm over each other's shoulder, the other under as we plastered ourselves together. We rubbed the sides of our faces together as if we wanted to pass our scent onto each other.

"I missed you so much," I whispered in his ear.

"Not as much as I missed you. C'mon, let's go."

MY FAMILY HAD BANDED around Dipti, Luke, and Sarah. Millie and Sarah were soon joined at the hip and reminded me of Val and Emily at the same age. Ken had Mia on his knee as she handed him book after book to read, glad for once Sarah had distracted her sister, leaving space for her to listen to Ken's mellifluous tones describing a much-loved koala. Boyd and Emily had taken Luke into the lounge and hooked up the old gaming console, and the two of them were racing around a track dodging mushrooms or something. My brother and his girlfriend were both big kids at heart, and I couldn't wait until they started popping out spawn of their own.

Val was back in Brisbane but had video-called through. She and Dipti were having a conversation, and I saw Dipti wiping tears from her eyes. It was going to be a challenge for them to settle in a new town and make new friends, but I was glad my family was around to help.

"Hi, everyone." Bridget blew in the front door, still in her pink scrubs. It was still a shock seeing her with short hair, but she was ever the pragmatist, telling me it would grow again. "Well, that was a fun afternoon. The dad did a Giles."

Giles had infamously fainted at Millie's birth.

"It was all the love rushing to my heart, sweet Bee." Giles greeted his wife with a kiss that showed exactly how loved up the couple were, even after six years together.

The doorbell rang a few minutes later, Lena not just entering as the family would, despite Hillary telling her she was more than welcome to just come in.

"Henry said you'd done some bookkeeping, and I heard of a position that I think might be perfect for you all." Lena sat next to Dipti over dinner. She had moved to Cassowary Point with Christian when he was Luke's age, escaping a situation not dissimilar to Dipti's. She'd worked as a housekeeper at a resort in town for years before becoming manager there. "The owner of the resort I work at also owns several smaller properties in the area. He was telling me last week he's bought a small apartment complex that he's turning into holiday rentals, but he can't find the right person to manage them. He wants someone on-site,

234

so it comes with a three-bedroom apartment. Check-in and out is all digital, but he wanted someone to make sure people have arrived and to place a welcome basket in each apartment. He also said something about figures, but I'll let him talk to you about that if you're interested."

"Is it safe?" Dad asked between forks of pasta. He and Mum had cooked up a feast. "I mean, no offence, Dipti, but I don't think I'd want Val, Emily, or Bridget telling people to turn the music down at 2 a.m."

"Charlie." Bridget was ready to thump her hand on the table, but Giles grabbed it and was whispering in her ear.

"It's not what we'd expect, no." Lena had thought this through. "Marcus, my boss, wants the police called. He doesn't want his employees to put themselves in the line of fire."

"Marcus, hey?" Mum wiggled her eyebrows at her friend as Lena waved her serviette in her hand, a blush coming to her cheeks. "What happened to Mr Debenham?"

"And it comes with accommodation?" Dipti asked in a soft voice.

"Absolutely," Lena said. "Initially, Marcus' daughter was going to manage them, but she's headed to Brisbane to complete her MBA. She's actually going to live with Val and her friend."

Things had a way of falling into place, it seemed. I could only imagine what an upheaval Dipti had experienced over the last few weeks. Ken had already suggested counselling for them all, and I'd grabbed some brochures from work.

Work. How things had changed. I thought back to my rotations in Brisbane and how difficult I'd found them. I didn't find the content difficult, but more like the characters involved. And that often included the patients. Now I was working in psych and loving it. A lot of our clients had awful backgrounds with stories that made me want to question humanity, but there was something about them that drew me to them. I felt like I was doing something worthwhile. Each day, I got up excited about work. I'd never felt this in medicine before.

As I looked around my parents' large dining table, I saw love. Mum and Dad smiled at each other at the ends of the table. Giles whispered in Bridget's ear as she gave him a light backhand across his chest. Emily and Boyd snuck kisses, both of them with their hands under the table, and it was good I couldn't see what they were doing. Then I saw Dipti hugging Luke as he told her something, and Lena was convincing Sarah to try some of the salad.

Finally, there was Ken. He sat beside me, his leg touching mine, as if was the most natural thing in the world, my arm around the back of his chair. My cheeks almost hit my eyes as my lips pushed them upward in a smile.

"I want to get you home," Ken whispered in my ear, causing my smile to grow. "It's been too long since you were in our bed."

"Our bed?" I asked as Ken leant over and kissed me on my cheek.

"It doesn't matter which room, and hey, your old bed might be smaller, and that might be better, but I want to sleep close to you as much as I can." Ken tickled his fingers along the base of my neck, causing me to shudder in delight.

"Uncle Ken kissed Uncle Hen!" Millie clapped her hands and shrieked as she bounced in her chair. "Are you getting married? Can I be your flower girl?"

"Are you going to have a baby?" Sarah's eyes were wide with excitement now as she ignored Lena and looked our way.

"How do two boys have a baby?" Luke looked puzzled.

"There are many ways," Dad said as he looked at Luke. "Neither of them can carry a baby, of course, but there's nothing wrong with two men in love raising a family."

Luke accepted Dad's explanation and went back to playing with some garlic bread. Dad looked over at us both and subtly raised his glass, a grin on his face. I'd never not been accepted by my parents, and knowing they loved Ken as much as I did— Wait, love? My chest grew warm, understanding that I was deeply in love with Ken. He was my person, and I was his.

"Mum messaged me and said that they're all awake and flipping pancakes. She said, and I quote 'You two stay in bed for the morning', followed by a winking face emoji." Ken and I were still a tangle of arms and legs as we lay in his bed after bringing each other to climax yet again.

"How about the market, and then I can cook for us all tonight?"

I pulled my head away and looked at a very contented Ken. "You want a repeat of last night?"

"No." He chuckled. "I was thinking more like your parents, Dipti and the kids, and us, but I'll never tire of your family."

"They're a lot." I ran my hand through my beard. It needed a trim.

"They're a lot of awesome." Ken snuggled into my neck. "Just like you. In fact, I don't want you to feel smothered, but I need to tell you something."

Ken swallowed before lifting his head and looking into my eyes.

"I love you," I whispered through my smile.

"Hey, that was going to be my line." Ken's face mirrored mine. "I love you so much. My heart is full, and I know I'm in the right place."

After separate showers—I tried to convince Ken to come in with me, but he promised he'd make it up to me tonight—we jumped in my jeep and made our way to the market. I didn't try to hide the music that talked of love and forever, because for the first time, I felt it inside me. I knew I'd found the love that the songwriters sang about.

"Have you heard from your mother?" I asked Ken as we circled for a park.

"We didn't part on good terms." Ken sighed. "She called me all manner of slurs and told me I was no longer her son."

Why hadn't Ken told me this earlier? Had we been lost in our own bubble? "Oh, babe. I'm so sorry. You know that's her issue, though?"

"Yeah. I spoke about it with Dipti last Friday night. She was just as dismissive of her, too. I mean, she's grieving for Appā, and I get that, but her downright hatred for the two of us is deeper than that. Dip and me actually spoke about changing our names. She doesn't want Gayan's surname, and neither of us wants our father's name."

"What will you do?" I asked, not even angry that another car had pulled into the park I was aiming for. I didn't mind driving around with Ken.

"I'm going to change my name formally to Ken Kandiah and Dipti is going to take Kandiah as a surname, too." Ken looked relieved at getting this in the open. "One day, I might even change it again and become Ken Kandiah-Hartman. And because you blurted out your love for me first this morning, I'm going to be the one to propose to you."

Fuck. This man. His words were like a balm to my soul. He wanted us as much as I did.

"And," Ken continued, "I'm going to finish my cardiology rotation, but then I'm going to ask for psych as my last rotation for the year. We can train together to become psychiatrists. I mean, if that's what you want."

I was waiting for a car to pull out, the driver loading bags of produce into the back as the passenger buckled a child into its car seat.

"I'd love that." I squeezed his leg as my phone rang. "You're on speaker, stinky."

"Good." My sister giggled. "I just spoke with Em, and she said the two of you were very lovey dovey last night."

"Hi, darl," Ken spoke to my sister before I could. "I didn't know there were cameras in our room, but what can I say? Your brother has an amazing cock."

"Fuck you. I just spat coffee all over my phone." Val was laughing. "Seriously, though, I'm glad you two worked things out. Oh, and Hen?"

"Yes, stinky?"

"Remember to communicate. It's really important."

"Yeah, thanks for that advice." I shook my head, even though my sister couldn't see.

"Hey, darl?" Ken piped up again. "You don't mind me calling you that, do you?"

"No, Kenny, I don't." She laughed.

"Good. I wanted to thank you for all you've done for Dipti and the kids. You've been amazing."

"Nah. All good." Val was never one to accept praise well. "Can you let Giles know, please, and remind him that if I had become a bloody doctor, I couldn't have sorted things out for you?"

"Well, we're at the market, and we finally got a park." I didn't mind talking to my sister, but I wanted to get Ken home again, and that meant shopping first.

"Ooh." Val let out an almost moan. "If the crepe man is there, make sure you try the caramelised pineapple. Although you two probably eat a lot of pineapple as it is." Val laughed before bidding us farewell and hanging up.

"Pineapple?" Ken asked innocently.

"It's meant to make your spunk taste better."

"Yours tastes fine already." Ken smiled as I grabbed the bags from the back. "C'mon, lover. I've got veggies to buy, food to cook, and I might even want to pop into cricket for a bit this afternoon to parade my boyfriend."

"Boyfriend, hey?" I grinned as he took my hand, and we walked towards the market entrance.

"For now, yes." Ken kissed me on the cheek as he squeezed my hand.

I was so far gone for this man, it wasn't funny. I may have thought that I was smothering him, but we were both on the same page now, and it was almost as if we couldn't smother each other enough. We were amazing together. It truly was a meeting of minds.

Epilogue

Ken

It was a gorgeous service. The bride looked stunning, and the groom wasn't bad either. He had nothing on Henry, though, who stood beside me in a crisp navy suit. He'd spent hours choosing the right tie and then complained when mine clashed with his, so he'd decided he needed to spend another hour choosing a matching one for me from his collection. Yes, he'd brought a collection of ties to Brisbane with him just for one evening.

"Henry Hartman, is that you?" A good-looking guy with blond, wavy hair and the bluest eyes drew Henry in for a bear hug.

"Jaxon de Vries! What are you doing with yourself these days?" Henry gushed, his hand lingering on Jaxon's arm.

"Plastics. I'll be a consultant by the end of the year, then I'll go out on my own and make my millions in breasts, as revolting as they are." Jaxon laughed. "What about you?"

"Psych. We've got about eighteen months to go." Henry looked at me and must have sensed my unease, as he threw his arm around my shoulder and pulled my head to his. "This is Ken, my better half."

"Wait, you're married?" Jaxon's jaw dropped, as if Henry had said he was running for Prime Minister.

"Not yet, but we will be," I answered as I kissed Henry's cheek. "We've been together almost five years now, and we've both been focussed on our training. Soon though. Billie looks lovely."

"Yeah. Um... Oh, hey, I've just seen..." Jaxon looked behind us and signalled he was off. There was no farewell or nice to meet you, Ken, or anything.

"He seemed..."

"Like a prick? Yeah, that's Jaxon, alright." Henry shook his head. We both understood the politeness of medicine, especially in social situations. "He always tried to get in my pants at uni, and I always said no."

"God, they look so loved up, don't they?" Billie and Micky approached us, still holding hands I doubt they'd dropped since they walked down the aisle at the end of their service.

"Look at you two." Billie finally dropped her husband's hand as she gave me a hug and a kiss on the cheek. "You know I take all the credit in getting the two of you together."

"I suppose you introduced us at the gala." Henry squeezed my side as, once again, he drew close to me.

"I was thinking of when I moved out." Billie grinned. "You know, I told Bridget I thought the two of you would make a gorgeous couple. How is she, by the way?"

"She's a consultant and living the dream," Henry said.

"Please say hi from me when you get home. I'm so glad you could both be here."

I'd kept in touch with Billie over the years. She heard my father had died, and she contacted me, telling me off for not contacting her when Henry did his ghosting act.

It was strange to think that Henry and I had been together for almost five years. Tomorrow night was the gala and would celebrate Hillary and Charlie's thirty-fifth anniversary. When Billie rang to say they were getting married over Valentine's weekend, I was scared I'd have to tell her we couldn't come because of the gala, but a Friday evening wedding made it all possible.

Henry was giggling as he pocketed his phone. "Val's sent another message. Mum isn't happy with the fairy lights and had Giles rehanging them. We're lucky we're not there."

I was enjoying the cocktail party aspect of Billie and Micky's reception. We could mingle and weren't forced to sit at tables with people Henry might know but I didn't. Sure, there were plenty of Jaxons who made their way over to boast about their achievements to Henry and show off their wives and girlfriends, but Henry and I could also stand back and people watch. It was lots of fun.

"I like the idea of a cocktail reception like this." Henry stroked my arm as I took another sip of champagne. "I don't like the idea of having to travel so far from the ceremony to the reception, though."

It had only been a fifteen-minute cab ride from the gardens the ceremony had been held in to the inner-city hotel where we stood on the rooftop terrace.

"I'm still not one hundred percent on the idea of a beach wedding, you know that, babe." I looked at Henry as I spoke.

"I know. I know." Henry rolled his eyes. "It's not that you've asked me, anyway."

I hadn't. We knew we'd get married, and that was a given, but we were in no rush. We'd both be consultant psychiatrists in the next eighteen months and were both still loving working in mental health. Sure, it might not have been for everyone, but it was for us.

Working with Hen had been amazing. We were never on the same team, which I could understand, and, often, our rosters still clashed, and we'd got a few weeks without being able to have a day off together, but I was the happiest I could remember.

My mother and Abha had stopped all contact with Dipti and me. I had some counselling at the beginning and came to realise that it was healthier for me to accept this break between us and move forward with Dipti and the Hartman family.

Dipti was amazing at managing the apartments. Luke and Sarah were thriving. Dip still hadn't divorced Gayan and accepted his refusal to pay child support, worried that if she pushed it, he would want to see the children. It's her life and her decisions to make. I'd love to see Dipti with someone who was truly worthy of her amazingness, but she claimed she's not interested.

"Boyd and Emily used the pool deck at home, but I think we'd have a few more people than they did at our wedding, no?" Henry was still focused on weddings.

"We'll work something out when the time is right." I kissed his cheek and squeezed his hand. "Now, the dancing is about to start, and I want to have an excuse to press my body to yours for the next however long."

Hen's smile lit up his face. "Dancing with you is never a hardship."

"It usually makes something hard," I whispered in his ear.

Henry sounded like a wounded animal as he groaned back at me. "Our room's only three floors down. We could head there now?"

"I thought you wanted to dance. Plus, there's still cake to come." I knew how much Henry loved cake.

It reminded me of that gala five years ago as Henry and I danced away. The music was upbeat and spoke of love. I could imagine Henry adding some of these to his ever-growing playlist.

"Hey, everyone." Billie had grabbed the microphone, her voice sounding as dishevelled as her hair looked after her wild dancing with her husband. "You know neither of us are that traditional, and we're only tossing the bouquet, so all the single folk, gather around."

Henry and I stood to the side, our arms wrapped around each other's waists. "Did you ever catch a bouquet or a garter?" I asked him.

"No." Henry laughed. "Bridget and Giles didn't do any of that, and most other weddings I've been to have been with you."

Neither of us were taking any notice of the group of people who gathered in front of Billie as she prepared to toss the small bunch of flowers. It came as a great surprise when I saw something from the side of my eye floating towards us. Henry was half a second behind me, but the flowers landed slap bang between us, to cheers from the crowd.

"But we weren't even in the mob vying for the bouquet." I laughed.

"It's a sign, you two." Billie came and threw her arms around us both. "Get hitched. It's lots of fun."

"One day, Billie, and you and Micky will be there. Don't worry." I kissed her cheek, hoping she could hear the frivolity in my voice.

"But I'm going to take this one downstairs now and have my wicked way with him, so we'll love you and leave you." Henry looked at me with sparkling eyes. How could I not love this man?

"WHAT ARE YOU LAUGHING ABOUT?" I asked Henry as the plane to Cassowary Point touched down the following morning.

"Just thinking of five years ago." Henry squeezed my hand. "First, a stripper tried to hit on me before we boarded, then Val told the flight attendant to keep her hands off me because I was all hers, then..." Henry paused to laugh. "A married man tried to chat both me and Val up and was upset when I told him I wasn't interested in a threesome with my sister."

"Sounds charming." Ken rolled his eyes.

"Yeah. Then I met the hottest guy I've ever seen and had the best kiss of my life, well, up until that point anyway, as I've had some phenomenal kisses since then, and he ran away from me."

"What a prick."

"Nah, he was scared, and I know why." Henry stood and passed me my cabin bag as we waited to leave the plane.

"Yeah, well, now he just wants to marry you." I threw it out there as I looked to see if Henry had heard.

"Are you..." Henry's hand went to his chest as I stood, and we started disembarking.

"What? Were you expecting dancing girls and a marching band or something? You told me you wanted to marry me five years ago. It's a given, anyway. I was going to wait until tonight, but Giles already did the whole gala engagement thing and, well, we don't have to tell anyone."

"That's more Boyd and Emily, though. Emily didn't even wear a ring, remember?"

We'd all been shocked when we arrived for dinner at my parents' to find out Emily and Boyd had planned a wedding around the pool as the sun set in the background.

"Well, for me, this is just a formality, I suppose. A social expectation." We walked into the terminal as if we hadn't just become sort of officially engaged. "I know you're mine as much as I'm yours and one day we'll get hitched, but we've got final exams coming up and lots of other things."

"Boyd's here to collect us. He's waiting out the front." Henry checked his phone. "I like that, you know. The idea of a low-key engagement."

"No, you don't, so don't lie. I'll ask again sometime, and I might even splash out and buy a ring."

To be honest, I wasn't sure where my proposal had come from. It wasn't like Henry had badgered me about it. It had been a given, a fait accompli, that it would happen. I'd just made it more official, I suppose.

It had been a bit of a letdown, though. I should have made it more special. Perhaps I needed a do-over, but that could wait. We had a gala to get through.

"How was the wedding?" Boyd asked as we climbed into his car. He was much more sombre than usual.

"It was fun." Henry sat in the front and turned to look at me, smiling as he did.

"Cool." Boyd's reply was clipped. "Get a fucking licence, you fucking prick!" he screamed at a driver who had the right of way. It was lucky he hadn't crashed into Boyd, as he pulled out without looking.

"What's got into you?" Henry asked as an obviously uptight Boyd flew down the road from the airport.

"It's nothing. Just stress." Boyd turned up the radio.

He and Emily had seemed uptight the last few months. They'd started their training programs—Boyd in paediatrics and Emily as a GP—but something was off. After Easter, they'd be heading to Brisbane for a year so Boyd could work at the Children's Hospital to get some experience. I knew Val was looking forward to this.

Boyd slammed on the brakes as he pulled up outside our town-house. We were still renting the same one we'd been in since I arrived at Cassowary Point but had talked about buying a place of our own. This was still super convenient to the hospital, and it was all we really needed.

"Want to come in for a chat?" Henry asked his brother, who simply rolled his eyes.

"I've got no idea what's gotten into him." Henry's brow furrowed as we watched Boyd speed down our street.

"He'll talk when he's ready. Now, have we got time for a rest before we have to get ready?" I asked as I squeezed Henry's gorgeous bum. He knew I wanted to rest as little as he did. I just wanted him naked in our bed.

"Well, you are my fiancé now. Perhaps we need to do fiancé things." Henry jiggled his eyebrows suggestively, causing me to laugh.

"You'll need to show me, because I'm so innocent about these things." I bit my lip and batted my eyelids.

"You may have been once, but not anymore."

"You corrupted me." I laughed.

We both knew we'd corrupted each other.

"HAPPY ANNIVERSARY, you two loved up crazies. And thank heavens you didn't go with a coral dress. It would have clashed with your colouring." Henry planted kisses on both of his parents' foreheads as we arrived.

"Thank you, my Hammy." Hills gave her son a hug before hugging me.

"That Blue is a very sexy colour on your mother." Charlie eyed his wife of thirty-five years suggestively.

"Are we first here?" Henry asked as he ignored his father.

"Emily's upstairs with Val redoing makeup or something. I think she and Boyd are fighting. Boyd's out by the pool with a beer in a foul mood."

I had no idea what was going on, but I let Henry go speak to his brother alone.

"You look lovely, Ken." Hillary handed me a glass of champagne as Giles and Bridget burst through the front door.

Henry had taken me to Brisbane after Christmas to buy a proper dinner suit. I couldn't help but smile when I remembered the morning at the shop he used to work at.

"Sorry we're late. Slight argument with an eight-year-old who thinks she should be at a grownup party. I don't pity Mrs McIntyre having to calm her down."

"Rosa will have her watching movies and eating lollies by now. I know she can't wait for Emily and Boyd to give her grandchildren of her own." Mum smoothed down Giles' tie after giving him one of her famous hugs.

"You're looking dapper, Ken. Where's Hammy?" Bridget asked as she curled her arm around her husband's waist.

"He and Boyd are by the pool."

I didn't think it was my place to speculate on what was going on with Boyd and Emily.

Val and Emily finally appeared in the kitchen. Val wore a black gown with a long slit up the thigh and Emily was in a vivid red, Emily looking like this was the last place she wanted to be.

"I need you to meet one of my new interns tonight, Valerie. He's extremely smart, good-looking, and an all-round lovely man." Hillary's lips extended up her cheeks as she told her daughter of her plan.

"Not Gerald?" Giles shook his head. "He's a suck-up. I think stinky would be better with Mo. He's a lot of fun."

Hillary and Giles went back and forth about the junior doctors they wanted to pair Val up with. I felt sorry for her being under this pressure and knew she felt it being the only non-doctor in the family. She was too busy talking with Emily, though, making sure she was distracted from whatever had been upsetting her.

"Fuck, babe." Boyd and Henry reappeared, Boyd's face lighting up when he saw his wife. "You look stunning. Clearly the sexiest woman here tonight."

I saw Giles squeeze Bridget, but he wasn't about to contradict his brother. Well, not publicly anyway.

"You look lovely, Emily. As do you all." Henry waved his hand around as he nodded to the women present. "So, Ken and I are getting married. We don't know when, but we'll let you know when we do."

"We won't hold our breath." Val gave me a hug. "And it's not like this is fresh news. I mean, we can all see how perfect the two of you are together."

Their brush-off of our announcement didn't faze me. Our

announcement wasn't that big of a surprise. I mean, we've lived together since we got together.

"Congratulations, boys." Charlie grinned as he raised his empty champagne glass towards us. "Now, the first bus will be here any minute, and we need photos."

This was my second gala, but my first seeing it from the Hartman side of operations. I hadn't bothered to have my photo taken five years ago when I was new to Cassowary Point. Now I couldn't wait to immortalise my evening with Henry. The marquee looked stunning; Hillary and her team chose a theme that mimicked being under the sea for their coral anniversary.

People were arriving, and the band was raring to go.

"I wish they'd hurry." Henry looked to where the guitarist was plugging in his gear. "I want to dance with my fiancé."

"Luckily, he wants to dance with you, too. But more than that..."

We weren't in a dark corner. We weren't alone. But this didn't matter, well, not to me. I didn't care who saw us. I leant over and gripped Henry's cheeks in my hand before bringing my lips to his. Our mouths opened, and, soon, we were engaged in a battle of the tongues, each of us wanting to be deeper inside the other.

"Get a room." Val appeared with Dipti by her side. "Look who I found."

Reluctantly, I broke away from the kiss, with Henry grabbing my wrist as I did, as if to hold me in place. Little did he know there was no way I was running from him tonight—or any other time, for that matter.

Henry was my person. He understood me and loved me despite my flaws. He made my life so much richer for being in it. Every day, he showed me how much he loved me, and I hope I did the same to him. I was excited to grow old with this man and was looking forward to many more adventures, and galas, together.

A Note from Jez...

This book took much longer than the first one to write. I suspect a lot of it had me looking at my own thoughts and beliefs and second guessing how I could write a story about two men in love when I hadn't experienced love as a man.

Thanks to my friends who talked me through it and suggested I'd written Giles already and I needed to get over the thought block of not feeling up to it.

I know there are many people who don't typically read MM fiction, and I understand this to some respect, but love is love. Henry and Ken deserve, in my humble opinion, to have their shared far and wide, and it is no less valid than the other Hartman siblings' stories.

If you're reading this, and were hesitant about picking up a gay romance, then thank you for giving it a go. I hope you enjoyed it as much as I enjoyed writing it (once I got my head out of my arse!)

There are some surprises in a few pages too! Boyd and Emily's story will release on Tuesday, 6th February 2024 and Val's story will release on Tuesday, 7th May 2024!

Acknowledgments

This should be the straightforward part, but I know I'm going to leave people out.

Thanks to...

My amazing assault team—the em-dash embracers! You know who you are and you rock! Also, the stunning Cygnets, brought together by the brilliant TL Swan, who are there to offer support, insight, and a kick up the bum when needed!

Sarah and Cheyenne, editor and proof reader extraordinaire. I'm trying not to use as many exclamation marks, I really am! Sam from Keir Editing and Writing Services, who offered more than simply a sensitivity read. Your input truly was invaluable. Also A and C, who I talked things through with and tried to get a gay man's insight before I put pen to paper, or finger to keyboard.

The cover- Kristin, you've done it again!

My ARC Readers, especially the support from the Books and Bitches Down Under crew- you rock! May your endings be happy and your books be ever spicy!

Not to forget my readers. The support and encouragement you offer with messages and emails is just lovely.

Finally, Dr N! You may still be reading The Heart Switch, but you also keep asking me what I'm working on and are there to make me coffee when I get up early to write. And my spawn... Mummy writes books with sex in them. You're old enough to know about this, but I think I'll refrain from telling you for a wee bit longer!

PS—Thank you for the review you've just written! It means so much to indie authors. Oh, you haven't yet? I'll let you do that now then!

About the Author

Jezabel Nightingale is an emerging author of contemporary romance. She wears so many hats, including nurse, mother, wife, writer, and scholar. In her spare time, you'll find her cheering on AFL football, in the kitchen baking a cake, or reading a spicy romance novel. It is not unusual to find a gin and tonic in her hand, or something chocolatey in her vicinity. She will blame these vices for her overuse of exclamation marks and commas, because, why not?

She lives on the East Coast of Australia with Dr Nightingale, her spunkrat of a husband, her cats, and her kids who keep popping home, despite officially having moved out.

After publishing short stories online through Liter0tica for several years, this is her second novel.

Also by Jezabel Nightingale

The Hartman Family Series
The Heart Switch

A Meeting of Minds

Kidding Around

Fiction v Reality

The Bayview Monarchs
Tackling Love Once More

Lovemore Gap
Finding Love

Coming February 2025

Standalone Titles
Secret Santa

Manufactured by Amazon.ca
Acheson, AB

15879108R00149